Her Nightingale

TARA CONRAD

HIS ONE HER ONLY PUBLISHING

Contents

To the love of my life- thank you for reminding me everyday that I may be bruised but I am not broken.

Alex

VIKTOR'S PICTURE FLASHES ON MY PHONE. HE KEPT HIS distance for so long that I was afraid he'd never come around. I'm thankful we've finally been able to repair our friendship. "Hello?"

"Hey. It's me."

"Yes, it is." I chuckle. "What's up?"

"I need your help. Your advice about a woman."

My coming back caused him so much suffering. I'm thankful he's finally healing enough to move forward. "You met someone?"

"Yeah."

"You've been holding out on me. When did this happen?"

"I guess a few months ago."

"That's great."

"I'm not the right man for her. Nothing good will come of this."

"Viktor, you have to stop thinking you aren't good enough—"

"Alex, I'm in love with Amelia Solonik."

There's no way he just said the words *love* and *Amelia* in the same sentence. "Can you repeat that?"

"I'm in love with Amelia."

It's a good thing I'm sitting down. Otherwise, I would've fallen over.

"You are so fucked."

"Thanks. You're such an encouragement."

"Does she feel the same?"

"I think so. We haven't actually said the words, but we've—"

"Please tell me you haven't had sex with Maxim's daughter."

"Not yet."

I'm relieved knowing he hasn't done something he can't take back—yet.

"I don't know what to do. I've told myself this isn't okay. That I can't fall for my boss's daughter, but it's too late."

My first instinct, as a father, is to tell him to stay the hell away from her. He's thirty-two. She's eighteen. If that were Rose, I'd kill him. But that's not going to work. The heart doesn't care about age or rules.

I run my hands through my hair. Think Alex. Is there anything I can do to ensure Maxim doesn't kill him?

"She's young, and she's never dated. You two spend a lot of time together. It might be puppy love or infatuation."

"Right," he replies. "Infatuation."

My intent wasn't to hurt him, but the sadness in his voice is unmistakable. Amelia's young and inexperienced in the area of relationships. She'd never hurt him on purpose, but if he goes all in thinking this is a forever thing, he's going to be devastated again.

"I'm not saying that's what it is. Just keep it in the back of your mind."

"I appreciate your concern. But I want this—with her. What do I do?"

"Go slow. Really slow. Amelia couldn't have set her sights on a better man." I chuckle. "But Max is going to blow a gasket when he finds out."

"Which isn't going to be anytime soon."

Natalie

"HI, SWEETHEART," I ANSWER THE PHONE. "HOW WAS your show last night?"

"It went really well. The A&Rs were impressed.." Amelia pauses. "I need to talk to you about something."

"Anything. What's up?"

"It's about the guy I've been telling you about." Amelia sounds hesitant. "Last night, things started to get physical."

"Was it consensual?"

"It was perfect, and then he stopped. He told me he didn't think he was the right man for me."

"I'm sorry, honey. That must've been really hard." My heart hurts for her. Relationships are all new to Amelia, and I can guess where her head went when she got rejected.

"It hurt. Especially because I know he's the right man for me. And he knows it, too. He's just scared of our age difference and what Dad will say. But I don't care. I love him."

"I'm a little confused. I thought we were talking about the band guy. I didn't know he was so much older than you."

"It's not the band guy. It never was." She pauses, and I hear her take a deep breath. "Natalie, please don't freak out. I'm in love with Viktor."

"Dobrow?" I ask.

"Yes," she replies, her voice barely above a whisper.

I'm in shock. Amelia's in love with Viktor. For months, she's been telling me about the sweet, thoughtful things her mystery man has been doing for her. It was apparent he cared about her but wasn't ready to take the leap. I assumed he was insecure. Knowing the mystery man is Viktor. It all makes sense.

"Natalie? Are you still there?"

"I'm here."

"I'm sorry." Amelia starts crying. "I just screwed up our friendship, didn't I?"

"Oh honey, it's nothing like that. I'm surprised, that's all."

And confused by the onslaught of emotions. Even though my heart and soul belong to Alex, I still feel possessive over Viktor. He was mine. I guess in the whirlwind of everything that's happened over the past year, I never really let go of him.

"I know how you feel about Viktor. I shouldn't have let this happen."

"Amelia, you've done nothing wrong. Yes, I'll always have a special place in my heart for Viktor. I'll always love him, but I'm not in love with him. My heart belongs to Alex—it always has."

"Are you sure?"

I wipe at my tears. Viktor and I were through so much together. He held me when my life shattered. I'll never forget what he meant to me, what he'll always mean to me. But it's time for me to let go of any what-ifs that may have been floating around in my head. Holding onto Viktor isn't fair to anyone.

"I'm very sure. Viktor's a wonderful man who deserves to be someone's first choice. That's something I could never give him," I explain. "Amelia, Viktor's had a difficult past. His heart's fragile."

"I know how hurt he was when he lost you."

"It goes far deeper than that. He's experienced a great deal of loss in his life. You need to be sure about this before you do anything with him."

"I know I don't have any experience with men. But I also know that I want to be with him. I'll do everything I can to guard his heart. The same way he does mine."

I have no doubt Amelia will treasure him. Then another worry pops into my head—Maxim.

"Does your father know?"

"No. I don't know how to tell him."

"Carefully and from a distance. Because he's going to totally freak out."

"That's what I'm afraid of."

"Obviously, there's a lot you and Viktor have to work out. I'm assuming he's struggling with your age difference as well as what your parents are going to say."

"And my past."

"What do you mean?"

"I think he pushed me away because of what happened to me."

"That doesn't sound like Viktor," I reply.

Amelia listens patiently as I explain that I think Viktor's afraid of triggering her by doing anything sexual. He overthinks things and is most likely trying to figure everything out. We talk until I can't put Rose's dinner off any longer.

"You can call me anytime," I assure her.

"Thanks, Nat. I love you."

"Love you too, Melia-bug."

I scoop up my little girl and bring her into the kitchen to get settled in her highchair while I make her lunch.

Alex comes into the kitchen and sits next to Rose.

"Wow." He runs his hands through his hair.

"What's wrong?"

"I just hung up with Viktor," he says.

I give Rose her sippy cup. "I just hung up with Amelia."

"So, you know?"

I nod.

"Does she have feelings for him?"

"She's in love with him."
"Those two have one hell of a hard road ahead of them."

Viktor

TALKING TO ALEX DIDN'T DO A DAMN THING TO MAKE this better. He was supposed to have the answers I needed, but other than going slow and wishing me luck with Max, he didn't have any other advice.

Amelia and I need to talk. After a quick shower, I go to find her. When I pass by her bedroom, I find the door open, but the room is empty. She's not in the kitchen or living room either. Where did she disappear to? Stepping onto the balcony, I spot her. She's in her swimsuit, lying on a blanket by the water.

I throw on a pair of swim shorts and head down to join her.

"You need to let me know if you're leaving the house."

"I needed some time alone," she says, pushing up on her elbows.

"We need to talk." I lower myself next to her. "What you said last night couldn't be any further from the truth."

"Then, why did you stop?"

"You were upset. It would've been wrong to take advantage of you."

"You weren't—"

"It wouldn't have been right. Not like that." I stare out at the water for a beat. "Amelia, there are so many things wrong with this. With us."

"But there doesn't have to be."

I wish that were true. That we lived in a world where we'd be accepted as a couple. Instead, we have everything going against us. Pursuing a relationship is crazy. The problem is, I don't want to walk away from this.

At the same time, I have no idea how to move forward. We're going to encounter a whole lot of hate. Hell, if Maxim finds out, and he eventually will, he's going to kill me.

Amelia studies me for a moment before she reaches out and threads her fingers with mine. "I want this. I want us."

Amelia

"I WANT THIS. I WANT US."

I know Viktor's scared. I am, too. The issues we're going to face won't be easy. Saying my parents won't be happy is an understatement. But I'm not a child. They don't get to tell me who I can be with.

"I called Natalie this morning. I told her everything," I confess.

"I called Alex." He cracks a smile. "I wish I was a fly on the wall. I can only imagine the conversation they had after talking to both of us." We share a laugh. "Seriously though, this—" He motions between us. "—isn't a good idea."

"What did Alex tell you?"

"That I'm fucked when your father finds out," Viktor says deadpan.

I guess that's one way to put it. Dad isn't going to be happy, that I'm sure of. But I think Alex and Viktor are being a bit over-dramatic. I'm sure he and Mom will be surprised at first, but they're open-minded. They'll get over it quickly.

"He also told me to be careful and to go slow." Viktor brushes sand off the corner of the blanket. "How did your call with Natalie go?"

Knowing Viktor was in love with Natalie makes this conversation difficult. I don't want to hurt him or make this any harder than it already is.

"I know what you're thinking. Yes, I was in love with her. Natalie and I will always share a special friendship. But that's all it is. She's with Alex, where she belongs, and I'm where I belong."

His words calm my nerves. "I was afraid she was going to hate me."

"Why would she hate you?"

"Because of all this. But Natalie reassured me that she wasn't mad. Then she warned me to be sure of my feelings before going further."

"Amelia, I'm not sure there should be an us," Viktor says quietly. "There's a lot you don't know about me."

"So, tell me. I want to know all of it.

Viktor

Telling Amelia about my past terrifies me. Once she knows the things I've done, the people I've hurt, she'll never look at me the same. Maybe that's for the best. Scaring her away will keep her safe.

"My past isn't pretty."

"My life hasn't been a fairy tale either," she says softly.

"This is different. What happened to you wasn't your fault. My life has been a series of bad decisions."

"Trust me. Tell me, and let me decide."

Opening up, I lay myself at her feet, baring everything. I share the good, the bad, and all the moments in between—the people I've loved and lost, the extent of my work with Maxim. Finally, I tell her everything about Natalie, and for the first time, it doesn't feel like my heart is being torn apart.

When I finish, I'm left feeling vulnerable. Amelia's watching me, but she hasn't spoken. I knew my story would scare her away. I move to stand up, intending to go back up to the house to give her space.

"Where are you going?"

"Inside."

She adjusts her position to her knees. "Don't go."

"I figured you wouldn't want anything to do with me."

Amelia moves closer, straddling my legs. "You've experienced so much loss. You didn't deserve any of that, and I'm sorry." She presses her lips against mine. "But nothing you said changes how I feel." She kisses me again. "You're gentle and caring. You're kind." Another kiss. "You're safe."

"Amelia, my life is dangerous. I have enemies who'd love nothing more than to hurt someone I care about to get to me."

"There are many things in life that can't be controlled. You may have enemies, but I don't doubt for a second that you wouldn't do everything in your power to keep me safe."

"What if I fail?"

"You won't." She cups my cheek. "I'm willing to take that chance if you are."

"I want to try." I put my arms around her, pulling her closer to me. "But I'm scared."

"You've been my rock when I'm afraid," she says quietly. "Let me be strong for you now."

"I can't say no to you." I rest my forehead against hers. "I don't want to say no."

✦

As the sun begins to set, we make our way back down to the water. Walking along the beach at dusk is a ritual we cherish, a moment of quiet serenity. The only sound is the rhythmic crash of waves against the shore, a soothing backdrop to our time together.

Tonight's walk is different. I'm free to hold Amelia's hand. To keep her close to me. We stay out until the sky turns dark, and we're treated to a sky full of twinkling stars.

"*Moya zirka*," I whisper and wrap her in my arms.

"What does that mean?"

"My star. You're my guiding light, the one who pulled me out of the darkness."

Amelia

Viktor opened up to me last night and told me everything about his past. His glacier-blue eyes were haunted as he recalled his parents' deaths and how he went back home to heal from losing Natalie, only to face losing his grandmother—his only remaining family member.

We share a similar pain. When my parents died, I had no one. At fifteen years old, I was an orphan. My sixteenth birthday, one that was supposed to be a milestone, was a nightmare instead.

Both Viktor and I have dark pasts. We have scars. We've both shared moments where we were ready to give up. But we didn't, and we made it through. I believe we survived because we were meant to find each other—to love one another.

We've agreed to try at this—whatever *this* is. Neither of us wants to put a label on us. Instead, we're going to take it one day at a time and see what happens.

Right now, the only thing that's happening is we're straightening up the house before we leave for the airport to pick up my mom and Lana. They've flown in for my chamber music recital on Monday.

"You ready to go?" Viktor pops his head into the guest room, where I'm putting fresh sheets on the bed.

"As soon as I finish this, I will be." Viktor comes into the room and helps me finish making the bed. "Thank you." I wrap my arms around his waist.

He holds me against his chest. It's my favorite place to be. I feel safe in his protective embrace. Then, he leans down and kisses me. "One last kiss before your family gets here."

I'm going to miss this new normal we've been living. One where we're free to touch one another. Free to show affection. Viktor doesn't want to rush the physical side of our relationship, so he's placed limits on what he'll do, which is no more than holding and kissing me. He also insists we sleep in separate rooms. But each evening, when he kisses me goodnight at my bedroom door, it gets harder to let him go.

The closer we get to the airport, the more nervous I get.

"Amelia, you have to relax," Viktor says. "Everything will be fine."

I wish I had his confidence. I've never lied to my mom or kept anything from her. I don't like not being able to tell her about us. But it's too soon for that. I'm just afraid she's going to see right through me.

"What if they find out?"

"Then, they find out, and we deal with the consequences sooner rather than later."

"How are you so calm?"

"I have to be, moya zirka." He glances my way. "It's part of keeping you safe."

The ding of a text alert interrupts my worrying.

Lana: We're here. We landed early.

"It's Lana. They're already here," I tell Viktor before texting her back.

Me: Viktor just took the exit for LAX. We'll be there in a few minutes.

LAX is like a city within a city. There's an intricate system of roads leading to numerous terminals, hotels, and restaurants. It's crazy confusing. I'm impressed with the ease in which Viktor finds his way. I don't think I'd ever be able to drive in here.

Finally, we come to a private tarmac, and dad's jet comes into view. Viktor drives past it and pulls the car into the private hanger.

"Ready?" he asks.

"Do I have a choice?"

"Not really." He cracks a small smile. "We've got this."

Thankfully, he moves his hand just as Lana pulls my door open and nearly drags me out of the car.

"I missed you so much." She squeezes me tight.

I hug her right back, not realizing how much I miss my family. "Me too."

"*Moya malen'kaya ptichka*," Mom says and wraps me in a hug. "The house is too quiet without you."

"I'm so happy you're both here."

"I see Viktor's his usual pleasant self," Lana says, motioning behind me where Viktor is standing by the car. "I don't know how you live with him. He's so moody he'd drive me crazy."

I look over my shoulder where Viktor's talking with Pyotr. "He's not that bad. We seem to do okay."

"You're a better person than me, little sis."

Viktor grabs their bags and gets them in the trunk.

"Are you ladies ready to go? The traffic's going to be terrible."

"How are we going to fit Pyotr?" Our car isn't that big.

"He's staying in L.A. The boss gave him a few days off."

Lana and I get settled in the backseat while Viktor helps mom into the front. Then, we make our way out of the airport and back onto the freeway.

"Are you hungry? We can stop for something to eat on the way home," I suggest.

"That would be lovely. Is that okay with you, Viktor?" Mom asks.

"Is there anywhere special you would like to go, Mrs. Solonik?"

"You can call me Irina. There's no need for all the formalities." Mom smiles and then looks back at me. "I don't know anything about the area. Where would you suggest, Amelia?"

"What about the restaurant by the bay we like?"

Viktor glances in the rearview. "That sounds perfect."

Viktor

Putting boundaries between Amelia and me is going to be more complicated than I thought. I already miss her next to me. Miss reaching out to touch her. I need to put distance between us, but we're stuck in the car in this ridiculous traffic. I thought New York City was bad, but it's nothing compared to the congested California freeways.

What should only be a half-hour drive takes nearly two hours, but finally, we're pulling into the parking lot for Bay Front Restaurant.

Once inside, I ask the hostess for two tables.

"You aren't going to eat with us?" Amelia asks.

"No."

"Oh." Her smile fades

Lana threads her arm through Amelia's. "He'll be fine. He's not great at conversation anyway."

"Thank you, Viktor," Irina says.

I watch as the three ladies are seated before I'm led to a separate table where I sit facing Amelia. Lana and Irina's backs are to me. A positive since they can't see me watching Amelia's every move.

The women laugh and chat throughout their meal, their

conversation lively and animated. I can only imagine Amelia filling them in on everything they've missed. A pang of longing hits me—I miss being the one she talks to like that, sharing her thoughts and stories with me instead.

It's still light when we pull into our driveway.

"The pictures don't do the house justice," Irina says. "It's beautiful."

"It's been like living in a dream," Amelia says. "I can't thank you and dad enough."

"Forget the house. I want to go down to the beach," Lana says.

"I'd like to see the inside and get settled first." Irina overrules her daughter.

"Fine." Svetlana shrugs. "Come on, Melia. Give us the grand tour."

"I'm going to give Viktor a hand with the bags."

"No, you're not. Viktor's a big boy. He can handle it."

Amelia glances over her shoulder and mouths the words *I'm sorry* as Lana drags her away from me.

I've known Svetlana since she was a little girl. Despite being raised in a strict home where showing respect was expected, Svetlana often acts like a spoiled brat. When she was with Brandon, he kept her reigned in. But the longer she's been without him, the more out of control she's become.

It's going to be a long few days with her like this.

Amelia

I KNEW IT WOULD BE HARD TO KEEP MY DISTANCE FROM Viktor, but I didn't realize how difficult it would be. We've gotten used to being close very quickly. And now we're forced to act like two people who are no more than roommates.

"Here's your bedroom, Mom." I open the door to our guest room.

"It's stunning. And look at that view." She walks straight to the balcony doors I left open, allowing the ocean breeze to drift in.

"Some days, it's hard to peel myself away from it. Come on, Lana. I'll show you to our room."

"Our room? Dad said this place has three bedrooms."

"It does. The other bedroom is Viktor's. I didn't want either of you to have to sleep on the sofa bed. And I didn't think you'd mind sharing my room for a few days," I say, uncertain.

"That's fine. It'll give us a chance to catch up."

We pass Viktor in the hall. He nods politely and keeps walking.

"What's the deal with you and Viktor? You never seem to have a nice thing to say about him."

Lana flops down on my bed. "He's always there. In your face. You know what I mean?"

"Umm. Isn't that kinda his job?"

"I guess. But most of the other guards hang back and give you some personal space. You would've been better off having Igor here. He'd give you much more freedom than Viktor ever will."

"He's not that bad." I sit cross-legged on the other side of the king-sized bed.

Lana grabs my pillow to prop her head on. "What's this?"

She holds up Viktor's t-shirt that I sleep with every night.

"Nothing." I reach out to grab it, but she pulls it away. "Let me have it. It should be in the laundry."

"It smells like a man's shirt." Lana raises her eyebrows. "Does my little sister have a boyfriend she's not telling me about?"

"No." I pull the shirt out of her grasp and toss it into my laundry basket. I'll have to get another one from him.

Lana tilts her head as she studies me. From the look on her face, I know she doesn't believe me.

"Didn't you want to go to the beach?"

"Smooth." She grins. "I need my bag so I can get my swimsuit."

I open the door to go in search of her bag and find it waiting in the hall outside my room. Viktor mustn't have wanted to interrupt us.

"Here ya go." I wheel it in and set it on the bed. "I'll grab my swimsuit and get changed in the guest bathroom." Anything to get out of here.

I change into my favorite black two-piece, which I know always gets Viktor's attention. Then, I slip my shorts on and grab a few towels before heading out to the living room, where I find mom and Viktor sitting on the sofa chatting. Viktor stops speaking mid-sentence when I enter the room.

"Looks like you and Lana are going down to the water," Mom says with a smile.

"We are. Are you coming down with us?"

"Not this time. I'm exhausted from the flight."

"What about you, Viktor?"

"I'll stay here and keep Irina company."

"Don't be silly." She pats his arm. "I'll be fine. Go with the girls. The ocean makes me nervous."

"Ready?" Lana asks when she comes into the room.

"Yep. Let's go." We start walking toward the door. Viktor gets up and follows us.

"You're kidding, right," Lana says sarcastically. "Amelia can't even go to the beach without you tagging along?"

"I asked him to go with you," Mom says, not giving Viktor a chance to respond.

"It's a private beach. We'll be fine," Lana complains.

"You know how I feel about the water," Mom says.

Lana rolls her eyes and walks out the door. I look at Viktor and smile, glad he's coming with us.

Amelia

The weekend seemed to fly by, and tonight's Chamber Music Recital is upon us. We're all enjoying a late lunch at the house when my phone dings with a text alert.

Mateo

We need to talk. Can I pick you up for the recital tonight?

I read the text and set the phone face down without replying. I haven't heard from Mateo since the disaster at the after-party the other night, but Sparrow and I have been keeping in touch. He told me Mateo had a few bad days after the incident, but he's slowly moving past it.

"Who's that? Could it be the owner of the T-shirt under your pillow?" Lana waggles her eyebrows. Viktor and I exchange a questioning glance. I don't think he knew I kept his shirt.

"It's a friend from school. He wants to pick me up for the recital tonight."

"Have you met someone special?" Mom asks. "I'd love to meet him while I'm here."

"It's nothing serious. We're just friends, really."

"Since when do you sleep with a *friend's* shirt under your pillow?"

"Svetlana, don't embarrass your sister."

I've created quite a problem for myself, and I don't know how to explain my way out of it. If I introduce Mateo to my mom, it'll send mixed signals, and I don't want to do that.

"I'd prefer you didn't ride with him." Viktor comes to my rescue.

"Seriously? Amelia's allowed to date."

"It's a complicated situation, Svetlana. One I'd rather Amelia not get involved in."

"I'm assuming you've run a background check?" Irina asks.

"I have, and there's nothing apparently wrong."

"But?"

"Overall, he's a nice guy. But he's dealing with some major issues," I interrupt. "He'd like to be more than friends, but I'm not interested in him like that." I pick up the phone to text him back.

Me

I'm sorry. My family's here from Russia. We're going to ride there together.

With that disaster averted, I push out my chair and stand. "I'm going to go start getting ready. We'll have to leave early if we're going to get there on time."

Lana follows me into my room and sits on my bed. She watches as I go into my closet and return, holding the black dress I wore to the wedding.

"I hate that you and mom have to leave tomorrow," I say as I go into the bathroom to get changed.

"A lot is going on at Jelena's Hope. It's been keeping her very busy. But you'll be home in a few weeks for Christmas break."

Once I'm dressed, I walk back into my bedroom.

"Holy shit. The pictures didn't do the dress justice. You look hot."

My cheeks heat from embarrassment. "Viktor gave me a hard —" I stop as soon as I realize what I'm saying.

"Gave you a what? A hard time?" Lana cocks her head to the side. "What's really going on between the two of you?"

"What do you mean?" I turn around and pretend I'm checking out the dress in my mirror.

Lana gets off the bed and stands between me and my reflection. "I see the looks you two exchange. And that T-shirt under your pillow smelled strangely like his cologne. I think there's more going on here than you're letting on."

"You're crazy." And way too perceptive. "We're friends. He's the only person I really know here, so we spend a lot of time together. That's all."

"Mhm." Lana disappears inside the closet before I can respond. She returns a few minutes later with her clothes in hand. "I'm going to take a quick shower."

My hands shake as I try to apply my make-up. They can't find out about us yet. It'd be a disaster. I finish my make-up in record time, hoping I can talk to Viktor before Lana's done with her shower.

I find him in his favorite spot—the balcony. "Viktor, we need to talk." He spins around to face me. My breath catches. Viktor's dressed in a black suit and a blue tie that matches his eyes. I've never seen him dressed in a suit. Oh my God, I didn't think he could be any more gorgeous, but I was wrong. "Wow." I take a few steps closer. "You look amazing."

A smile spreads across his face, making my insides feel all tingly.

"And you, moya zirka, look stunning. Although I'd still rather you not wear this dress out in public." He leans in, placing a gentle kiss on my lips. "I'm sorry, I couldn't help myself."

"We need to be more careful. Lana's on to us."

"What do you mean?"

"She was questioning me about the T-shirt and the way we are together. She suspects something's going on."

"What T-shirt?" He asks, a playful smile on his face.

"After everything I said, you're only concerned about what T-shirt?"

"Don't worry about Lana. She's all about the drama. If we don't give her a response, she'll drop it."

"Are you sure?"

"I'm positive." Viktor runs his knuckles down my cheek.

"Aha," Lana exclaims. "I knew it."

Viktor

AMELIA'S EYES GO WIDE, AND HER FACE TURNS GHOSTLY white. I'm afraid she may pass out. Shit. I should've known better, but I couldn't not touch her.

"There's nothing to know," I say, hoping to control the situation before it gets out of hand.

"It's not what it looks like," Amelia spins around. "I was about to have a panic attack. Ania's worked with Viktor on ways to ground me—to avoid a full-blown panic attack. One of the techniques is physical touch." Amelia's speech is hurried, giving away her nerves. She pauses and looks back at me before returning her attention to Svetlana. "My face is the most sensitive and grounds me quickly."

"What's going on out here?" Irina appears in the doorway.

This is the moment. Lana's either going to call us out or at least pretend she believes the story Amelia came up with.

"Amelia's really nervous about the recital," Lana says, not taking her eyes off me. "Viktor and I were just telling her she's going to do terrific." She smiles at Amelia, and I breathe a sigh of relief.

"Of course, she's going to do great." Irina walks over to Amelia and embraces her. "I'm so proud of you, sweetheart."

"Thanks, Mom. I have to get my shoes, then I'll be ready to go." Amelia hurries off down the hall.

"She responds so well to you," Irina says, her eyes filling with tears. "Maxim and I are very grateful you're here."

"If my presence makes this transition a little bit easier for her, that's the least I can do."

"It looks like she's flourishing to me. I can't wait to tell Maxim. He's been so worried about her."

"I'm ready," Amelia announces as she walks back into the room. "Mom, why are you crying?"

"Look at you." Irina dabs at her eyes. "You look so grown up."

Amelia kisses Irina's cheek. "That's because I am."

"Enough of the kiss and cry," Lana says and rolls her eyes. "If we don't leave, we're going to miss Amelia's recital."

Irina and Amelia walk out the door together. I move to follow, but Lana steps in front of me.

"Don't think you two are fooling me for a second, Dobrow. You do realize she's only eighteen, right?"

"I'm aware of her age."

"And that my father's going to kill you if he finds out something's going on between you."

"Then we're in luck. There's nothing for him to find out." I move to walk around her, but Lana grabs my arm.

"I love my sister." She softens her voice.

There's no sense in continuing to deny this. Svetlana clearly knows what's going on. "That makes two of us."

"Don't do anything to hurt her, and I won't say anything."

"I give you my word."

✧

Once we arrive at the theater, we bring Irina and Lana to the main entrance. Amelia was able to secure front-row seats for her family.

As soon as they're safely inside, I escort Amelia around the back of the theater building to the stage door.

She places her hand on my chest, stopping me from following her inside. "This is where we say goodbye."

"I'm not leaving you."

She hands me a ticket and then stands on her tiptoes to place a gentle kiss on my lips. "The stage door locks from the inside. And unless you're on his list." She points to the young man standing outside the door with a clipboard in his hand. "You don't get access. I'll be fine. I want you to sit in the audience like any normal boyfriend-type."

I can't help the smile that spreads across my face. "I've never been anyone's boyfriend before."

"I'm glad."

"Promise to keep your phone on and text me if you need anything?"

"I promise."

"Break a leg."

I watch as she disappears behind the stage door. Then, I make my way back to the theater's main entrance, where I'm handed a program on the way to my seat.

"You aren't staying with her?" Irina asks when I sit next to her.

"Nope. She refused to allow me backstage." I shrug. "She wants me to be in the audience to enjoy the recital."

Irina studies me—too closely. It's as though she's peering into my soul and extracting all my secrets. I struggle to keep a neutral outward appearance. Because inside, I'm terrified she'll see right through me.

"She's a special young lady. Always thinking of others."

"Yes, she is."

Thankfully, the house lights dim, and a gentleman I recognize as Amelia's music professor steps onto the stage, announcing the start of the performance.

When the curtain opens, my eyes are immediately drawn to

the young woman behind the grand piano. Like every Death Rat performance, she searches the audience until she spots me. I know the second she does because a beautiful smile graces her face.

Before I knew Amelia, I had never been interested in the arts. This is the first time I've been to an event like this. When I was young, my mother encouraged me to listen to classical music and to appreciate ballet. But I never gave it a real chance. Teenage boys didn't do such things.

Now, I wish I had cared less about my friends and more about the gift my mother was trying to give me. Because tonight, I find myself enthralled with the music being produced by this small group of talented musicians who are playing selections from various composers. Some songs are vaguely familiar, yet I couldn't tell you their names. Others I've never heard, but all are entrancing.

After the last song in the program, the conductor turns around to address the audience.

"Ladies and gentlemen, on behalf of myself and my students, we hope you've enjoyed our performance this evening." The audience's applause interrupts his speech. "This year, our university has had the pleasure of welcoming a very talented student who comes to us from St. Petersburg, Russia." He motions to Amelia, whose cheeks turn as red as her hair. "Ms. Solonik is majoring in classical piano with a minor in vocal studies. She's agreed to perform a classical piece from her country. I hope I say it correctly, *Dve Siyayushchiye Zvezdy*—Two Shining Stars."

Amelia, accompanied by the rest of the chamber orchestra, begins playing the familiar song. Everything and everyone disappears when *moya zirka's* angelic voice fills the auditorium.

"Viktor," Irina whispers. "Did you know about this?"

I shake my head, unable to speak.

When the song finishes, Amelia receives a standing ovation from the audience.

While the audience is still applauding, I excuse myself. "I'll meet you outside the main doors," I say to Irina. I need to get to the box office before the audience makes their exit. The people inside have their backs to me, so I knock on the glass. A woman turns around, and I point to the bouquet of flowers on the table. She grabs them and motions for me to meet her at the door.

"Viktor?" she asks.

"Yes, ma'am."

She passes me the beautiful bouquet.

"Whoever's getting these is one lucky young lady."

"She's extraordinary."

With the flowers in hand, I step outside and wait for Irina and Lana to make their exit from the auditorium.

"Wow," Lana says when she sees the flowers. "That's a little over and above your job, isn't it, Vik?"

"Oh, Lana, leave him alone."

"It's her first recital. I wanted to make it special for her."

"I think it's a lovely gesture."

My heart feels like it's going to explode while we wait for Amelia. I struggle to keep my emotions in check, afraid I'll give away our relationship.

Amelia

"Amelia, wait up," Mateo calls as I head for the door. "Can we talk?"

I know we need to talk, but this isn't the time or place. Right now, the only thing I want is to get outside to Viktor and my family.

"I'm kinda in a hurry."

"Dad's going to be contacting everyone, but I wanted to be the one to tell you." Mateo runs over to me. "The A&R rep called. We got an offer."

"What does that mean?"

"We've been offered a contract to go on tour this summer with Zapped Euforia."

"Oh my God, that's so exciting. What happens next?"

"We have a meeting with our agent and attorneys next Monday afternoon. Can you be there?"

"I should be able to. Text me the info."

Mateo's smile fades. "Amelia, I'm sorry about what happened at the party. I want to explain—"

"Now isn't a good time."

One of my classmates walks around us and opens the door.

"There she is," Lana says excitedly.

"I have to go." I hurry outside.

Lana rushes over and throws her arms around my neck. "You were amazing."

"Thanks, Lan."

"Is this your sister?" Mateo asks.

I was hoping we didn't have to do this, but there's no avoiding it now. "Svetlana, this is my friend, Mateo."

"It's nice to meet you. Amelia's told me a lot about you," Mateo says.

"I see." Lana looks at me with a raised eyebrow.

"There's my girl," Mom says, wrapping me in a hug. "You were incredible."

"Thanks, Mom."

"Hi. I'm Mateo. I'm one of Amelia's band—"

"Mateo's in the chamber orchestra with me."

"It's a pleasure to meet you," Mom says.

"Congratulations." Viktor hands me an exquisite bouquet of flowers.

"Thank you." I bring the fragrant bouquet to my nose. "They're beautiful."

We stand in the middle of the walkway, facing one another. Several people grumble because they're forced to walk around us.

"We should all go and grab a bite to eat somewhere," Mateo suggests.

"I don't think—"

"That would be lovely." Mom smiles and slips her arm through mine. "You didn't tell us you met a boy," she whispers to me as we walk down the sidewalk.

"Mateo? He's just a friend."

"The way he's looking at you says he likes you as more than that."

And that's a problem because friends are all we'll ever be.

Mateo sidles up next to me. "How about we go to Snack and Shake?"

I look at him, eyes narrowed. "I'm kinda tired and would prefer to go home."

"Amelia, it's our last night here. I'd love to get to know your friend before we leave."

"You can ride with me—"

"No," Viktor and I say in unison.

Mateo raises his hands in surrender. "Can't blame a guy for trying."

The four of us squish into one of Snack and Shake's small booths. Once again, Viktor chooses to sit in the booth behind us.

"Do you and my sister have classes together?"

"Yep." Mateo takes a bite of his burger. "We have a few classes together."

"What instrument do you play?"

"Guitar."

I'm finding it hard to eat the loaded fries I ordered. Instead, I push them around on my plate. Viktor watches me carefully from his seat. I know Mateo won't do anything to hurt me, but I'm still uncomfortable. I see the game he's playing, and I don't like it. He's hoping to get my mom to think we're a couple or at least have promise as one. And she's falling for it.

When he's done eating, Mateo slides his arm around me. My body stiffens in response. His move puts Viktor on high alert. He meets Mateo's stare, but Mateo doesn't back down. He's playing with fire, and he's going to get burned.

"What do you want for dessert, Mel?" Mateo asks.

"I'm not feeling well. I want to go home," I say loud enough for Viktor to hear.

He jumps from his booth. "I'll settle the check, and we'll get out of here."

After the bill is paid, we walk out to the parking lot.

"It was nice meeting you, Mateo," Mom says, hugging him.

"I'm really happy I was finally able to meet Amelia's family." Mateo smiles. Although I believe his excitement is genuine, the whole situation feels wrong.

"I enjoyed spending the evening with you, too." Mateo turns to me. "Text me about next week, okay?"

"I will." I get into the car, but Mateo grabs my hand, stops me, and kisses my cheek."Good night, everyone." Mateo gives a small wave as he turns and makes his way to his car.

"He seems like a sweet boy," Mom says.

"He's nice. But we're only friends."

"Some of the best relationships start as friendships, dear," she says as she slides into the car.

"What was that all about?" Lana asks quietly.

"It's a long story."

"And once we get home, you'll have all night to tell me everything."

Amelia

THE RIDE HOME IS FILLED WITH MOM ASKING ALL sorts of questions about Mateo. She assures me Dad's going to insist on meeting him. Once she's satisfied with my answers, she moves on to quizzing Viktor about Mateo's background check. Fortunately, he leaves out the parts about Mateo's drinking and drug use.

As soon as we pull into the driveway and Viktor turns the car off, I jump out. "I'm going for a walk."

"By yourself?" Mom asks.

"I'll come with you." Lana links her arm with mine.

I was hoping Viktor would join me, but I know Lana and I need to talk—away from Mom.

"Give me your flowers. I'll put them in water for you," Mom offers, and I pass her the bouquet.

"Be careful," Viktor adds. "I'll be watching from the house."

Lana and I ditch our heels on the steps and make our way through the cool sand until we get down to the water.

"Are you ready to tell me what's going on?"

"I could ask the same for you?" I give her a cheeky smile.

"Give it up, little sis. I already know something's going on with you and Viktor." She stops walking. "What I can't figure out is where this Mateo kid fits in."

I allow the warm ocean waves to lap over my feet while I consider how much information I should divulge. "Do you promise not to say anything to mom and dad?"

"Do you really think you have to ask me that?" Lana puts her hands on her hips. "Now, spill it."

I take a deep breath and start telling her the saga of Mateo. In her defense, she listens quietly and withholds any judgmental looks or comments, especially when I get to the part about how I fell for Viktor.

"He came into my room to check on me after the whole Mateo mess. Things got pretty heated between us. Nothing happened that night. Viktor put a stop to it. But that's how I ended up with his T-shirt."

"Wow. You've been busy."

"It wasn't anything we planned." I shrug. "It just happened."

"I don't want to sound all preachy, but you do realize how much older Viktor is, right?"

"Yes, I can count." I roll my eyes.

"Ha ha," Lana mocks me. "I'm just worried—"

"Worried that my past is going to cause problems."

"Yes and no." Lana splashes her foot gently in the water. "Viktor has a lot more experience with life in general. You're just starting out. Especially in the world of relationships."

"I understand your concerns, but my life hasn't exactly been sheltered. I'm not into parties or dating around. Heck, I never thought I'd trust a man enough to let him near me." I stop and look up. A thick cloud cover is blocking the usually star-filled sky. "Lana, I love him."

"Dad's going to lose his shit when he finds out."

We both share a laugh.

But on the inside, I'm terrified of just how bad Dad's reaction will be.

Viktor

From my spot on the balcony, I have an unobstructed view of the girls who are standing at the water's edge. Part of me is jealous. Walking on the beach at night is our thing—Amelia and me. But I know she needs time alone with her sister.

A short time later, Irina joins me on the balcony. "It's nice seeing the girls together. I think Svetlana misses Amelia more than she expected."

"Yeah." I don't take my eyes off them.

"Now that we're alone, I'd like to get your real thoughts on that Mateo boy. Something tells me you disapprove."

Despite being in Max and Irina's lives for most of my adult life, I've not spent much one-on-one time with Irina. I'm surprised at how perceptive she is. "His background check came back clean."

Which is true. However, it left out a lot of important information. I hated having to call in a favor, especially since our friendship was on rocky ground. But I didn't want to miss anything that could put Amelia in danger.

Dimitri agreed to do it since it was for Maxim's daughter. But, when he dug deeper, he uncovered Mateo's adoption records that his hotshot attorney father had buried so deep the average person wouldn't find them.

"Amelia only sees him as a friend, but the kid doesn't take a hint too well." I feign annoyance.

"I'm glad she has you looking out for her."

"I'm just doing my job."

"You're going to think I'm crazy. When we got here Saturday, I saw a look you and she exchanged. For a minute, I wondered if something was going on between you." Irina laughs softly.

I freeze, afraid she'll see the truth.

"I realize what a silly notion that was. She feels safe and is able to let her guard down with you. Amelia's obviously not ready to enter the world of dating yet. I'm not complaining. It's one less worry."

"Whatever she chooses, I'll look out for her safety."

"Maxim and I both appreciate what you're doing." Irina pats my arm.

A gentle breeze blows from the water, and I return my gaze to the girls. They've been down there for nearly an hour.

"I can't wait for them any longer." Irina stands up and yawns. "I'm going to head into bed."

"Goodnight."

I'm left alone with my thoughts. Thoughts about the beautiful girl who's finally walking back toward the house. A few minutes later, the door opens and closes.

"I'm heading to bed."

"I'll be in shortly," Amelia replies. Then she steps out onto the balcony. "Do you mind company?"

"From you? Never."

She starts to sit in the chair next to me, but I stop her and pull her onto my lap. She nestles her head against my chest.

"I miss being alone with you."

"Me too." She draws circles on my chest with her finger.

"I hate when you wear this dress, you know that?"

She picks her head up. "I thought you liked this dress?"

"I do."

"But?"

"I don't like other men looking at you in it." I lift her chin with my finger and kiss her.

She adjusts her position so she's straddling my legs. Her dress slides up, exposing too much of her. But I don't care. No one apart from me can see her out here. Our kiss quickly becomes heated.

I pull back, breathless. "We need to stop."

"Why?"

"Your mother and sister are in the other room."

She sighs. "I guess."

I lift her from my lap and adjust my prominent erection before standing. "We should get some sleep. Tomorrow's going to be a long day." She threads her fingers with mine as we walk into the house. "What do you have to text Mateo about?"

"Oh my gosh, I almost forgot. The band was offered a contract to open for Zapped Euforia on their summer tour."

"For real?"

"Yes. For real."

I want to be happy for her, but this news only further complicates an already very complicated situation.

"You know we'll have to tell your parents about Death Rat?"

"I know." She sighs. "I don't want to say anything while Mom's here. I'll wait until she's home and then call them. They're not going to be happy that I won't be home for the holidays. Hopefully, they'll understand why."

"Here's hoping." We stop outside her doorway. "This is where we part ways, moya zirka."

She stands on her tiptoes and places a gentle kiss on my lips. "Goodnight. Sleep well."

Amelia opens the door a crack and slips into her room. I wait until the door closes softly behind her before going to my room.

I'm glad Amelia had a good visit with her family. I know she's missed them. Unfortunately, the timing wasn't ideal. We're just beginning to figure out whatever this is between us. It'll be nice to be alone again to continue exploring our feelings for each other.

Amelia

Mom says. "Jelena's Hope has been so busy. I can't be gone for too long."

"It's okay. We weren't really planning on doing anything special. Were we?" I look to Viktor for an answer.

"Whatever you want to do is fine with me." Viktor shrugs.

"Come here, let me hug you once more." Mom squeezes me tight.

"You're going to break her," Lana says. "It's not like we won't see her again. She'll be home in a few weeks."

Viktor and I exchange a knowing glance.

"I'll be counting the days." Mom dabs at her eyes.

"Are you ready to board, Mrs. Solonik?" Pyotr asks.

"Yes." He takes her arm and leads her up the steps into the plane.

"Are you coming home during break?"

"That's a long story. But there's no time for it now."

Lana gives me one last hug. "The flight home is over eighteen hours. Text me your *long* story." With one final goodbye, she disappears inside the jet.

Viktor and I walk back to where our car's parked. We watch

the jet taxi down the runway, gaining enough speed to safely lift from the ground. A few stray tears spill from my eyes. Viktor puts his arm around me, and I rest my head against him.

"Are you up for a little adventure?"

"What are you thinking?"

"I had an idea about something fun we could do while we're up here." He opens the car door for me. "You game?"

"Sure."

Viktor grins as he rounds the car and slides into the driver's seat. He starts the drive out of the airport, but instead of heading south, he gets on the freeway to go north.

"Do I get any hints?"

"Nope."

While we're on the road, my phone dings with a text message.

Mateo: Do you have plans for Thanksgiving?

Me: I think we're just going to hang out at home.

Although we're living in the States, with neither of us being American, it's not a holiday we typically celebrate.

Mateo: My parents asked me to invite you to our house for dinner.

Me: Please thank them, but I'm going to have to pass.

Mateo: We still need to talk.

Me: Soon. TTYL.

I turn my phone off and slide it into my pocket. I want my full attention to be on Viktor and me.

We're pulling into a parking lot almost an hour later, and Viktor's surprise is revealed.

"Santa Monica pier," I exclaim. "I wish I brought my swimsuit."

"You did. I packed for us while you were busy with Lana and your mom."

We get out of the car, and Viktor grabs the bags from the trunk. Then, we find a public changing room.

"I'll meet you back here."

"Where do you think you're going?"

"To get changed." I point to the ladies' changing room.

"I don't like the idea of you going alone."

"It's not like you can come in with me," I say and roll my eyes.

Viktor doesn't move, but I see the wheels in his head spinning.

"Go get changed. I'll be out in a minute." I don't give him a chance to say anything before I disappear into the changing area.

I find an empty changing area and go in. Opening the bag, I see Viktor packed my black two-piece. There are also towels and sunscreen. Being fair-skinned with red hair, I burn easily. I change into my swimsuit and cover-up and go back out to find Viktor.

He's waiting for me a few steps away. Seeing him in only his swim trunks causes unrecognizable feelings to come to life.

"Oh my God. Check out the guy." Two girls stand next to me, talking to one another. "He's gorgeous."

"I know what I'd like to do with him." They both giggle.

That green-eyed monster called jealousy rears its ugly head. Now I know how Viktor feels when he says he can't stand if another guy looks at me. It takes a lot of self-control to not say anything rude to the girls. Instead, I walk over to my man, who puts his arm around me as we walk away.

"Was there a problem back there?" Viktor asks in a playful tone.

"Yes. I don't like it when other girls look at you."

"Are you jealous, *moya zirka*?"

"Very."

"There's no reason. I have eyes only for you."

We stop at the car to put our extra bag in. Then, hand-in-hand, we walk down the boardwalk and grab some fried food.

After we eat, Viktor rents an umbrella, and we find a spot on the beach. While Viktor digs the umbrella into the sand, I spread our blanket.

"Come here. Let me put sunscreen on you." I slide my cover-up off, and Viktor ensures every inch of my skin is properly protected before he puts his own on.

"Turn around. I'll get your back."

I squeeze some sunscreen into my hand and rub it over the taught muscles of Viktor's back. "What kind of bird is this?" I run my finger over the bird tattooed on his back.

"It's a Nightingale."

I move around to his front. "What does it mean?"

"Most people think of the bird as a shy bird that sings a beautiful song," he explains. "But when it's dark, the Nightingale sings its most beautiful melodies—ones that scare away its enemies."

I study his beautiful face for a moment. "That's you," I whisper. " My Nightingale."

He stands, offering me his hand. "Come swim with me."

I place my hand in his and follow Viktor into the cerulean blue ocean water. He leads us to where my feet can no longer touch the sand beneath us. But he never lets me go. Viktor pulls me to him, and I wrap my legs around his waist. I feel his arousal as he holds me against his body. Everything else fades away. It's just him and I riding the waves together. We stay in the water until the tips of our fingers are wrinkled before we make our way onto the sand.

Using my towel as a pillow, I lay back and relax. Viktor remains sitting.

"Lay down with me."

"I'm good."

I lean up on my elbow. "Don't you ever relax?"

Viktor looks down at me. "When I relax, people get hurt."

"That can't always be the case."

He doesn't answer. Instead, he returns to scanning the beach. Between the late night and the long drive today, I'm exhausted.

Knowing my Nightingale is watching over me, I let my eyes close and drift off to sleep.

Viktor

I'm thankful Amelia isn't weighed down by the scope of the potential danger that's always lurking in the shadows. I don't want her to live in fear, always looking over her shoulder. I want her just as she is—relaxed.

The late afternoon sun is now shining directly on Amelia, who's still sound asleep on her back. I put my towel over her exposed skin so she doesn't burn. A wave of fear washes over me while I watch my sleeping angel.

People I get close to have a habit of getting hurt or, worse, dead. Because of my inability to keep them safe, they end up leaving me. I brush a lock of hair from her face. I will not allow this woman to get hurt, but do I really have the power to stop it? Somehow, I must do better than I ever have. I have to prove to myself and everyone else that I'm capable of keeping my loved ones safe.

"Hey," Amelia whispers. "What's wrong?"

"Nothing." Which is true. At this moment, everything's right in my world.

She sits up. "Your face tells another story."

"Does it now?" I tilt my head. "Tell me what the story is."

Amelia adjusts her position to face me and studies my face closer. "There's worry and sadness. Fear."

"Why?"

"What do you mean, why?"

"Why so much fear?"

Where do I start? Most people look at me and see a heartless killer. Few people have cared enough to look past the façade. To see the man behind the mask. The man who also experiences normal human emotions and feelings. In one sentence, my soul's been ripped open and bared before her. I don't know if I should flee in fear or bow at her feet for actually seeing me.

"*Moya zirka*, we have so much to be afraid of."

She reaches out and takes my hand.

"Don't you see? As long as we're together, there's nothing that can hurt us."

With everything I am, I want to hold onto her words and pretend they're true. But I know they're not. In addition to the danger of being connected to Maxim, we also face a certain amount of danger from Maxim himself.

Lana finding out was one thing. She challenges her parents at every turn. Lana's never opposed to fighting her father for what she wants. My concern is whether or not Amelia will be able to handle Maxim's wrath when he finds out about us.

"Are you dry?" I ask in an attempt to lead the conversation to a different topic.

"Yes."

"Good, let's go get changed."

"We're leaving already?" Amelia pouts.

"No. We're just on to the next part of our adventure."

"What is it?"

I point to the pier's amusement park, where the lights start to turn on as the sun begins to set.

"We're going on the rides?"

"As long as you're okay with it."

"Yes." Her smile spreads across her face. "Lana took me to my first amusement park, and I loved it."

Together, we pack up from our afternoon on the beach. After we change out of our swimwear, we stroll down the boardwalk in search of the ticket stand, where we purchase several books of tickets.

"Can we ride the roller coaster first?"

"We can do anything you want."

We spend the next few hours riding all the rides, including the famous solar-powered Ferris wheel. Unfortunately, it's already late, and we still haven't done everything I had planned.

"How about we spend the night?"

"Really?"

I nod. Amelia's smile and happiness are infectious. They spark unfamiliar feelings inside me.

This dating thing is new to me, too. I've been with women, yes, but never for more than a few nights. I never met anyone worth keeping around until Natalie. And as much as I cared about her, in my heart, I knew she'd always belong to Alex. She would've learned to love me, but I'd always be her second choice.

But with Amelia, I'm her first choice. Something I see reflected in her gaze. Feel in her touch. All she wants is me. I hope she sees those same emotions reflected back at her. She's my future—my forever.

After a quick internet search, I find us an oceanfront room at a hotel a few beaches down. It's not too far out of the way, but at the same time, far enough from the pier that we won't be disturbed by the noise from the boardwalk.

This place is magnificent. Although it's a modern hotel, the chosen décor makes the rooms feel more like a bed and breakfast. We don't have direct beach access, but the open floor-to-ceiling arched windows allow the cool night breeze to flow through the room.

The dark walnut four-poster bed is on the wall across from the windows, so the first thing we'll see when we wake up is the glistening water of the Pacific Ocean. A cozy sitting area with two Chesterfield chairs and a small accent table is off to the side.

"Wow," Amelia says as she explores. "This is stunning." She opens the door to an attached bathroom with a large glass-enclosed walk-in shower and a huge soaking tub. "This is the only thing our house is missing." Amelia runs her hand along the tub. "I miss taking a long, hot soak."

"Why don't you do that now, and I'll order room service. I'm starving."

"Dinner sounds good."

"Is there anything special you'd like me to order?"

"I'm not picky. If you choose it, I'm sure I'll love it."

"Don't drown in there, okay?" I grin and close the bathroom door behind me.

Amelia

I turn the tap on and adjust the water until it's pleasantly hot. Then I pour in some of the lavender vanilla-scented bubble bath that's on the sink. While the tub fills, I strip out of my clothes and rinse the sand and sunscreen off them in the shower. I leave them to dry on the retractable clothesline.

With the tub nearly full, I lower myself into the bubbly water and practically moan in delight. Nothing beats soaking in a tub. I rest my head back and relax. Today's been so much fun.

"Amelia," Viktor calls from the other side of the door. "Dinner's here."

"Okay, be out in a minute." Regrettably, I let the water out of the tub and dry off with one of the soft, fluffy towels. Then it hits me. Viktor only packed for the day and the stuff I was wearing is currently still dripping in the shower. I slide on one of the hotel robes and join Viktor in the main room.

"Umm. We don't have any clean clothes."

"I didn't think about that. If you don't mind, we can wear the same outfits tomorrow. We spent most of the day in our swimsuits anyway."

"I don't have a problem with that, but I rinsed my clothes off." I hesitate. "I have nothing to wear to bed."

Viktor's eyes sparkle with mischief. "You can wear my T-shirt if you want."

"That'll work."

He pulls his shirt off, exposing his chiseled muscles. Part of me wants to forgo dinner, but my stomach grumbles in protest.

"Let me throw this on quick, and then we can eat."

Once again, I disappear into the bathroom. His T-shirt is soft and worn in, but the best part is that it smells of bergamot and citrus—Viktor.

When I open the door, Viktor's standing by the table where there are two place settings, glasses of sparkling water, and a lit candle in the center. Soft music plays from Viktor's phone.

Viktor's in the middle of lifting cloches off the plates. "I hope you like Sea Bass."

"Fish is one of my favorite meals."

The food is exquisite. I close my eyes and savor the flavors. All the while, Viktor watches my every move.

"What?" I ask with a smile.

"Sorry." He actually blushes. "I didn't mean to stare. I was just." He stops. "Nevermind."

"Just what?"

"Nothing."

It's the push and pull we've been playing at the past few weeks. Viktor's usually guarded and tense. Every now and then, he drops his guard and allows me a glimpse at the man behind the walls, but it never lasts for long. He quickly puts those walls back up, and I find myself on the outside once again. We finish dinner in awkward silence, and Viktor wheels the makeshift table outside our door.

"I'm going to take a quick shower," he says.

While he showers, I relax on the bed and pull out my phone. I see a missed text.

Natalie: How was your visit with Irina and Lana?

Me: We had a good time. Lana knows.

Natalie: It's usually hard to keep stuff from her. How did she take it?

Me: She was concerned about our age difference, but other than that, she seemed okay with it. She warned me that Dad was going to blow a gasket. Hopefully, we can keep this from him for a while longer. I'm not ready for that conversation yet.

Natalie: That's walking a fine line. The longer you keep it from him, the more betrayed he'll feel.

Me: I didn't think about it that way. We'll tell them soon, I promise. Guess what?

Natalie: What?

Me: Viktor surprised me with a trip to the Santa Monica pier. We ended up staying here overnight so we could go to the aquarium tomorrow.

Natalie: That sounds like fun.

Me: Viktor just finished his shower. Gotta run. TTYL.

When Viktor comes out of the bathroom, he's wearing nothing but his boxer shorts, and wow, he looks mouthwateringly delicious. Parts of my body I feared would never work correctly have sprung to life.

He doesn't say anything as he walks across the room to the bed, where he sits next to me.

"I like the way you look in my shirt."

"I like the way you look out of your shirt." I trail my fingers down his exposed chest, letting them go lower and lower until his hand captures mine.

"Amelia, I don't want to rush this."

"Right." I pull my hand away and sit up, turning my back on him. "We should've taken a room with two beds."

"Amelia."

"I get your hesitation. Your disgust because I'm not a virgin. I've been raped by more men than I can count. I don't have any idea how to be in a relationship or how to please you in bed." Tears fill my eyes. "If you're worried, I'll get you sick. I won't.

When I was at Jelena's Hope, they made sure I didn't have anything." Viktor walks around the bed, stopping in front of me. "And I'm on the pill, so I won't get pregnant."

"Look at me," he orders, but I refuse. He stoops down to my level and takes my face in his hands. "What happened to you was not your fault, and I'm not disgusted by you in any way. I don't ever want to hear you say that. Those bastards took your body without your permission. They may have taken the physical signs of your virginity. But in my eyes, until you willingly give yourself to a man, you're still a virgin."

He uses his thumbs to wipe the tears that are streaming down my cheeks. "I want you, Amelia. I want you so damn much, but I don't want your first time, our first time, to be rushed. You need to be sure this is what you want."

"Viktor," I murmur. "I've never been more sure of anything. I want to be with you."

He stands to his full height and walks over to the window. "You can't say that. You don't know me."

"Then, tell me." I follow, standing behind him. "I want to know everything about you. Show me. Let me see who you really are."

He turns around. "I like to be in charge, and I'm not gentle."

"Are you into that BDSM stuff too?" I've never been interested, but if that's what I need to learn to be with Viktor, I'm willing.

"No. But I do like certain things in the bedroom." He runs his hand over his head. "You're so young, and you've been through so much."

"That's in the past. It's over." I take a step closer to him, our bodies nearly touching. "This is now. We're now." I reach my hand out to touch his face. "Teach me how to be with you."

"I can't say no to you, Amelia."

In one move, he lifts me, and I wrap my legs around his waist. His lips are on mine. The kiss is intense and full of need. Both our needs. He doesn't break our connection as he walks to the bed, where he slides me down his front, setting me on my feet. "I'll be as gentle as possible," he says as he grabs the hem of his shirt, pulling it over my head. His eyes scan my naked body. "You're beautiful. Perfect."

He takes a step closer, and the back of my knees hits the bed. I lay back, propping myself on my elbows. I can't take my eyes off his body and the erection tenting his boxers.

"Lay back."

When I do, he spreads my legs, baring me to him. No one's ever given me a choice. I've only ever known violence. No man's ever looked at me with the same mix of lust and love that's on Viktor's face. It's an internal struggle, and I fight the urge to close my legs and hide my nakedness.

"Don't go there, Amelia. You're here with me." He lowers himself to his knees, and feathers kisses up first one leg and then the other. "If you're uncomfortable, tell me to stop. We will not do anything you don't want. Okay?"

When I don't respond, Viktor stops abruptly.

"Amelia, you have a choice in what we do or don't do. Let's try this again. This time, I need you to use your voice." He looks at me expectantly. "We will not do anything you don't want. If you're uncomfortable, all you need to say is stop."

"I understand, and I don't want you to stop."

He rewards me with a stunning smile and returns to kissing my leg, moving to my inner thigh, and then his tongue finds my center. I've never had a man's mouth on me. The feeling is unlike anything I've known. Viktor explores each part of me before his tongue finds my clit. He teases it gently with his tongue. I squirm from the intense pleasure, but he steadies me with his hands on my hips. Then, he increases the pressure, sucking and nipping at the sensitive area.

An unfamiliar sensation begins to build from somewhere deep inside. Sounds of pleasure escape my mouth. Then, he adds his fingers, moving them in and out while his tongue flicks my clit. My back arches as the feeling inside grows stronger.

The sensations are so overwhelming. It feels like I no longer have control over my body, and I experience a moment of panic.

Viktor must sense my fear. "That's it, *moya zirka*. Don't be afraid. Let it happen."

He nips my clit once more, and I shatter in his arms. An orgasm washes over me, taking control of every nerve ending in my body, and I cry out in pleasure. Viktor doesn't stop. He continues his licking and sucking, drawing out the intense pleasure. Just when I don't think I can handle it a second longer, he stops.

"You taste exquisite and look beautiful when you come for me," he says as he stands and positions himself over me.

I can't speak. My senses are overwhelmed by the high I've just experienced. Then, he kisses me, letting me taste my essence on his lips.

"Was that your first?"

"Yes."

"It won't be your last." He smiles. "Are you sure you're ready?"

"Yes, please. I want to feel you inside me."

He leans back and takes his rigid length into his hand. Then, he slowly breaches my entrance and stills.

"Are you okay?

"I've had men inside me, but never willingly. All the way back to Seth, no one ever asked or cared if I was okay. Instead, they derived pleasure from my pain. My past and present collide. I swallow over the lump in my throat, trying my best to not be overcome with emotion. "Yes. I'm okay."

I hold onto his arms as he slowly pushes himself further in. His piercing blue gaze locks onto mine. His eyes say what words don't—I'm not alone. We're here together, and he'll never hurt me.

Viktor's my rock as I fight against the horrific memories trying to claw their way into the forefront of my mind. I can't let them win. They have no place in this moment.

Once he's fully sheathed inside me, he stops again. This time, lowering his forehead to mine. He's allowing my physical body to adjust to the new sensations.

Then, ever so slowly, he begins moving his hips. The gentle friction reignites my senses, and I feel that same tingling building up again. Viktor lowers his head, kissing me passionately. My hands roam his chest, shoulders, and arms, reveling in the feel of his toned muscles that flex with each move.

This is the first time I'm willingly giving myself to a man. I want to experience every move, feel every sensation to its fullest, and commit them to memory. Viktor never stops touching or kissing me. Never breaks our physical connection.

"Come for me again," he says, his voice deep and gravely.

"I don't know how," I whimper.

His hand goes between us as he rubs my clit, bringing me closer and closer.

"Just like that. Don't be afraid. I'll catch you when you fall."

His reassurance was what I needed to let go. To allow pleasure to take over my body, knowing I'm safe to fall apart in his arms.

Viktor keeps his movements still slow and gentle, but I feel the strain in his muscles. He's holding back.

I cup his cheek in my palm. "It's okay. You don't have to be so careful."

"I don't want to hurt you."

"You could never hurt me. I want to feel you—all of you."

With my permission, Viktor picks up the intensity of his movements. With each thrust, my body welcomes him deeper. I didn't think it was possible, but I feel another orgasm building.

"Come with me, moya zirka."

He thrusts one more time, and I let go. Viktor follows me over the edge. His body pulses inside mine. I'm overwhelmed by both the physical sensations and emotions of the moment. The feeling of our bodies and hearts joining together. Tears stream down my face.

"Did I hurt you?" Viktor asks nervously and tries to move off me.

"No. You didn't." I hold him as tight as I can. "Please don't move yet. Let me feel you for another minute longer."

He lowers his mouth to mine and gently kisses my lips. "I love you, Amelia Solonik."

"I LOVE YOU WITH ALL MY HEART, VIKTOR DOBROW."

Her words burrow deep inside me to a place of vulnerability I hide from most people. But instead of keeping her out, I let her in.

I've only told one other woman I loved her, but she couldn't return my affection. The hurt and loneliness that resided deep inside didn't abate.

But tonight, Amelia's love fills the deep void I've carried with me for years. For the first time in my life, I feel like a whole man. A man worthy of the love Amelia's so freely giving.

Carefully, I withdraw from Amelia's body and position myself next to her. I keep my arm wrapped tightly around her, and she nestles herself against me. She lays her head on my chest, and I rub lazy circles on her back as we bask in the afterglow of what we've just shared.

At some point, we fall asleep, our bodies entwined with one another.

The sun shining through the window wakes me, and for the briefest of moments, I fear last night was nothing more than a dream. But then, I feel her breath on my chest. Amelia's still here in my arms.

"Good morning," she whispers, her voice sleepy.

"It's the best morning." I smile.

"Is it now? Why?"

"Because you're here, next to me."

"I think I can make it even better."

I'm already hard as she pushes herself up, straddling my body. I steady her as she lowers herself over my erection. Her head falls back with a quiet moan, and I take the opportunity to appreciate every inch of her perfect body.

When she opens her eyes, I see the fear. Her body tenses. "What do I do?"

"Move yourself up and down. Like this."

With my hands on her hips, I lift and lower her gently.

"This is so much more intense. I feel you everywhere."

She continues the movement on her own. As she experiments with the pace, I slide my hands up her abdomen to her breasts and roll her hard nipples between my fingers. Then, lifting my head, I take one into my mouth, sucking and nipping. She mewls in pleasure.

"I'm so close already."

I want to come with her. I lift my hips, pushing myself deeper. She fumbles with the new rhythm. I hold her hips, taking control of the pace.

"You feel so good, Viktor."

"You feel us, *moya zirka*. We're perfect together." I thrust hard. "You were made for me. You. Are. Mine." As soon as the words leave my lips, I come hard. Her orgasm squeezes my body, drawing out our shared pleasure.

She lays forward on my chest. "I am yours. Always."

As much as I want to spend the rest of the day in bed

worshiping her body, we have to get up. I purchased tickets to visit the aquarium this afternoon.

"Shower with me." I take her hand and lead her into the bathroom.

After I adjust the water, I step aside to let her enter first. We stand under the rainhead shower, letting the warm water fall over us. I know we should get on with the shower, but I can't help myself. I lift her, and she instinctively wraps her legs around my waist. I back her up against the tiles as I slide into her. She holds onto my shoulders as I take her hard and fast.

"Oh my God, Viktor. You feel—"

"Is it too much?"

She squeezes her legs tight. "No. Don't stop."

The pulsing of her body sets off my orgasm. My muscles tense as I spill into her. I hold her tight against me until her breathing returns to normal. Then, I carefully lower her until her feet touch the shower floor.

Amelia reaches around me to grab the body wash, squirting some into her palm. Then she washes my body. Her petite hands rub over my chest and down my sides. Amelia lowers herself to her knees as she tenderly washes my legs and my cock, which is hard and ready to take her again.

When she's through, I help her to her feet and take my turn washing her. Our caring actions transform a regular shower into an intimate and profoundly connecting experience.

Amelia

Last night and this morning were more than I could've ever hoped for. My past experiences with sex have been unwilling and violent. They were full of pain from forceful taking.

Viktor was none of that. He was gentle and giving. I've never had a man's mouth explore my most intimate areas. I've never been granted pleasure. And when he finally penetrated me, it wasn't to gain some sick power over me. It was a consensual joining of two bodies—two souls.

Viktor told me he likes to be in control in the bedroom. That he's not gentle. Which makes last night even more special. Everything he did was for me. He set aside his own wants and needs to ensure my first time was perfect.

I was afraid to open my eyes this morning. Scared when I did, I'd realize everything was a dream. But it wasn't. Viktor's arm was still wrapped around me. My legs tangled with his, and my head on his chest, listening to the steady beat of his heart.

"I almost don't want to go back home," I say as I finish toweling off after our shower.

"Don't think about it right now. Let's focus on enjoying

today." He passes me my clothes, which thankfully dried overnight. "Are you hungry?"

"I'm starving."

"I'm sorry. I shouldn't have been so selfish."

"I'm not sorry. I enjoyed every second." I smile. "I hope we do it again."

Viktor wraps his arms around my waist and pulls me up against him. "I can promise you we'll do it again. But right now, we're going to eat."

We found a cute little café with outdoor seating, where we enjoyed a delicious lunch. Now, we're at the aquarium learning about the area's wildlife and the aquarium's efforts to ensure the watersheds in the region remain a clean and healthy environment.

Viktor's like a little boy at the touch tank. He can't contain his smile when a hermit crab crawls over his hand, and he's surprised by the softness of the chocolate chip starfish. He's shocked to learn there's something called a sea cucumber and that some people consider it a delicacy.

Before we leave, we aquadopt a Swell Shark pup. On our next trip back, we'll be able to schedule a private feeding with our adopted animal. Then, we do some souvenir shopping before walking back to the car.

"Thank you for today."

"You don't have to thank me."

"I don't have to. I want to."

"I intend to give you the world, Amelia."

"All I want is you."

"I don't deserve you."

I hate that he feels unworthy of love. "You deserve every good thing in life."

And I plan to prove that to him.

Amelia

VIKTOR AND I DECIDE TO CELEBRATE THANKSGIVING BY ordering pizza and cuddling up on the couch to watch movies. We're halfway through *Son-in-Law* when Viktor's phone rings with a video call request.

"It's Natalie," he says, tapping the green button on his screen connecting the call.

"Happy Thanksgiving," Natalie says. "I hope we didn't interrupt your dinner."

"We didn't do the whole turkey thing. We ordered pizza."

"Pizza for Thanksgiving?" Alex asks, shocked.

"You forget, neither of us are born and bred American," Viktor says with a smile.

"How are you feeling, Nat?"

"Nauseous."

"Being pregnant doesn't sound appealing at all." I scrunch my nose.

"It's all worth it when you get that new baby."

"I guess."

"Rose has been asking to talk to you both," Natalie says. "Hang on while I get her."

She lays her phone down, and our view switches to the ceiling while they try to corral their daughter. I hit the mute button. "Are you okay with this?"

"I am." Viktor grabs my hand. "What's more important is if you're okay with it?"

"Alex and Natalie mean a lot to both of us. I want them to be a part of our lives. As long as you do."

"They're like family to me, but I know Natalie and I have a complicated history," Viktor says. "I don't want you to be uncomfortable."

"You were Natalie's rock when her life was in ruins. I know what you mean to one another and that you'll always have a special bond. I'd never ask you to change that."

Viktor cups my face in his palm before kissing me. "Your compassion and understanding amaze me, *moya zirka*."

"We've got her," Alex says, the camera view returning to them.

I take us off mute.

"Hi there, Rosie-girl. Auntie Melia misses you."

"I miss you too, Auntie Melia." Rose's voice melts my heart.

"Guess who's here with me?"

"*Dedushka?*"

"Nope, even better." I turn the phone, so she can see Viktor.

"Friker," Rose squeals.

"*Privet, printessa. Ya skuchayu po tebe.*"

"*Ya tozhe soskuchilsya,*" Rose answers.

"Wow, her Russian's coming along really well." I'm impressed.

"She picks it up so easy," Natalie says. "I wish I could do it as well as she does."

"I wish you guys could come out for a visit."

"We can try to plan something after you're back from Christmas break."

I look at Viktor. "I'm not going home for break. The band has a few shows over the holiday."

"Have you told Max yet?" Alex asks.

"Nope." There's a lot I haven't told him yet.

"I'm assuming he doesn't know about the two of you yet?"

"We're not in a rush for that conversation," Viktor says.

"You two are set on this relationship?"

Viktor puts his arm around me. "Yes."

"You have our full support," Natalie adds.

"Thank you. That means the world to us."

Natalie shows us her ultrasound photos. The baby looks like something from an alien movie, but I tell her how adorable they are anyway. Regardless of its current alien status, in a few months, it will be my adorable little niece or nephew.

"It's been great talking to you, but we have to get going," Viktor says. "We're in the middle of a movie marathon."

"We'll plan a get-together soon."

We say our goodbyes and get back to our movie.

The weekend goes by way too quickly. We spent most of it exploring one another's bodies. But today, we have to go back to the real world. We're meeting the guys at Mr. Hart's office to discuss the contract Death Rat's been offered.

I spent hours last night trying to decide what to wear. As usual, Viktor said everything looked great. After the fifth outfit, he was done with the fashion show. He scooped me up and carried me to his room, where he spent the rest of the night showing me how much he prefers me without clothes. The memory makes me smile.

It took a bit, but I decided to go with my denim skirt and a black tank top that exposes my mid-drift. I pull my hair back into a ponytail and put some make-up on. Then, I grab my black Chucks and am ready to go.

As usual, Viktor's ready to go before me and is waiting on the balcony.

"Ready?" I ask as I step outside.

"I am, but you're not."

"What do you mean? I love my outfit." I give a quick twirl.

He pulls me onto his lap. "Every man in that room won't be able to take his eyes off you, which will bring up violent urges in me."

His overprotectiveness and jealousy are a turn-on. "But the only man in the room I care about is you."

"Can I convince you to put on a different outfit? Something that covers some more skin?"

"Nope." I hop off his lap. "Now, let's go, or we'll be late."

Viktor

As I suspected, all eyes are on Amelia when she walks into the meeting room. Mateo gets up from his seat and gives her a hug.

"You look great." He doesn't hide his perusal of her body.

"Um. Thanks." She walks around him to an empty chair. I take a seat beside her.

Mateo's father, the band's attorney, sits across from me.

"It's nice to see you, Amelia," Mr. Hart says.

"You too, sir."

"Amelia, this is Jennifer Carlisle. She's the attorney for Zapped Euforia."

"It's very nice to meet you."

"You too," Jennifer says, turning her attention to me. "And you are?"

"Viktor."

"Are you Ms. Solonik's personal counsel?"

"Yes."

Amelia squeezes my leg under the table. I grab her hand and thread my fingers with hers.

"Now that we're all here. Let's get started." Jennifer picks up a stack of papers. "Please take a copy and pass them around. Mr.

Hart, you've already had the opportunity to go over these. Are there any changes you'd like made?"

"No. Everything's been written up as we discussed. Death Rat." He stops and clears his throat. "Will be the opening act for Zapped Euforia for the duration of their nationwide stadium tour. There will be a total of twenty shows."

"When does the tour start?" Viktor asks.

"It kicks off the first weekend in May."

"That's before the spring semester is over."

"Will that be a problem?"

"No, it won't," Amelia answers before I have the chance to speak.

I give her a questioning glance but don't say anything. How's she going to manage school, the spring recital, and traveling with the band? Unless. No. She wouldn't consider quitting school, would she?

"Mr. Hart, can you review the contract details before we make a final decision?"

"Everett, please. And certainly."

Over the next twenty minutes, he explains each detail of the pending contract, including show dates, travel expenses, and compensation.

"Do you feel this offer is in the band's best interest?"

"It's a fair offer and an incredible opportunity for them." He looks at the boys and Amelia. "If you're all comfortable with this, we can sign today."

They offer a resounding yes. Despite my reservations, Amelia joins the rest of the group in signing the contract.

"Congratulations," Jennifer says as she gathers her things and stands. "Rowan Ford, Zapped Eupforia's rep, will be in touch with you in the next few weeks."

"I'll see Ms. Carlisle out," Everett says. "I'll be back in a few minutes."

Once they leave, the boys start high-fiving each other and hugging Amelia.

"This is our big break, guys," Quincy says. "Next tour, we'll be the headliners."

The five of them chat excitedly, making plans for an updated set list and a rehearsal schedule. From the sound of it, most of Amelia's holiday break will be filled with band activities.

Everett Hart returns to the room, closing the door behind him. "Congratulations. You've all worked very hard for this. I'm proud of you. My secretary's making copies of your press schedule. There are photo shoots, interviews, and several other events scheduled over the next few months."

"Interviews, for what?" Mateo asks.

"Press interviews to hype up Death Rat for the tour."

"Cool."

"We need to leave," I whisper to Amelia. "There are a few things we have to discuss."

"If there's nothing else, we have to be going," Amelia addresses the room, then we excuse ourselves.

It's a quiet walk back to the car. I'm trying to keep my temper under control—something that's proving rather difficult at the current moment.

"You're mad," Amelia says once we're on the road.

"Mad? I'm more than mad." I grip the steering wheel tighter. "How do you plan on finishing your semester and going on tour?"

"I'm not going back to school in the spring."

Amelia

"Th at's not an option," Viktor says through gritted teeth.

"Excuse me?"

"You're not dropping out of school." He raises his voice.

"I'm the one who gets to decide that, remember?" I cross my arms. "What am I going to do with a degree in classical music other than maybe teach?"

"What's wrong with teaching?"

"Nothing's wrong with it. But I don't want to teach." I turn slightly in my seat. "Being in a band was never on my radar. Heck, there's a lot in my life right now that was never on my radar. But I love the direction I'm headed."

"What if this band thing doesn't work out?"

"I'll figure that out then."

Viktor's silent for several minutes. His hands relax on the steering wheel, which is a good sign. I understand this decision seemed sudden, but it's something I've been thinking about for a few days.

Sparrow texted last week with a heads-up about the tour dates. I didn't say anything right away. I wanted the chance to think through everything on my own. When the subject came up today, I already knew my answer.

Playing in this band has been a dream come true—a dream I didn't even know I had. But one I'm not ready to walk away from. I'm confident Viktor will come around. My parents? They're going to take some more convincing.

Viktor still hasn't said anything when we pull up at home. Unfortunately, the rest of the conversation is going to have to wait. I have an online class in ten minutes.

I grab my earbuds and laptop and head out to the balcony. There's no reason not to enjoy the afternoon sunshine while I'm in class.

My thoughts drift while the professor lectures. If I can take more classes online, I can possibly stay in school part-time while we're touring. That might smooth things over with everyone. But is that what I want?

Life's going to be crazy with rehearsals, shows, and traveling. I want to make sure there's time for Viktor and me to spend together as well. If I stay in school, that's going to significantly decrease my free time. I decide to stick to my plan of dropping out. Everyone else will have to get used to it.

Before I know it, class is over, and I'm bringing my laptop back to my room. Viktor stops me on the way.

"I packed us a picnic. How about we have an early dinner by the water?"

"That sounds perfect. I just have to put this away first."

This is a good sign that he's ready to talk. I hope he sees things my way. I'm going to need as many people in my corner as possible.

Viktor

WHILE AMELIA'S IN CLASS, I KEEP BUSY IN THE kitchen. Cooking gives me something to focus on besides my anger. Amelia made a major life decision, something that will affect us both, without even mentioning it to me. If this is going to work, we need to have better communication.

My timing is perfect. I finish packing the cooler just as Amelia steps into the kitchen.

"I've packed us a picnic. How about we have an early dinner by the water?"

"That sounds perfect. I just have to put this away first."

It only takes a few seconds before she's ready. She grabs the bag, I take the cooler, and then we head to the beach. After we get the blanket laid out, Amelia opens the cooler and sets out our food. It isn't anything extravagant. We're having tuna sandwiches and a salad.

"I'm sorry for not telling you about the tour dates and my decision to quit school," she says. "There's no excuse. I was wrong."

"If we're going to be together, we have to talk about these things before making a decision."

"I was afraid you'd say no."

"Amelia." I take her hand. "I'll always be in your corner. But I'm not going to lie. I'm starting to worry about how your parents will handle all this."

"Me too. It's going to be a shock, but they'll get used to it."

"What idea are you referencing? Us or quitting school?"

"Both." She gives me a small smile.

"You're going to have to tell them about holiday break soon."

"I'll call them tomorrow," she sighs. "I'm not looking forward to it."

"We'll call it a warm-up for when we tell them about us."

"Hey guys," Amelia says, looking over my shoulder. "What are you two doing here?"

I turn around and see Sparrow and Mateo walking toward us.

"You forgot your copy of the contract," Mateo says. "And I thought maybe we could talk."

I know Mateo wants to talk to her about what happened at the party.

"Sparrow and I can take this stuff back up to the house," I suggest. "If that's okay with you."

Amelia nods.

I lean close to her. "I'll be watching from the house and can be here in seconds if you need me." Then, I stand and grab the cooler. "Come on, Sparrow, there's extra sandwiches in the house."

Amelia

"Here's your contract." Mateo hands me a manilla envelope.

"Thanks." I set it down on the blanket next to me.

"We can't keep ignoring what happened."

"There's been a lot going on." I shrug.

"I went too fast. I realize that. I know something bad happened to you," Mateo says. "Will you tell me what it was?"

This is something I've worked tirelessly on in my sessions—telling my story. I knew it'd eventually come up in conversation with someone at some point. But I also knew no matter how much I prepared for this moment, it wouldn't make it any easier. Ania has stressed that I'm in control of what details I share. Not everyone is entitled to know everything.

"I was fifteen when my parents died. Within a matter of hours, I became an orphan and a foster child."

Most people would think that was the worst part of the story, but it only goes downhill from there.

"While I was in foster care, I was raped." Mateo listens quietly. Although the circumstances were different, our stories share a lot of similarities. I skip the parts about being trafficked. It's not something I feel comfortable sharing with him. "I ran away and lived on the streets. Eventually, I met Max and Irina. They're good people. They've given me a home and a family. I was lucky."

"Lucky? Shit, Amelia. There's nothing lucky about any of that."

"I'm not saying my story was all rainbows and unicorns. My past will always taunt me, but I do my best to not let it rule my life. I'm in a good place now." I glance toward the house and see Viktor and Sparrow sitting on the deck.

"Sparrow told me you know about my past."

"I do."

"You and I are so much alike." Mateo gets on his knees. "We're made for each other."

"Mateo—"

"Wait." He puts up his hand. "I know you aren't in love with me right now, but I think if you give it some time, give us some time, I'll prove that I'm worthy of your love."

"You don't have to prove anything to me. You're worthy of love." I take a deep breath. "But time isn't going to change anything. I'm in love with someone else."

"Don't tell me. You think you're in love with Viktor?" He lets out a frustrated breath. "You have to realize he's way too old for you. What could you possibly have in common?" He takes my hands in his. "My family has money. I can give you the world, Amelia. You just have to let me."

"I'm so sorry. I don't want to hurt you."

"Then don't." His grey eyes fill with tears. "Give me a chance, please."

Mateo's pleas are sincere. I have no doubt about that. I don't want to hurt him more than he's already hurting. But I can't give him what he's asking.

"Please try to understand. There's nothing wrong with you. You're a nice guy. But all we'll ever be is friends."

Tears are now pouring down his face. "If you give us some more time, I'll show you—"

"Viktor and I are together."

"There's no way he can make you happy," he spits out the words.

"I get it if you need some time and space. I want to stay friends."

Mateo stands up. His sadness has shifted to anger. "A friend, that's all I'll ever be to you. Well, that's not enough for me," he yells. "I need you to love me, not him." He points toward the house.

Viktor and Sparrow both jump from their chairs.

I get to my feet. "Mateo, please calm down. You're a nice guy. You'll find someone—"

"I don't want *someone*. I want you." He grabs my hand. "Come with me. Let me show you."

"Let me go." I try to pull my hand away.

"I want to take you out. Show you that I'm the right man for you, not Viktor. He's twice your age. He can't make you happy. He—."

"Take your hands off her." Viktor comes from nowhere and pushes Mateo away from me. He holds my trembling body close to his. "Can't you see you're scaring her?"

"I'm sorry, Amelia," Mateo cries. His anger is gone, replaced once again by grief. "I don't want to scare you. I just want a chance. Can you give me a chance?"

I tuck myself into Viktor's side and cry.

"Mateo, come on." Sparrow tugs on his arm. "It's time to go."

"Sparrow, tell her. Tell her I'm not going to hurt her."

"She knows that."

"Then why won't she love me?" Mateo grabs Sparrow's shirt. "Why won't she love me?"

"You can't force someone to love you. I know that all too well," he says quietly. "Come on, let me take you home."

As Sparrow leads Mateo away, he keeps repeating, "Why won't she love me?"

I may not love him the way he wants me to, but I do care about him. I don't like seeing him hurting.

"He'll be okay," Viktor reassures me.

"Are you sure?"

"It might take him some time to process everything. But I'm sure."

Viktor

Watching a distraught Mateo being led away by Sparrow is a gut-wrenching sight. I've been in his shoes and understand the heartache he's experiencing. Loving someone who doesn't love you back is a hard road to walk. But Mateo's young, and he has a strong support system. I'm confident he'll be okay.

Amelia's shaken up by the whole situation. Once they're out of sight, I scoop her into my arms and carry her into the house. She keeps her head tucked against my chest as I walk past what used to be her room and lay her on my bed. I lay beside her and open my arms, allowing her to curl up next to me. I kiss the top of her head but make no move to do anything more. Amelia needs the intimacy of the moment to feel safe and cherished.

Amelia's ringtone wakes me up, and I slide the phone from her pocket. The clock on her lock screen shows it's nine p.m.

"Amelia, wake up." I shake her shoulder gently. "It's your father."

"What?" She blinks her eyes a few times as she wakes up.

"It's Max. You better answer it." I pass her the phone.

She puts the call on speaker. "Hello?" Her voice is groggy.

"*Moya malen'kaya ptichka*, did I wake you?"

"I was watching television and didn't realize I fell asleep."

"Are you feeling well?"

"Yes," she says and sits up. "I've been studying for finals and had a big paper, that's all."

"And that is why I am calling. Your semester ends next Tuesday, correct?"

"Um. Yeah." She looks at me, her eyes wide.

"I will have the jet at LAX early Wednesday morning."

"There's something I need to tell you," she says hesitantly.

"Go ahead."

"I'm not coming home for the holiday break."

We hold a collective breath and wait for his response.

"I see. And why not?"

"I have some big performances coming up in the spring. Several of us decided to stay back to rehearse over the holiday break." She's walking a fine line with the truth.

"Your mom will be disappointed."

"I know, and I apologize. But this is really important to me."

"I applaud your dedication to your craft."

Amelia lowers her head. I know she feels guilty for not telling him the whole truth.

"Is Viktor around? I want to speak to him."

"Yeah, he's right here." She takes the phone off speaker and passes it to me. "Dad wants to talk to you."

"Hey, boss. What's up?"

"Did you know she was not coming home for the holiday?"

"She mentioned it to me, yes. But she requested I allow her to tell you." And right now, I'm questioning if I should've insisted she tell him the whole story.

"I see." Although I can't physically see him, I can hear the gears turning in his head. "These kids she is rehearsing with. Have you done background checks on them?"

"Yes, boss."

"And they are, okay?"

"They're good kids."

"I am expecting you to keep her safe."

"Yes, sir. She's never out of my sight."

Amelia smiles at me, and I see mischief dancing in her eyes. What is she up to? My silent question is answered a second later when she slides out of bed and takes off her clothes. My body responds immediately, and I struggle to keep my composure.

"Is she doing well otherwise?"

"She's doing terrific."

After her sexy strip tease, she crawls across the bed and works at the button on my jeans.

"She's adjusted to California life just fine."

I lift my hips so she can pull my pants off. My erection juts from my boxers. She looks at me and smiles before she licks across the slit where there's already a drop of pre-cum. It takes every ounce of willpower I possess not to groan in pleasure. Amelia's never done this before, and she chooses right now?

"Is there anything she needs?"

"Nope." I cough as she takes the tip into her mouth. My head drops back as she takes more of my cock.

"Is she there? I would like to say goodbye to her."

"Sure."

"Your dad wants to say goodbye," I say with a wicked grin.

She sits back on her heels and takes the offered phone.

Two can play this game, *moya zirka*.

"Hi again."

I pull her to me and take a nipple in my mouth.

She gasps. "No, Dad. I'm fine. I almost dropped the phone."

While my mouth gives one breast attention, my free hand moves between her legs and finds her already wet.

"I miss you too." Her voice squeaks. "Dad, I'm exhausted. I

want to turn in early tonight." She pauses while Maxim speaks. I can't make out what he's saying. "I love you too. Give Mom a hug for me."

She doesn't wait for him to say goodbye before she disconnects the call and tosses her phone to the side.

"You played a dangerous game, *moya zirka*."

"Did I?" She bites her bottom lip and feigns innocence. "What are you going to do about it?"

Challenge accepted.

Amelia squeals when I flip her onto her back without warning. I continue teasing her clit with my fingers. Sweet sounds of pleasure slip from her lips as I worship her body.

"I want you." She tries to wrap her legs around me.

"Not yet."

She groans, and I add a second finger, sliding it into her. She has no idea how fucking sexy she is as I bring her to the edge of orgasm and then stop.

"Viktor, please."

"I love hearing you beg for me," I say a second before thrusting into her. "Is that what you wanted?"

"Oh my God, yes."

I'm not gentle as I thrust in and out. "Tell me to stop if it's too much."

"No, please don't stop." She pants.

I take her mouth, needing to be connected to her in as many areas as possible. She holds onto my shoulders and meets me thrust for thrust. Her body begins to tense—her orgasm is close. I see the nervousness in her beautiful brown eyes that often happens. The loss of control she feels at that moment is a struggle for her.

"That's it, *moya zirka*. I've got you. Let go." I thrust hard and deep, and she shatters beneath me. "Fuck, Amelia." Her body tightens around me, and I release with a forceful, shuddering climax deep within her.

Amelia

I'VE SPENT THE LAST WEEK CRAMMING FOR MY FINALS. As happy as I am that the semester's over, I know when I leave the campus today, I won't be returning. It's bittersweet saying goodbye to this short chapter of my life, but I'm also excited about what lies ahead.

Christmas is only two weeks away. Growing up in Australia, Christmas was during our summer, so I was used to a warm weather holiday. However, living in Russia for the past few years, I quickly got used to a cold holiday season. Somehow, the snow made everything feel more Christmas-y. Now, I'm back in a warm weather climate for Christmas, and I'm finding it challenging to stir up the holiday spirit.

We're driving home when I ask, "Can we get a Christmas tree?"

"Of course. You don't have to ask."

"I didn't know how you'd feel about it."

"Do you want an artificial tree or a real tree?"

"I'd love a real one." I have many lovely memories of childhood Christmases with my parents in Australia. After I was adopted by Max and Irina, we celebrated twice—the traditional

Christmas for me and the Orthodox Christmas they were used to celebrating. "But we don't have any decorations."

"Sounds like we need to go shopping. You up for it today?"

"Sure."

Before we go home, we hit the stores and pick up lights, ornaments, and tons of decorations for both inside and outside the house. The next stop is a Christmas tree lot where we pick out the most beautiful Frazier Fur I've ever laid eyes on. I take pictures while Viktor ties it to the top of the car. I've learned nothing in life is permanent, so I try to capture every memory in photos.

It's been a long day, and neither of us feels like cooking. So, we order Chinese take-out. We're sitting on the living room floor, eating at the coffee table, trying to decide the best place to put the tree.

"How about we try it in front of the windows?" I suggest

While I clean up from dinner, Viktor lifts the seven-foot tree and sets it in front of the windows. Standing back, I examine it from all angles.

"It blocks the view of the ocean."

"How about the corner over there," Viktor suggests.

"I feel bad putting something so beautiful in a corner." I crinkle my forehead.

"It's not like we're hiding it." Viktor chuckles. "It'll be visible as soon as you walk into the house and won't block the view outside."

"Let's try it and see."

He lifts the large tree again and carries it across the room, where he sets it down in the corner. After he straightens the tree in the stand and makes sure it's secure, he steps out of the way.

"What do you think?"

"I think I love it." I smile.

Viktor strings the lights on the tree, wrapping them around each branch to ensure an even distribution. When he finishes, we hang the ornaments together. While I make popcorn to string, Viktor puts lights around our windows. In a matter of a few hours, we transform our house into a Christmas wonderland.

Viktor

THE HOLIDAYS BRING UP A LOT OF MEMORIES FOR Amelia. She's been struggling with missing her birth parents. Since my parents died, I've only celebrated Christmas one time with Natalie and Rose. With both of us having a hard time getting into the Christmas spirit, I thought I'd plan something fun for us to do. A way we can begin to make happy memories. So, while I'm outside hanging lights, I make the necessary arrangements.

When I come back in, I find Amelia sitting cross-legged on the sofa, stringing popcorn. I grab a handful from the bowl and sit next to her.

"Hey. That's for the tree, not your stomach," Amelia scolds me.

"It's for eating too." I feed her a piece. "I made plans for us for the next few days. You're going to need to pack a bag."

"Where are we going?"

"South."

She freezes. A look of terror blankets her face.

"What's wrong?" Amelia doesn't move or answer. With one word, I've triggered her panic. I take the needle and string from her hand and drop them into the bowl, which I put on the coffee table. Then, I turn her to face me. "Amelia, you have to talk to me."

"Mexico." The word is barely audible.

"No, *moya zirka*." I pull her onto my lap. "I would never bring you to Mexico. We're going to San Diego for a few days."

It takes a minute, but she finally relaxes in my arms.

"I'm sorry," she whispers. "I ruined your surprise."

"Don't apologize. Nothing's been ruined. You still don't know what we're doing there." I plant a quick kiss on her lips.

"I guess we need to finish this popcorn garland if we're to pack tonight." She points to a second needle next to the bowl on the table. "Let's get moving."

We're both still learning her triggers. And thanks to Ania, I'm also learning better ways to help ground her when she panics. I don't want anything we do to cause her stress.

The drive to San Diego should only take about two hours, but this west coast traffic is worse than New York. It ends up taking us nearly three and a half hours before we pull up to the resort located on Coronado Island. We're met by the bellhop who takes our luggage. The valet is right behind him, waiting to park our car. With Amelia's hand in mine, we go to the check-in desk to get our key cards.

We're staying in a luxury beachfront villa that reminds me of the one I stayed in while I was in Grenada. The open plan features a high-end kitchen, a sitting room with modern furniture, and a fireplace. The wall of floor-to-ceiling windows offers an unobstructed view of the ocean.

The separate bedroom boasts a California King facing the oceanfront view. A set of French doors open to a private balcony with loungers and a hot tub. The ensuite bathroom boasts a marble shower big enough to fit several people.

"Wow. This place is incredible.."

"You deserve only the best, *moya zirka*." I wrap my arms around her.

"I don't care where we are as long as we're together."

Amelia's the daughter of a man with an endless amount of money. Yet none of that seems to matter to her. Unless she's forced, she doesn't buy extravagant things. That makes it even more special to bring her to these places because she truly appreciates the beauty of everything around her.

"So," She turns in my arms to face me. "What are our plans for tonight?"

"Tonight, we're staying in."

"Oh?"

"I have plans that involve only you and me tonight." I push a stray curl behind her ear. "But let's not waste the day. Want to go to the beach for a while?"

"Absolutely."

We may live on a beach, but I don't think either of us would pass up a day on the sand by the water. We'll miss oceanfront life when it's time to leave Long Beach for her tour.

Amelia

I DIDN'T THINK A BEACH COULD BE MORE PRISTINE L than the one we live on, but it is. The sand here literally sparkles in the sunlight, and the water is the most beautiful shade of cyan. I could lie here, entranced by the hypnotizing sound of the waves lapping at the sea's edge, and I'd never tire of the sound.

Coronado Island offers the best of both worlds with its magnificent sunrise and sunset views. And right now, we're being treated to a sunset show as the sky turns shades of pink, orange, and yellow. Just like our first night in California, we stay on the beach until the sky turns dark and the stars come out. Then, we make our way back into our villa.

Viktor doesn't know, but a few weeks ago, I bought lingerie. It's a black lace chemise with a matching thong. While I was held at Moreno's, I was forced to wear lingerie that was humiliating and degrading. Thinking about it brings back the memories of being raped. I bought this with the hope of taking back something else that was stolen from me. I've had it tucked away in my drawer, trying to get the courage to wear it.

Thankfully, Ania can't tell my parents anything we talk about. She's been a constant source of support for me when it comes to this new relationship. I told her about the lingerie and my fears surrounding it. Replacing the traumatic memories with new, happy memories is something we've been working on. She said I'd know when the right time was, and I think tonight's it.

"I'm going to take a quick shower." I grab my pj's with the lingerie balled up inside.

"Do you mind if I order dinner?"

"Please do." I smile and disappear into the bathroom to wash away the sunscreen and sand.

After drying off, I look at the options for getting dressed. I can put on my usual pair of sleep shorts and Viktor's T-shirt, or I can overcome my fear and wear the lingerie. I stand in front of the mirror wrapped in a towel, weighing my options for what feels like an eternity. Finally, I reach out and grab the lingerie.

Tonight's the night. Then, with one last deep breath, I open the bathroom door. Viktor's lounging on the bed, looking at something on his phone. He looks up when I close the door.

"Amelia," he says my name almost reverently and sits up. "Wow. You look— Umm. You look incredible." He sets his phone aside and motions for me to go to him.

"You like it?" I ask as I walk around the bed and stand between his spread legs.

"Like it? I more than like it." He puts his hands on my hips and pulls me closer to him. "I love it."

My heart starts beating furiously. Voices from the past push their way to the surface. Flashes of faces—Seth and the men in Moreno's compound flood my senses. They're laughing with one another as they talk about what they're going to do to me. Hands grab the fabric, tearing it from my body.

Someone bends me over and kicks my legs apart. A hand wraps around my neck, holding me down. The men take turns violating my body. Some, one at a time. Others take me in different places at the same time.

"No. Stop, please," I yell. "Get away from me." I kick and punch at whatever is in front of me, desperately trying to stop the attack. I don't want to be hurt anymore.

Strong arms wrap around my waist, and I fight harder. We begin to fall, and I brace myself. I'm expecting to hit hard, but my landing is cushioned. The arms don't let go even as I continue struggling. I fight with everything I have until, finally, I break free. I scurry away on my hands and knees. I pull my knees to my chest to make myself small and hide between the bed and the wall, hoping not to be found.

Viktor

I DON'T KNOW WHAT HAPPENED. ONE SECOND, AMELIA was with me. The next, she was screaming and fighting against an invisible enemy.

"It's me, Amelia," I say while holding onto her. "I'm not going to hurt you."

"Let me go. Stop. Please," she screams, tears pouring down her face.

She's unable to see or hear me. Amelia's lost in her memories where she's fighting for her life. She kicks and punches with all her might. I'm not worried about getting hit. I'm concerned about her hurting herself. I keep my arms wrapped tightly around her as I desperately try to reach her and calm her.

"*Moya zirka*, stop fighting. You're safe," I say, sliding us down to the floor. That only seems to make her fight harder.

My heart shatters seeing the terror on her face. Reluctantly, I open my arms and let her go. I don't know what else to do. The second she's free, she crawls away from me as fast as possible and hides between the bed and the wall.

I stay on the floor where I am for a few minutes. I'm struggling to make sense of what's happening and what I can do to get through to her. Wetness coats my cheeks as she continues to cry.

"Go away. Please don't hurt me."

My beautiful girl, I'll never hurt you. But how do I reach you right now? How do I bring you back to me? Slowly, I stand up and walk across the room.

"*Moya zirka*, it's just me, Viktor," I say quietly and sit on the floor beside her, but I don't reach out. "No one's going to hurt you. You're safe here. Come back to me, please."

The scene is heartbreaking. Amelia curled up, her knees to her chest and her arms wrapped around her legs. She's sobbing while repeatedly begging not to be hurt. I'm afraid to touch her. Scared to send her back into fighting mode.

"Sweetheart, can you look at me?" She doesn't lift her head. "What do I do?" I think back to when I was a boy and would wake from nightmares. My mama would sit in my bed and sing to me until I fell back asleep.

So, that's what I do. I know how much Amelia loves "Just Give Me a Reason." She sings it at all her shows, and she added it to my playlist. I didn't realize it that first night, but when Amelia sang those words, she was singing to me. She already had feelings for me, but I wasn't there yet.

Although my voice is nothing like my angel's, I hope the words penetrate the fear that's taken her away from me and speak to her heart. Amelia's not broken. Our hearts are meant for one another. Amelia taught me how to love again—we're one another's destiny.

When I get to the chorus, I hear her voice, ever so softly, singing with me. That's my girl, fight through the darkness. My tears fall unbidden, watching her slay her demons and return to me. I stop singing and listen to her finish the song.

"Viktor?"

"Yes, *moya zirka*. I'm here."

"Hold me, please."

When I open my arms, Amelia climbs onto my lap and lays against my chest. "You're safe. I've got you." I close my arms around her in a protective embrace. "You're safe. I promise no one will ever hurt you again."

Amelia

Fear, paralyzing fear. Faces. Voices. Pain.

Then, somewhere in the distance, I hear a different voice. A comforting voice—a song. Little by little, it gets closer. As it does, it chases the bad things away until all that's left is this new voice. Viktor.

It all comes back to me.

I'm here with Viktor. He'll never allow anyone to hurt me.

"Hold me, please," I beg.

He opens his arms, and I climb onto his lap and press my head against his chest. The sound of his steady heartbeat is calming. The feel of his arms around me is grounding.

"You're safe. I've got you. You're safe," he murmurs. "I promise no one will ever hurt you again."

"I'm sorry. I ruined tonight."

"Do not apologize. You're okay, and that's all that matters to me."

We stay huddled together on the floor until we hear a knock on the door.

"That's our dinner. Is it okay if I answer it?"

I nod.

Without letting me go, Viktor gets to his feet. He sets me gently on the edge of the bed. "Stay in here. I'll be right back."

While he's gone, I grab a robe from the bathroom and slip it on. Then, I get my phone and text, Ania. It's morning in Russia, and I know she usually starts her day early.

Me: Are you awake?

I get a response right away.

Ania: I am. Are you okay?

Me: Not really. Can I call you?

I don't get a chance to pull up her number before my phone rings. I touch the green circle connecting the call.

"What's wrong?"

"I had a panic attack," I say. "It was like I was right back in the room with those men.

"Are you ready to—" Viktor stops when he gets to the doorway. "I'm sorry. I didn't know you were on a call." He turns to walk away.

"Please stay."

"Are you sure?" he asks.

"Yes."

Viktor sits next to me, and I explain to Ania about the flashbacks I started having when I came out of the bathroom. "I know what I was experiencing, but I don't know what was happening in reality. All I remember is hearing Viktor singing to me."

"May I ask Viktor to tell me what happened?"

I nod. I'm scared to hear it, but at the same time, I need to know.

"As Amelia said, she'd just come into the bedroom. I told her how beautiful she looked and called her over to me." He stops and looks at me for permission to continue.

I nod, letting him know it's okay.

"When I reached out to touch her, she started screaming."

Viktor continues telling Ania how I yelled and fought him physically. How he held me, but I got more agitated. He didn't know what to do, so he finally let me go. It wasn't until he began singing that I came around.

"You had a trauma reaction."

"I feel like I lost all the ground I've worked so hard to gain." A tear drips down my face.

"You stumbled, but we've talked about that. It's okay, and something I anticipate will occasionally happen," Ania reassures me. "Now, we're going to devise a plan to minimize how often it happens until it doesn't happen at all. And we'll give Viktor some more tools to help if it does."

"Viktor knows a lot of my story. He knows I was raped. But I haven't told him what happened that night."

"Is that something you're comfortable doing now?"

"It's not something I ever look forward to talking about. But if I don't, it'll continue to come between us. To have power over me. I don't want to give it that much power anymore." I turn slightly on the bed, facing Viktor. "Moreno had a few *special* clients he'd bring to the house. Sometimes, one at a time, but more often, he'd have a party. There'd be a group of men. Those nights were awful, but not the worst." I stop and take a breath. "The worst was the night you came to rescue Natalie and Alex. There were five guards. The power went out, and they knew something was up. One of them grabbed me and brought me into Moreno's panic room. The other four guards followed us. They didn't care about their boss's orders anymore. They laughed as they talked about what they were going to do to me."

"I tried to get out, but the door wouldn't open. One held me still while another took his knife and cut off the black lingerie I was wearing." I close my eyes, reliving the horror of that night. "They started by taking turns with me. But as they grew more aroused, they grew bolder. If there was a hole, they made sure one of them was filling it. My body tore from their violent intrusion. I thought they were going to kill me."

Viktor's beautiful blue eyes look tortured as he struggles to hold my gaze.

"I fought. I fought so hard."

"It's my fault," he says.

"It's not your fault. The people to blame are those men and Moreno. And they're all dead. If it wasn't for you, they would've killed me."

Ania allows us to process at our own pace. Then, she reaffirms what I told Viktor, that none of what happened was his fault. Once we're ready, we'll make a plan to move forward.

She suggests wearing lingerie a few times without doing anything physical so I can get used to wearing it and associate it with new, positive memories. She encourages Viktor to check in with me frequently to gauge where I'm at and if we need to stop.

"Amelia, I think it would be beneficial for you and Viktor to establish a safe word or gesture. You need to feel empowered when you're in a vulnerable situation," Ania explains. Then, she gives a final piece of advice. "For now, try a color other than black. Something that isn't associated with the past."

By the time our emergency session is over, Viktor and I are both feeling more confident moving forward.

"Why don't you get changed, and then we'll eat," Viktor suggests.

I stop on my way into the bathroom. "I'm sorry for ruining your plans tonight."

"Seeing you terrified was hell for me, but I'm sure it was worse for you reliving that nightmare." He walks over to me. "Please don't apologize. We're here. We're together, and you're safe. That's all that matters to me."

Taking his face in my hands, I stand on tiptoes and kiss him. "I love you, Viktor."

"And I love you, *moya zirka*."

Amelia

Last night started in the worst possible way. It was no surprise that I was raped, Viktor already knew that, but he didn't know the specifics. Especially from that last night. I've been afraid to tell him. Scared that when he found out, he'd run in the other direction. But that's not what happened. If anything, telling him strengthened our bond.

"Are you ready to go?" Viktor pops his head into the bathroom, where I'm trying to get my unruly curls up in a bun.

"As soon as I get my hair to cooperate, yes."

Viktor stands behind me. Our reflections stare back at us. "You're beautiful, no matter what your hair does."

"You're sweet but crazy." I laugh and finish securing my hair. "I'm ready."

We're going to see the San Diego Parade of Lights. It's something I've learned is a holiday tradition here. Viktor drives us back over the Coronado Bridge to the pier. It's supposed to be the perfect spot to watch the water parade.

While he drives, I take pictures of this incredible five-lane bridge and the other beautiful sights as we make our way up the coast of Southern California. We pass a marina filled with boats of all different sizes, and I smile, thinking about the dinner cruise we took when we first moved here.

"Look at the ship," I exclaim as we pass the USS Midway Museum. "How in the world does something that big even float?"

"It's pretty impressive."

Viktor glances at it quickly and then turns into a parking lot on the pier. It seems like an odd place to watch the boat parade, but I'm sure Viktor knows what he's doing. As I get out of the car, my phone rings. It's Sparrow.

"Hello?"

"Hey. Do you have a minute?"

"Sure. What's up?"

"It's Mateo."

The tone in Sparrow's voice makes my heart stop. "Is he okay?"

"Not really. God, I don't know how to say this, Mel."

I put the phone on speaker so Viktor can hear, too. "You're scaring me, Sparrow."

"The day after he flipped out on you at your house, he overdosed."

"What? Why didn't anyone call me?"

"The first few days, he was in bad shape. They weren't sure he was going to make it. Once he crossed the major hurdles and woke up, I was going to call you, but he asked me not to."

A mix of emotions hits me all at once. Fear. Sadness. Guilt. "I didn't realize things were that bad."

"None of us did. Mateo learned how to function while he was high or drunk."

"I don't know what to say." I'm concerned for Mateo and Sparrow. I know how much he cares for Mateo.

"Mateo finally hit rock bottom. He told his mom he needed help, and his parents arranged for him to go to a rehab center. He's been there about a week."

"Have you talked to him?"

Sparrow's voice cracks. "No one's allowed to contact him until he's fully detoxed."

"I'm sorry. I didn't mean for this to happen."

"His overdosing isn't your fault," Viktor adds.

"Viktor's right, Mel. None of us is responsible for Mateo's actions."

"If we don't go, we're going to be late," Viktor says quietly.

"Sparrow, can I call you tomorrow?" I don't want him to think I'm blowing him off. "Viktor brought me to San Diego. We're about to watch the Parade of Lights."

"I'm leaving for Aspen tomorrow. I'll text you after we get settled. Don't worry about Mateo. He's safe now. You go and have fun. You're going to love it."

"Thanks for letting me know about Mateo."

The call ends, and I close my eyes, trying to wrap my head around everything Sparrow just told me. "Wow."

"That was a lot. Are you okay?"

I turn my head to look at Viktor. "Are you sure this isn't my fault?"

"*Moya zirka*, Mateo had substance abuse problems long before he met you. His actions are his and his alone." Viktor takes my hand in his. "Hopefully, he takes this opportunity seriously."

"I hope so, too."

"Do you still want to do this tonight?"

I sit back up. "Yes."

"Let's go then." Viktor smiles.

In true Viktor style, nothing about tonight is done halfway. We aren't just watching the Parade of Lights from the shore. We're taking a dinner cruise in the harbor to watch the parade.

This year's theme is A Tropical Christmas, and the lights are spectacular. The owners have taken the theme to the extreme. There are inflatable palm trees and Santas in Hawaiian shirts. When I think it can't get any better, the next display is even more impressive. There's a whole island on one of the boats. I wish the parade could go on all night, but eventually, it ends, and our boat sails back to the pier.

"Thank you." I thread my arm through Viktor's as we walk back to the car. "This was one of the best things I've ever seen."

"I'm glad you liked it, *moya zirka*." He slides his arm around me. "I love making memories with you."

Viktor

The unexpected phone call from Sparrow left Amelia and me a bit shaken. The good thing is Mateo is safe and in a place that can help him get well. I offered to take Amelia back to the hotel if she wasn't up to our date. I can't lie. I was glad she didn't take that option. The Parade of Lights was an incredible spectacle to watch, but what I found even more special was how Amelia's eyes sparkled as the boats slowly sailed past.

"I think we should get a boat," I suggest as we drive back to the resort.

"Us? We don't know anything about sailing."

"We could learn."

"You're serious? You want to get a boat?"

"Yes. Then we can go out on the water whenever we want."

"Okay, Captain Vik." She giggles.

I make a mental note to check out both boats and sailing lessons.

Amelia fell asleep about fifteen minutes after we started driving.

"*Moya zirka.*" I run my knuckles gently down her cheek. "Time to wake up."

"I didn't realize I fell asleep." She stretches and then unbuckles her safety belt. "You should've woken me sooner."

"You looked too pretty."

She smiles as we enter our villa. "You're a silly man."

"You call it silly. I call it head over heels in love."

"Whoever you're in love with is one lucky girl." She bats her eyelashes at me.

"Is she now?" I step closer to her.

"Yes." She takes a step backward.

"Maybe I should show her just how lucky she is?" I grab her by the waist, pulling her against me.

"I think she'd like that."

I lift her, and she wraps her legs around my waist. I attack her mouth as I walk her into the bedroom and kick the door closed behind us. She slides down my body. The friction only makes me harder.

"Are you okay? Do you want me to keep going?"

"Yes, please."

"Raise your arms," I command.

When she does, I pull her shirt over her head and toss it to the side. Her shorts follow a second later. Amelia stands in front of me in her pink lace bra and panties. I'm in awe of how perfect she is.

"You're overdressed." She smiles seductively as she toward me. Sliding her hands up my chest, she pulls my shirt over my head. I remove my pants and kick them off to the side.

"Better?"

"Much."

"Lie down." Amelia lies on her back with her head on the pillows. "Can we try something different?"

"Like what?"

"Stay there." I go into my bag in the closet. I'm a little nervous about how she'll react to my idea. When I return, I have a small silver vibrator and a bottle in my hand. I hold them up for her to see. "I'd like to watch you make yourself come for me. You can say no if you're uncomfortable." I don't want to push her too far out of her comfort zone.

Without speaking, she shimmies her panties down her legs and drops them onto the floor.

"Is that a yes?"

She nods.

I take a step closer to her. "*Moya zirka*, you know I need more than that."

"Yes. I want to try."

"Open your legs." I can already see her arousal, but I still apply a generous amount of lubrication. Then, I pass her the vibrator.

She turns it on and pushes the button several times, familiarizing herself with the different vibrating patterns before lowering it between her legs. She gasps when it makes contact with her clit. While she explores and finds her rhythm, I push my boxers off, freeing my erection. Then I join her on the bed, sitting on my knees between her spread legs. Leaning forward, I pull the cups of her bra down, exposing her breasts to me. Her nipples are hard and begging for attention.

"Oh my God," she moans in delight.

As much as I enjoy teasing her, I let go of her nipple with a pop and sit back on my heels. I squirt some lube in my hand and slide it up and down my erection while I watch her pleasure herself. Her eyes lock onto what I'm doing. "Do you like this?" I ask.

"Very much." She clicks the button on the vibrator, turning it up to the highest intensity. "This feels so good."

"I want you to come for me."

She closes her eyes.

"Open your eyes. I want you looking at me when you come."

Her eyelids flutter open, and her gaze locks on mine. "I'm getting close."

I don't want to come yet, so I switch my attention to Amelia and slide two fingers into her opening. Her body readily accepts them as I pump them in and out. "Are you ready?"

She nods.

I push my fingers in and curl them. As soon as they find her G-spot, she explodes. Her body squeezes my fingers as a gush of wetness coats my hand.

"What was that?" she asks, her eyes wide in panic.

"That was a fucking good orgasm," I smirk.

Without wasting another second, I crawl over her and slide my erection into her welcoming body. I take the vibrator out of her hand and press it on her overly sensitive clit. Her back arches as another orgasm rips through her body.

"Do you think you can give me one more?"

"I don't know," she pants. "It feels so intense—"

I lean forward, pressing our bodies together to kiss her. Then, I pull out.

"Please don't stop," she begs.

"There's not a chance that'll happen. Turn over."

She rolls over onto her hands and knees. Without warning, I slam into her.

"Oh God, Viktor."

"Tell me if you want me to stop."

"Don't stop, please."

Holding her hips to keep her steady, I pull back and thrust in as far as possible. My rhythm is fast and hard. Her breathing increases as she chases another orgasm.

I'm close, but I want her to come with me. I grab the vibrator that's lying next to her and press it to her swollen clit. Amelia's orgasm is almost violent in its intensity. Her arms give out from under her. I drop the toy and use my arm to hold her up. I thrust into her one more time before I follow her over the cliff. Our shared climax seems to last forever.

When the pleasure finally wanes, I pull out slowly. "That wasn't too much, was it?"

"No," she says and wraps herself around me. I was nervous at first. I've never done anything like that. But when I saw the way you looked at me and how turned on you were, that gave me the courage I lacked." She signs in contentment. "I like exploring new things with you."

"I'm glad." I hold the woman who's become my entire world against me tightly.

"So." She pushes up on her elbow. "I planned something for us tomorrow. I wanted it to be a surprise, but since I don't have my license yet, I have let you in on it."

"Okay." I grin. "What's your plan?"

"I'll tell you tomorrow." She reaches over and kisses my cheek.

Amelia

"You wait here. I'm going to put the address into the GPS." I'm doing everything possible to keep our destination a secret for as long as possible.

"Whatever you say, boss." Viktor laughs.

I hope he enjoys this and doesn't think it was a childish idea. When I was growing up, I wanted to be a zookeeper. My parents took me to the Australia Zoo several times a year. In one of my photo albums, there's a picture of me with Steve Irwin taken a few months before he passed away. Being a good steward of our planet and wildlife has been instilled in me since I was a child.

Before they adopted me, Mom and Dad learned of my love for animals. They brought me to the Leningrad Zoo, the oldest zoo in Russia. That place has quite a history. Dad's not a fan of animals and wouldn't let me get a pet, but each time we went, he adopted an animal at the zoo in my honor.

I was even happier when they told me Jelena's Hope would incorporate pet therapy into their services.

"All done." I pop my head into the villa. "We're good to go."

It's a short ride from the island to downtown San Diego. Before too long, signs for the zoo start popping up on the sides of the road, and Viktor begins laughing.

"What's so funny?" I'm sure he thinks going to the zoo is a stupid idea.

"After you fell asleep last night, I bought zoo tickets. I wanted to bring you before our trip was over." He glances my way. "I guess great minds think alike."

"I guess they do." He doesn't know that there's more to this surprise trip than I've told him.

Fifteen minutes later, we're parked in one of the zoo's parking lots and heading for the main entrance.

"We need to go to the will call. The Christmas lights won't come on until this evening, so I made some other plans for this afternoon."

"Oh?"

"I guess I can let you in on them now. We're going to be taking a private safari. I hope that's okay."

Viktor stops walking and turns to face me. "No one's done anything like this for me in a very long time."

"I want to give you the world, too."

Right there, in the middle of the sidewalk, he kisses me. And not just a peck on the cheek. A passionate display of affection.

"What did I do to deserve you?" he whispers. I go to answer him, but he puts his finger to my lips.

"Next," the lady behind the window calls.

"That's us."

After I give the woman my name, she makes a call and points to a bench where she says our tour guide, Dante, will meet us in about ten minutes.

The rest of the afternoon and early evening is spent on the

adventure of a lifetime. If I didn't know we were in California, I'd swear we were somewhere on the African savannah. As we drive, we're treated to sightings of giraffes that come right up to the vehicle. Dante hands us some Acacia leaves to feed these gentle giants, who gladly wrap their tongues around the offered treats. We continue on and observe elephants, rhinoceros, cheetahs, and so many more animals who wander freely.

Part of our afternoon includes a sit-down lunch with Dante. While we eat, he gives us in-depth information on the various habitats and the zoo's efforts in conservation and protecting the futures of the animal species they're privileged to host.

The last stop on the safari includes a very special up-close encounter with several rhinoceros. He explains that the animals are never forced to interact with safari guests, but today, we're in luck. These pre-historic-looking creatures wander over to the vehicle and allow us to feed and touch them. It's an unbelievable privilege that neither Viktor nor I will forget.

"This isn't part of the usual tour," Dante says. "But when I heard you were originally from Australia, I thought you might enjoy a taste of home."

I'm shocked when he drives us to the Walkabout Australia part of the zoo. He leads us behind the scenes, where we get a first-hand look at what the zookeepers do daily to provide a safe, natural environment for the many endangered Australian animals housed here.

While we talk, a female employee enters the room with one of their animal ambassadors, an echidna named Orange. Although we aren't able to hold her, it's a thrill to see an animal I'm so familiar with.

Before we leave the area, we're brought back outside to a staff-only area.

"We're gonna sit here for a few minutes and see what happens." Dante leads us to some large rocks. "Here she comes."

I can't believe my eyes. A wallaby hops over to us and allows us to pet her. Several minutes later, a female kangaroo also makes her way to us.

"She has a joey," I say quietly so as not to scare her.

She eyes Viktor warily as she hops past him and stops between the tour guide and me.

"You can pet her if she'll let you. Put your hand out."

Slowly, I move my hand and place it in front of her with my palm up. She lowers her head to check out my hand. I'm shocked when she allows me to touch her fur. She sits in front of me and doesn't move.

"It appears as though Polly likes you," Dante says with a smile. "She letting you see her joey."

"Is it a boy or a girl?"

"It's a little boy who, up until recently, didn't have a name."

"He has a name now," Viktor says. "His name is Mel."

"What?" I ask, shocked.

"While you were in the restroom at lunch, Viktor arranged for this extra part of the tour," Dante says. "It happened very quickly, but Viktor arranged to adopt Polly and her joey. The director also agreed to name the baby after you."

I look at Viktor, too stunned for words. "This was supposed to be my surprise to you."

"I added a little something extra, that's all." He shrugs.

We feed Polly some vegetables. When she's through visiting, she hops away.

"This has been a wonderful treat." My voice cracks from trying to hold back my tears. "I miss Australia so much. Thank you both for this." I swipe at a tear that escapes.

We finish up just as the sun's beginning to set. Hand-in-hand, Viktor and I take a slow walk through the zoo. As darkness settles in, the lights turn on, transforming the zoo into a Christmas wonderland. Performers and musicians take their places, entertaining the passersby. It's magical.

What's even more special is that Viktor's let his guard down. I've enjoyed seeing him smile and hearing him laugh. He hasn't been scanning the horizon for some unknown threat. He's been present in the moment with me. The safari and seeing the animals up close were fun, but seeing him so carefree is the best part of my day.

Before we leave, Viktor insists we stop in the souvenir shop. We buy some stuff for ourselves and a stuffed animal to send to Rose. We also adopt two more animals. A gorilla and an African elephant.

"We're going to have adopted animals all over the world if we keep this up." I giggle as we walk back to our car.

"It's like leaving a piece of us everywhere we go. A kind of legacy."

"I like that idea." I enter the car and watch as Viktor walks around the front and slides into the driver's seat. "We're helping to make a positive difference in the world."

And in the end, that's all one can hope to do—leave things just a little better for future generations.

Amelia

Since my parents' deaths, holidays have been bittersweet. I have so many wonderful memories, but with those memories comes a reminder of everything I've lost. I know it's the same way for Viktor. Our mini vacation was exactly what we needed. Getting away and making new holiday memories has helped relieve some of the sadness we've both been struggling with.

On our way home, we stop at a small store to grab a few fresh groceries. We're unpacking the bags when Viktor finds the surprise I snuck in.

"What's this?" He holds up a little plastic bag.

"Mistletoe." I smile. "You should hang it up so we can try it out."

"Where do you want it?"

"How about over there." I point to the doorway that leads to our balcony, knowing we'll get to use it often.

Viktor secures it to the doorframe and then opens the doors. "Come here. We need to try it out. Make sure it works."

"Do we now?" I cross the room slowly.

As soon as I'm within his grasp, he puts his hand around my waist, pulling me against him. "I think the mistletoe's working too well." I drag my fingers up the outline of his erection. "What do you say we remedy this?"

Lust swirls in his blue eyes as he leans down and kisses me. My hands move to unbuckle his belt.

"What the fuck is going on?"

I jump back. "Dad? Mom? What are you doing here?"

My father storms across the room. "I believe I asked a question."

Viktor takes my arm and pulls me behind him. "Calm down, Max. Let's talk about this like rational adults."

"Calm down?" he yells even louder. "What were you doing to my daughter?"

"He wasn't doing anything *to* me," I say as I try to step out from behind Viktor's protective stance. "It was consensual."

"Hush, Amelia. I want to hear it from him." Dad pokes a finger into Viktor's chest.

I look over Dad's shoulder and see Pyotr and Igor rush in. Mom stands back, a look of shock on her face.

"Well, I am waiting for an explanation," Dad says. "No. I do not want to hear what you have to say. It does not matter. You are fired."

"You can't do that," I argue.

"I can, and I did. Get your things and get the hell out of here."

"Stop. Please." I hold onto Viktor's arm. "I don't want him to leave. Can't we take a few minutes to calm down and talk?"

"There is nothing to discuss."

"Mom." I hurry across the room to her. "Can you tell Dad to calm down and talk to us?"

"Your father is in charge. I will not go against his wishes."

Although I'm standing in the room with three of the people I love most, I've never felt so alone. I'm confused and scared. I don't know what to do.

"I'll go pack my things," Viktor says and turns to walk away.

I rush over to his side. "If he leaves, I leave too."

"No." Viktor doesn't hesitate with his response. "You need to stay with your family. I won't let you lose them over me."

"I don't want to lose anyone." Tears cloud my vision. "Why do I have to choose?"

"You aren't choosing, *moya zirka*." Viktor cups my face in his palm. "The decision's already made."

I'm paralyzed by fear, anger, and hurt as I watch Viktor walk down the hall and disappear inside his bedroom.

Spinning around, I look at my father. "You're not really going to let him leave, are you?"

"Yes." He takes a step toward me. "You are young. You do not know what you want. He has no business going anywhere near you. Once he is gone, you will see I am right."

"No, I won't. I hate you," I yell and run to my room, slamming the door. I don't care what he says. Nothing is going to change my mind.

Me: Please don't leave.

Viktor: I have to.

Me: Stay and fight for us.

Viktor: For now, that's not the right choice.

Me: So, you're giving up?

Viktor: No. I'm giving Maxim some space before I try to talk to him. Right now, he wouldn't hear anything I have to say.

Me: I'm going with you then.

Viktor: Walking away without you by my side will be the hardest thing I've ever done. But it won't be forever. I love you, *moya zirka*.

Me: I love you, too.

My heart's shattered into a million pieces. How am I supposed to do this without him? I pull up Natalie's contact and hit the green call button.

"Hello?"

"Natalie, I need your help." I manage to get out between sobs.

"What's wrong? Where's Viktor?"

"Mom and Dad showed up. They caught us together."

"Oh, honey."

"Dad freaked out. He kicked Viktor out. He won't listen to either one of us."

"We figured he wasn't going to take the news well. I'm sure walking in on something unexpected made it even worse."

"What do I do?"

"First, you need to take some deep breaths and try to calm down. Where's Viktor right now?"

"In his room packing. He's leaving."

"I know it's not what either of you wants, but for the current moment, it may be for the best. Max isn't going to calm down if Viktor's there. He needs some time and space."

"But what about me? What about what I need?"

"Right now, you need to be strong. For you and Viktor. I'm sure this is killing him, too."

"I hate Maxim, Natalie."

"You're angry, but I know you don't hate him."

"I do."

"I won't argue with you because there were times I felt the same way about my parents—especially when they forbid me from seeing Alex. I know from firsthand experience this isn't going to be easy. Max isn't going to want to hear anything about you and Viktor. Don't push. Give him some time to process the information."

"What if that doesn't help?"

"We'll cross that bridge if it comes to that." Natalie's quiet for a moment. "I know this is hard, but if you and Viktor are meant to be, it'll work out."

I hope Natalie's right because I won't give up being with Viktor no matter what Maxim says.

Viktor

In a matter of seconds, my world came crashing down around me. Maxim gave me no warning he and Irina were coming to visit. It's not like he's required to clear it with me, but he always gives me a heads-up. The fury on his face. I've seen that look directed at other men but never at me. And especially never toward Amelia.

The pain in her eyes when she begged to come with me was too much. I almost said yes. She's eighteen and doesn't have to stay. But that would've only enraged Maxim more. There's no way he'd let me out of the door with her. If we were to have gotten out together, he'd hunt us down and kill me—he may still kill me.

Right now, I'm trying to spare Amelia as much of the anger and violence I'm sure is heading my way. I finish packing my bag and return to the living room, where Irina's sitting on the sofa. Max is on the balcony talking with Pyotr and Igor.

"Boss. I'm leaving now."

Maxim doesn't turn around or show any signs of acknowledging my presence. His lack of action cuts deep. Maxim's been like a father to me for most of my adult life. I knew he wouldn't take the news about Amelia and me well. I have to believe if we had the chance to tell him rather than him walking in on us, it might've gone over a bit better.

When it's clear Max isn't going to respond, Igor looks up at me and nods.

I walk over to Irina. "I don't expect you to side with me or even speak to me. I need you to know I love Amelia. I would never do anything to harm her."

Irina looks up. Her dark blue eyes are filled with tears. "I think I've known that since I saw you and her together." She glances behind her to Max, whose back is still turned. "Please understand. My hands are tied."

"I understand." I hear Amelia's door open, but I don't look back. I'm afraid if I see her, I'll lose my self-control and do something we'll both regret. So, instead, I hurry to the door and leave.

With each step away from the house, breathing becomes more difficult. My heart physically hurts, and I wonder if it will fail. "I'm coming back for you, *moya zirka*," I whisper.

I stop at the coffee shop a few blocks from our house. I need to find a hotel for a few nights. Once I find a room, I text Amelia so she knows where I'll be staying.

I may only be a half mile away from her, but I may as well be on the other side of the world. Being without Amelia feels like a piece of myself is missing. I'm lying on the bed, trying to figure out what to do next, when my phone rings.

"Hello?"

"Natalie told me," Alex says. "Are you okay?"

"No."

"Amelia's no better."

Hearing that is what bothers me most. I don't want her to hurt.

"How do I fix this?"

"Max needs a few days to wrap his head around everything. But I'm sure he'll come around." Even as he says it, I hear the uncertainty in his voice. He's no more sure of that than I am.

"Alex, I can't lose her. As long as she wants me, I refuse to walk away from her."

"I know."

Amelia

I didn't sleep last night. Instead, I sat up and contemplated packing my things and leaving. The only reason I didn't is because I'm afraid for Viktor's life if I do—that's too high a price.

Unfortunately, things aren't going to get any better today. I still haven't told my parents about Death Rat, and now time's run out. We have practice in less than an hour.

Me: Can you pick me up for rehearsal?

Sparrow: Of course. Where's Viktor?

Me: It's a long story. I'll tell you on the way to Quincy's. Text me when you get here. Do not come to the door.

Sparrow: Why not?

Me: My father, the Russian mob boss, is here.

Sparrow: Enough said. I'll text you when I get there.

I take my time getting ready in my room. The less time I spend with my father right now, the better. Then, with a deep breath, I turn the handle and pull my door open. Mom and Dad are both in the kitchen. Mom's cooking while Dad's sitting drinking coffee.

"Good morning, Amelia," Dad says. "Sit and eat."

"I can't. I have somewhere I need to be." My phone buzzes. When I check, it's Sparrow. He's outside.

"Where are you going?"

"Music rehearsal."

"Will you be at the school?" Mom asks.

"No. It's at a friend's house. I have to go. He's outside waiting."

"Outside waiting?" Dad sets his coffee down. "He will need to come to the door like any decent young man."

"Seriously?" I cross my arms. "We're not dating. There's no need for the formalities."

"It is obvious you are not dating anyone your own age," Dad quips. "Before you leave this house, I will know who you will be with and where you will be. And Igor will accompany you."

I roll my eyes as I pull out my phone.

Me: My father's being a jerk. Can you come to the door?

Sparrow: Um. Yeah.

I half expect Sparrow to drive away rather than having to come face to face with Maxim, but a minute later, the doorbell rings. I pull it open and find a terrified-looking Sparrow.

"Don't worry, it's not you he's mad at," I whisper. "Dad, this is Sparrow. Sparrow, these are my parents."

"It's nice to meet you both." He puts on a brave face.

"Have you eaten yet?" Dad asks.

"No. Amelia and I were going to grab a bite to eat on the way to Quincy's."

"Quincy?"

"He's the lead—"

"We have to go, or we'll be late." I interrupt and grab Sparrow's arm, hoping to make a quick exit.

"The lead what?" Mom asks.

"There's something I need to tell you, but first, you need to promise not to take your anger out on Sparrow."

Dad raises an eyebrow.

"I told you I had music rehearsals over the holiday. That much is true, but it's not for school." I take a deep breath. "I'm in a band, and we're going on tour this summer." While I'm at it, I may as well tell them the rest. "I'm also not returning to school in the spring."

Mom stops what she's doing and spins around to face me. Dad pushes back his chair so fast it nearly falls over before turning to face me. When he does, that same look of fury I saw yesterday is again there.

"You are not returning to school to play in some band?" Dad asks.

"Sparrow, you should go ahead without me."

"I think that would be a very good idea, young man," Dad says flatly. "My daughter and I have much to discuss."

"Are you going to be okay here?" Sparrow asks quietly.

I nod. "Tell the guys I'll be there Friday for the show."

"Will do." Sparrow looks back and forth between my father and me. "It was nice meeting you both." He turns and hurries out the door.

"Irina, please excuse us. We will be late for breakfast."

"Yes, Sir. I'll keep it warm."

"Let us go for a walk," Dad says, heading for the door.

He doesn't say a word as we walk through the warm sand down to the water. However, I can feel the anger rolling off him in waves bigger than the ocean's. Once we get to the water's edge, Dad stares at the sparkling crystal water.

"I know there's a lot I've been keeping from you, and I'm sorry you had to find out this way." He remains silent. "I was planning on telling you, but to be honest, I was struggling to find the words."

"Being open and honest is the one thing we have asked for, and it is the one thing you have not done since you came here."

When he finally looks at me, the disappointment in his eyes is almost too much. It takes me a few seconds to compose myself.

"I'm sorry," I say. "I'd like the opportunity to explain what I was thinking."

"Go ahead."

"How about we sit." I point to the lounge chairs Viktor and I keep down here. "This is probably going to take a while."

He follows me over and takes a seat.

"Where do I start?"

"How about the beginning," Dad suggests.

That's where I start—the beginning. How when we first got here, I started having panic attacks again. And how Viktor began attending sessions with me to learn how to help me manage them. Then, I move into meeting Mateo.

"Viktor ran a background check, and everything looked good on paper. Even still, he never let me go anywhere alone with him."

"That is what I pay him for."

"Well, sometimes background checks aren't enough," I say, unafraid to meet his penetrating stare. "Mateo's how I got involved with the band. He wanted to be more than just friends."

"But you did not?"

"I tried, but I didn't care for Mateo as anything more than a friend."

Dad listens while I tell him about the day Mateo showed up here and how Viktor had to jump in.

"I found out a few days ago that when Mateo left, he overdosed and almost died."

"How did Viktor miss a drug addiction?"

"No one knew how bad Mateo's problems really were. He was a functional alcoholic and drug user."

"And where is this boy now?"

"He's in a rehab facility. He wants to get his life together before Death Rat goes on tour."

Dad's eyes open wide. "Death Rat?"

"That's our band."

"You are in a band that calls themselves Death Rat?"

I can't help the giggle that slips out. "We just signed a contract to be the opening act for Zapped Euforia on their summer stadium tour."

Dad looks at me, confused.

"Do you know how big of a deal that is?"

"No, I do not."

"It's the chance of a lifetime."

"What about school?"

"I'm not going back. I've already decided that."

"Because of this tour?"

"Yes. The tour starts the first weekend in May. Between now and then, we have some shows, rehearsals, and press events," I explain. "I don't want to pass up this opportunity. Anyway, it's a done deal. The contracts are signed."

"Contracts can be bought out."

"But this one won't be. I'm going on tour, Dad. And I'd really like your support." I stop and search his face for a reaction but find none. "We have a show this Friday. I hope you and Mom will be there."

"Igor will need the information to clear the place."

"Viktor's already done that. He cleared the list as soon as we got it."

"I do not want to hear that man's name."

"You're going to have to because I'm in love with him."

"That is not possible. You are a child, and he is a full-grown man. You are not in love with him." He balls his hands into fists. "Viktor had no business touching you—something he will reap the repercussions of."

"If you lay a finger on him, I'll never forgive you."

"Amelia, please. Whatever you thought was going on between the two of you was wrong. It cannot be allowed to continue."

"You're wrong. Viktor's kind and respectful. He didn't touch me until he was sure I'd thought it through and was confident I knew what I was getting into."

"Touched you? He better not have—"

"We've had sex."

"No. That is impossible."

"Why is it impossible?" I jump up. "Do you think I'm so damaged that I can't make a decision about my own body? Or that I'm too broken to fall in love?"

Maxim

AMELIA STORMS OFF, AND I GO AFTER HER. WE ARE NOT finished with this conversation.

"Amelia, stop. That is not what I was saying."

She spins around, and I see fire in her eyes. "Then, please explain it because that's sure what it sounded like."

"You are not damaged or broken." I reach out to take her hand, but she pulls it away. "And I know you can make decisions about your body. But Viktor is much older. He has more experience. He has no business being with you."

"Yes, he's older, and yes, he's been with other women. Viktor and I have talked about it all. But his past and who he's been with has nothing to do with him and me now." Amelia takes a deep breath before continuing. "Viktor knows all about my past as well. He knows the horrible things that were done to me—stolen from me. I didn't think a man could look past all that. But he did. Viktor loves me." Her hand goes over her heart.

"Do you know what that means to me? Viktor was the first man to show me kindness and tenderness. He didn't take from me. I willingly gave myself to him."

"You will not see him again."

"You can't stop us from being together."

"I can, and I will. Viktor is going back to Russia."

"He's a grown man, remember? He doesn't have to follow your orders."

"If he wants to remain alive, he will."

"If you want me to remain your daughter, you'll have to learn to accept us together. If you force me to choose. I choose Viktor." With that, she turns and walks away.

I watch until she disappears inside the house. I am a man who is used to being in control. To people following my orders. How did things go so wrong with Amelia? Obviously, I am not going to get through to her, but I know someone who will. I pull my phone out and call Svetlana.

"Hi, Papa," she answers. "How's everything in sunny California?"

"Terrible."

"I see."

"You know about Amelia and Viktor, do you not?"

"I do."

I feel betrayed by the amount of secrecy from my daughters.

"And you did not tell me?"

"No, I didn't. That was for Amelia and Viktor. When they were ready."

"Well, they had no choice when we walked in and found them kissing. I am just glad we got here when we did. She was about to—"

"They're in love," Svetlana interrupts me.

"That is ridiculous."

"We knew you wouldn't be happy, but you're going to have to get used to it. They have the real thing going on."

"I will get used to no such idea. If Viktor goes near her again, I will kill him myself."

"Be reasonable, Papa." Svetlana raises her voice. "You can't go around dictating who she can love."

"It will not be him."

"Papa, it's already him. You'll lose her if you harm him or try to keep them apart."

"I do not know how you can be so okay with this. Amelia is just a child."

"No, Papa. Amelia hasn't been for a very long time."

Svetlana and I do not often see eye-to-eye, but considering her views on men as of late, I was confident she would be on my side. But no, of course, she must oppose me. Before I end up in a fight with her, too, I say my goodbyes and disconnect our call.

I am the boss. The one in charge. I always have the answers, but this time, I find myself searching for guidance. "What am I going to do?"

Amelia

Tonight's the last show until after the holidays. Mom and Dad are in the audience, albeit reluctantly on Dad's part. I'm sure he's only here to tell me how much he hates it and that I have to quit. To make matters worse, they sent Igor to babysit me backstage. At least Viktor acted like a normal person. Igor's standing there stoically with his legs spread and arms crossed.

Viktor: I'm outside the stage door. Who did Max put backstage?

Me: Igor.

Viktor: Come let me in.

Viktor doesn't have to tell me twice. I won't pass up any opportunity to spend time with him. I push the door open, and the sight of him takes my breath away. Viktor's wearing tight jeans and a blue T-shirt that makes the depth of color in his eyes even more striking.

He's barely through the doorway when I launch myself into his arms.

"I miss you so much."

"*Moya zirka.*" He holds me tight. "I miss you, too."

"Viktor, what're you doing here?" Igor appears behind me.

"Please don't tell my father."

Igor's currently in a stare-off with Viktor and ignores my plea.

"I have strict orders to tell the boss if Viktor shows up," he finally says without breaking eye contact.

"Yury," Viktor says calmly.

I look between the men, not understanding who Yury is.

After a few seconds, Igor's shoulders drop. "Don't get caught, or my head's on the chopping block too."

"We'll be in the green room," Viktor tells Igor, then takes my hand and leads me through the busy hallway. Once we're inside the room, Viktor locks the door.

"Who's Yury?"

"Don't worry about that right now." Viktor sits on the sofa. "Come here. I need to feel you."

I straddle his lap and wrap my arms around him. "I don't know how much longer I can go without you."

My lips meet his, and the erection jutting from between his legs makes me wish I didn't have to be on stage in five minutes.

"Are you going to stay for the show?" I ask between kisses.

"I can't. It's too dangerous. If Maxim or Pyotr comes back-stage, we'll be in for bigger problems than we already have."

"How much longer do we have to be apart?"

"I don't know."

"Amelia, are you in there?" Sparrow calls from the other side of the door.

"I want to ignore the world and stay with you."

"Me too. But we can't do that." He stands up and sets me on the floor in front of him. "This show's important. You need to get onstage."

"Amelia," Sparrow calls again.

I unlock the door and crack it open. "Is it still only Igor out there?"

"Yeah. Come on. We need to get on stage."

"Text me later." Viktor kisses me. "You didn't see me," he says and makes his way to the stage door.

I bring my finger to my lips and watch until he's gone.

"Your dad still won't let you see him?"

"No."

Sparrow throws his arm around me, and I rest my head on his shoulder. He and I have become very close since the night of the party. It's like I finally have the older brother I always wanted.

"Everything's going to work out. I'm not sure how, but it will." He gives me a quick peck on the cheek. "Now let's get out there and give this audience one hell of a show."

This is the first concert Viktor's missing. Even though I know Viktor's not here, I can't stop myself from scanning the audience for him. He's always front and center with a gorgeous smile on his face, except for tonight. Tonight, my parents sit in his place. It's not that I'm not happy they're here. I guess I'm selfish. I want them and Viktor to be here.

The light's come up, and I'm forced to stop feeling sorry for myself. Since Mateo's still in rehab, Tristan's stepped up for lead guitar and vocals. He loves being the center of attention and is currently hyping the audience up—not that they need much help. News of our upcoming tour has already increased our popularity. I can't believe we've gone from playing small local bars and clubs to being set to go on a major stadium tour in such a short time. I'm realizing a dream I never knew I had.

We're on our last song, "Just Give Me a Reason." Since Mateo and I sang this duet the first night, it's become so popular that now, we close each show with it. Since Mateo left, Sparrow and I have been performing it together. He steps up to the mic.

"Our final song of the evening is very special to both Amelia and me." He glances back at me. "We'd like to dedicate it to the two people who've stolen our hearts."

He grabs his acoustic guitar and sits on the stool next to the piano. My emotions almost get the best of me several times during the song, but somehow, I manage to make it to the end before the tears fall. While the audience is applauding, Sparrow wraps me in a hug.

"We'll get them both back. I promise."

Maxim

AMELIA'S AN ACCOMPLISHED MUSICIAN OF THAT I HAD no doubt. Until tonight, I have only heard her play classical pieces. But it is clear her talent extends far beyond that.

"Max," Irina says and touches my arm softly. "I think you need to give her this. She looks happy on the stage."

"Yes. She does." I place my hand over Irina's. "But no daughter of mine will be in a group called Death Rat."

"You'll tell her we support her with this?"

"That is what you would like us to do, is it not?"

"Very much."

I lean over and kiss my wife's forehead. "Then, that is what we will do."

"And Viktor?"

"I will not discuss him."

A well-dressed man walks toward where Irina and I wait for Amelia.

"You must be Amelia's parents," he says. "I'm Everett Hart, Mateo's father and legal counsel for Death Rat."

"I am Maxim Solonik, and this is my wife, Irina. It is a pleasure to meet you." I extend my hand. "How is your son doing?"

"He's doing better, but he still has a long road ahead of him."

"We wish him the best." Recovering from an addiction is never easy on the person with an addiction or their family. Unfortunately, we see it a lot at Jelena's Hope. "I would like to discuss the name of this band with you."

"Death Rat." Everett chuckles. "I don't know where the kids came up with that, but it'll grow on you."

"No, it will not. If Amelia is to remain with this band, the name will have to change."

"That's not up to us. And Amelia is already under contract."

"I will buy out her part of the contract." I am not playing games, and I am not joking. "Either the name goes, or Amelia does."

"What did you guys think?" Amelia comes bouncing out of the stage door.

"You amaze me, *moya malen'kaya ptichka*," Irina says and hugs our daughter.

"What about you, Dad?" she asks hesitantly.

"You were superb, Amelia." I smile proudly at my daughter. Our relationship has been on shaky ground since we arrived. I hope this helps bridge the gap between us. "As I was just telling Mr. Hart, If you plan on staying with this group, the name will have to change."

"You can't be serious."

"I am very serious."

"This is ridiculous. It's one thing to try to control my relationship—"

"Amelia." The young man who came to pick her up the other day touches her arm. "Changing the name isn't a big deal. Actually, I think it's a good idea. The three of us never liked it anyway. It was something stupid that came up in a random name generator."

"For real?" She smiles.

"Yep. How about the four of us talk about it and come up with something else." He turns to Mr. Hart. "Would you be able to run it by Mateo for us?"

"He's still in the blackout period. We can't communicate with him for at least another week. But I'm sure he'll go along with whatever name change you come up with," Mr. Hart says. "Let me know what you pick something, and I'll make sure it gets switched on all the legal documents."

"Are you sure, Sparrow? You don't have to do this."

He puts his arm around Amelia. "I'm positive. We aren't going to lose you over a silly name."

She rests her head on his shoulder, and I make a mental note to speak with my daughter about this young man. The two appear comfortable with one another, and he is much closer to her age than the alternative.

"Then, we have a deal," I say. "Looks like you are going on tour, Amelia."

The drive back home is quiet and fraught with tension. Amelia stares out the window as if we are not in the car. Irina and I exchange glances several times, but neither of us attempts to get our daughter to talk.

After an agonizingly long drive, Igor turns into the driveway and puts the vehicle in park. Amelia does not wait for the ignition to turn off before she jumps out and runs into the house.

Our relationship feels strained, much like when she first came to live with us. I do not like it.

"Irina, please get Amelia," I say as we enter the house. "I would like to speak with her."

"Yes, Sir."

"I will be on the balcony."

It takes a few minutes for Irina to return with a clearly unwilling Amelia by her side.

"Thank you, *moye schast'ye*." I turn to Amelia and motion

to the chairs. "Please sit." I grab a chair and move it so I am facing her. "Tomorrow is Christmas Eve. "What would you like to do?"

"Nothing. I don't feel like celebrating."

"That is not like you."

"I was planning on spending the holiday with Viktor."

"Amelia," I warn. "We have already taken care of that situation."

"No, we didn't. You kicked Viktor out and refused to even discuss the subject."

"I do not want to have this same argument again."

"Neither do I. I'd like to have a conversation where you also listen instead of barking orders at me like I'm one of your men."

"Is that what you think?"

"Yes," she says matter-of-factly.

"And you, Irina?" I glance back at my wife.

"Do I have permission to speak freely?"

"Yes, you do."

"Amelia, understandably, your father and I were shocked when we walked into the house and saw you and Viktor," she says calmly. "We had no idea anything was developing between you two." Irina looks at me. "Well, I had a suspicion but brushed it off as nothing."

I look at my daughter, but she refuses to make eye contact with me.

Irina continues, "You must try to see it from our perspective. The age difference between you and Viktor is concerning. He has much more life experience. He's more settled, and I'm assuming looking to settle down with one woman."

Irina touches Amelia's hand. "You are just beginning to live your life. You deserve to experiment with dating. You need time to learn what you're looking for in a partner. You shouldn't be tied to one man."

"I've tested those waters and quickly realized they're not for me. I'm not tied to one man out of coercion or desperation—I chose only one man." Amelia looks at Irina. "Why is it so difficult to believe that Viktor and I want the same things?"

"What about that young man, Sparrow?" I interrupt. "He seems nice and very interested in you."

Amelia laughs. "Sparrow is one of my best friends. And he's gay."

"I see." That did not work out as I had hoped.

Amelia

"I know you both think I'm too young to be with Viktor. But you fail to remember that I haven't lived a *normal* life. From the day my parents died, I was forced to grow up real fast." I swallow over the lump in my throat. "Did you know my father was ten years older than my mother?"

A look of shock registers on Dad's face. "I was unaware."

"They were soulmates. Everyone who met them recognized it." I swipe at a tear that escapes. "It was only right they died together. They wouldn't have been able to live apart."

"That does not mean it is okay for you and Viktor, who is fourteen years older, to be together."

"Why not? Who decides that? Who makes up these rules?" I look between my parents. "It's not what most people do. So what? You and Dad don't have the most traditional or what most would call a *normal* relationship. But you respect and love each other. Don't I deserve the same thing? To be loved by a good man?"

"Your father and I understand what you're saying, but honey, Viktor's lived a hard life."

"That makes two of us."

"He has a dangerous job. Your life would be at risk being with him." She takes Dad's hand. "We don't want that for you."

"I know what Viktor does. We—"

"You do not know the full extent of Viktor's job. If you did, you would not be arguing about this with us."

"Yes, Dad. I do. Viktor and I talked about it—all of it. I know what he's done and will have to do in the future. He expressed his concern for my safety. Heck, he fought me on this. He didn't want to put me in danger."

"That is the first sensible thing I have heard since I arrived here."

"If I recall correctly, he does these things at your command." I meet my father's stern gaze. I'm not afraid of him, and I refuse to back down. "I'm going into this with my eyes wide open."

"My answer is still no. That will not change."

I get up, walk to the balcony rail, and look out into the darkness. "And if I continue seeing him?"

"If Viktor goes against my orders, he will face the consequences."

I know they're concerned for me. But how do I get them to see I'm not a child? Just like I understand who and what Maxim is, I also understand who and what Viktor is. I have complete faith that he'll always protect me—with his life if necessary. And I would do the same for him. That's what love is.

"Now, Christmas, what do you want to do?" Dad asks again as if he hasn't heard a word I've said.

I turn around slowly. "I want to see Viktor. There's no reason for him to spend the holiday alone. Even you couldn't be that cruel." My words come out harsh.

"Amelia," Dad warns.

"You'll all be here to ensure we don't do anything you wouldn't approve of."

"Fine. I will allow him to spend Christmas Day with our family."

Me: Dad will be calling you tomorrow. He's letting you come over for Christmas.

Viktor: Igor just texted me to let me know.

Me: I can't wait to see you. I love you.

Viktor: I love you, *moya zirka*.

Viktor

I DON'T KNOW WHAT AMELIA SAID, BUT SOMEHOW, SHE got Maxim to relent and let me spend Christmas Day with them. I'm not holding out any hope that this is anything more than an obligatory holiday invite. There's no way he's backing down and giving us his blessing.

Regardless, I can't wait to get there. I miss her so much. My life with her had a purpose. When she looked at me, her eyes were filled with nothing other than pure love—for me. Somehow, Amelia penetrated the walls I built around my heart and quickly became my whole world.

I don't know how we're going to get Maxim to change his mind. What I do know is he better be prepared for a fight because I'm not giving her up.

I grab the two gifts I have for her and go down to the lobby. Igor texted a few minutes ago, letting me know he's outside.

"Merry Christmas," he says when I get in the car.

"Yeah, something like that." I fidget nervously with the gifts on my lap. "What am I walking into today?"

"Amelia's been trying to convince the boss to accept you two. There's no chance of that happening." He glances at me.

"How long are they staying?"

"They're leaving tomorrow. I'll be staying behind until Max finds a new security team for her."

"Fuck." I run my hand over my head. "It wasn't supposed to happen this way."

"What were you two thinking?"

"We didn't plan it. It just happened."

"What are you going to do?"

"It's not like I can stop loving her. I'm not willing to walk away from this. I have to find a way to get through to him."

"Good luck with that."

"I'm gonna need it," I mumble. "How's Yury?"

"He's good." Igor's face lights up. "He flew in yesterday. We plan on seeing each other after the boss leaves."

"I'm happy for you."

"Weren't we supposed to do a double date?" Igor grins.

"I heard something about that."

I follow Igor into the house and immediately feel the tension in the air. Just a few days ago, this was my home with Amelia. Today, it feels like I'm an unwelcome stranger until Amelia, who's setting the table, looks up.

"Merry Christmas," she says, a smile gracing her beautiful face.

The temptation to wrap her in my arms is strong, but I have to resist. I'm not exactly welcome here as it is. "Merry Christmas."

"Viktor," Maxim says my name.

"Thank you for inviting me."

"It was only because of Amelia's insistence that you not be alone for the holiday."

"I understand." I set my gifts under the tree.

"Dinner's ready," Amelia calls from the kitchen. "Igor. Pyotr. That means you, too."

From the outside looking in, we'd appear to be a happy family as we gather around the table for the holiday meal. Igor and Pyotr sit to my right and left. Amelia sits across from me.

Irina makes Maxim's plate. After he's been served, we take turns passing the serving platters as we make our plates.

"Natalie gave me her lasagna recipe." Amelia's brown eyes meet mine. "I hope you like it."

"It is delicious, *moya malen'kaya ptichka*," Maxim says. "You have done an excellent job."

When we got here, Amelia had no cooking skills. One of her goals was to be able to cook meals for us. She's been practicing for months. She watches me expectantly as I take a bite.

"It's delicious," I compliment her. "I know you could do it."

"Thank you," she says quietly.

"Since we are all here, it is a good time to inform everyone of our plans," Maxim says, obviously meaning to interrupt us. "Irina and I will be returning to Russia first thing in the morning. There are several projects we need to wrap up before the new year. Pyotr will be accompanying us. Igor will remain here until Amelia's new security detail is put in place." Then, he turns his attention to me. "I expect you to arrive at my estate in forty-eight hours."

"You can't force him to go back to Russia." Amelia comes to my defense.

"He is still my employee and under my protection. If he expects to continue as such, he will do as he is told."

Amelia sets her fork down. "My friends used to whisper about you behind my back. They talked about what a cruel and heartless man you are. Maybe they were right all along."

Maxim's relationship with Amelia is important to him. It's clear from the shocked look on his face that her sharp words affected him.

"It's okay, Amelia. Your father's only doing what he feels is best for you."

"No, it's not—"

"Let's not fight during our meal," Irina interrupts."

"My wife is right. Today is for celebration."

Amelia looks at me, and I see her firey temper ready to explode. I give her a slight shake of my head. Having this fight today will not accomplish anything other than causing more hurt. We'll have time to come up with a plan after her parents leave.

Trust me, *moya zirka*. I'm not letting you go.

Amelia

AFTER MOM AND I CLEAR THE DINNER DISHES, WE JOIN everyone in the living room. I grab Viktor's gift from under the tree.

"This is for you." I hand him the wrapped box. "If I knew you guys were coming here for Christmas, I wouldn't have mailed your gifts."

"It is okay. Spending time with you is present enough," Dad says.

I resist the urge to roll my eyes and turn my attention back to Viktor. "Go ahead and open it."

Viktor carefully tears the paper open and lifts the lid off the box. For the first time today, some of the sadness disappears, replaced by a smile. "I love it. Thank you."

"What is it?" Mom asks with genuine curiosity.

Viktor holds the gift up to show her. It's a silver photo frame with a selfie of us from our first night here. The frame is engraved with the words *Her Nightingale*.

"That's beautiful." Mom smiles.

"I have something for you too." Viktor sets the box on the table and grabs the presents he brought. He passes me the first one.

"This paper is too pretty to tear." Carefully, I work at the tape, trying to preserve the vintage-looking gift wrap. I gasp when I see what's inside. "Are these?"

"Yes," Viktor says quietly. "They're the Matryoshka dolls *Babusya* and I made for Mama and Papa." Viktor's voice cracks.

I take my time opening them one by one. They're exquisite. "I don't know what to say."

"You don't have to say anything. I hope you like them." He quickly wipes a stray tear.

"Viktor," I say softly, longing to comfort him. "I'll treasure these always."

"There's one more." He hands me a small gift.

"I don't need anything else."

"Open it." He smiles.

I tear off the paper and find a small jewelry box. When I open it, I can no longer hold back the tears. "I don't know what to say."

"What is it?" Dad asks.

I turn the box so he can see the silver chain with the star made from diamonds.

"That is quite an extravagant gift."

Ignoring Dad's comment, I ask Viktor, "Will you help me put it on?"

Turning around, I lift my hair. Viktor's hands tremble as he puts the delicate chain around my neck and does the clasp.

"How does it look?" I turn and ask him.

"It's perfect, *moya zirka*."

"Isn't it beautiful, Mom?"

She examines the necklace. "It's lovely." She turns to Viktor. "It's a very special gift."

"Amelia's a very special young woman."

Mom can't hide the softness in her eyes. But when I look at my father, his eyes are still cold and heartless. I know his line of work often requires him to do things others consider violent and cruel. But, he's always done a good job of keeping that part of himself separate from the man he is at home—until now.

Many of my Russian friends believe my father is nothing but a cold-blooded killer. They don't know or care to understand what he does and why. But I know. I'm alive today because of my father and his efforts. He and his men, including Viktor, kill. They snuff out the lives of men, if they can even be called that, who steal and destroy innocent people's lives.

I've defended him on many occasions. I've lost friends because I've defended his actions. It never bothered me because I believed my father was doing the right thing—I still do. I choose to turn a blind eye to the methods he employs because his mission is important. The traffickers don't care who gets hurt. They prey on those who are weak or vulnerable. My dad works endlessly to wipe them from the face of the earth.

But this past week, I've witnessed another side of him. A cruelty I didn't believe he was capable of. He's taken the anger and hatred he usually reserves for the animals he hunts and turned it on his family.

He's come just short of threatening Viktor's life for what? Because we fell in love? Only someone with no heart would do that.

Amelia

"Are you sure you won't come home? Even just for a few days?" Mom asks for the hundredth time this morning.

"I'm positive. I need some space away from Dad." Who's outside on the balcony going over his orders for Igor.

Dad wanted to leave Pyotr with me, but there was no way he'd let me see Viktor. My father's still concerned with my comfort level around men, so it was easy to convince him to leave Igor. Especially after Viktor told me he and Igor have an agreement and that at least until the new security detail arrives, we'll be okay.

"Amelia, you know he only wants the best for you."

"I thought I knew that. But after this week, I'm not so sure."

"Please don't say that. You and he have come such a long way. I don't want to pry, but have you considered discussing this situation with Ania?

The conversations in my therapy sessions are private. I'm hoping by divulging some information, my parents will see how serious Viktor and I are about each other.

"Ania knows about Viktor."

"Oh," Mom says, surprised.

"I told her about my feelings for him long before he knew.

Ania and I discussed the pros and cons at great length," I explain. "Then, after a particularly difficult night when I had a major breakdown, he sat in on an emergency session. He wanted to learn how to help me avoid a full-blown panic attack and how best to help me if I have one. We've also done several sessions together, working through some of my issues with intimacy."

"You and Viktor have had sex?"

"Yes."

Mom takes a deep breath. "I didn't realize you two were that serious."

"If you listened to me and if anyone let Viktor talk, we could've explained all this together."

"May I tell your father this information?"

"If it's going to help him change his mind, you can tell him. But he better not go after Viktor because of it." I'd never forgive my father. "Mom, this isn't just infatuation or a crush. I love him. And he loves me. We want a future together."

"I saw the way he looked at you yesterday. I do believe he loves you very much."

"Then please convince Dad to back off."

"I'll talk to him, but in the end, it's his decision."

Dad and Igor walk back into the house. "It is time to leave, Irina."

Mom leans over and gives me one more hug. "I love you, and I'll do what I can," she whispers.

"Thank you."

"Amelia," Dad says. "I do not want to leave with this negativity between us."

"All you have to do is agree to accept Viktor and me together."

"That I cannot do."

"I hope you both have a safe flight," I say and start walking to my bedroom.

"Maxim, please don't leave things like this," Mom begs.

"Irina, do not overstep."

Once I'm in my room, I pull out my phone to text Viktor.

Me: They're leaving now. I'll let you know when Igor gets the message that their plane has left.

Viktor: I can't wait to see you.

Viktor

Yury and I are waiting at a coffee shop a few blocks from the house. We're excited to see our loved ones, but neither of us is willing to take the chance to go there until we know Maxim is safely in the air and on his way back to Russia.

When I was invited to the house for Christmas, I naively held onto the hope that perhaps Max was coming around, even slightly. I was wrong. He only did it to appease Amelia for the day. Now I'm facing the inevitable, I'll have to return to Russia in less than two days. That doesn't mean I'm giving up. My return to Russia is for one reason—to change Maxim's mind about us.

Amelia

Igor assures me he watched Dad's jet leave the ground. You and Yury can come over as soon as you're ready.

Me: We'll be there in about ten minutes.

"Ready to go?" I ask Yury.

"I was born ready." He grins.

With our bags in hand, we walk from the café to the house.

"Wow," Yury says when we get there. "This place is incredible."

"Max only buys the best."

Before we get all the way up the sidewalk, Amelia bursts through the door.

"I missed you so much." I drop my bag as she launches herself into my arms. "Don't ever leave me again."

My world rights itself when I wrap my arms around her. I want to give her the assurances she seeks, but I can't until after this trip to Russia.

Hopefully, I'll be successful at convincing Max. But if he still refuses, I'm going to have to call in a few favors of my own to ensure Amelia and I are protected. Because I'm coming back to get her one way or another.

"Get a room, you two," Igor jokes as he bypasses us to greet Yury.

"Let's take this inside," I suggest.

Once we're safely in the house, I make the introductions.

"Amelia, this is Yury. Yury, this is Amelia."

"I've heard a lot about you," Yury says as he gives her a hug. "I'm glad we're finally getting to meet."

While Igor takes Yury to their room to get settled, Amelia and I go onto the balcony.

"There's something you're not telling me," Amelia says once we're alone.

"What do you mean?"

"You're giving in and going back to Russia, aren't you?"

Fuck. I don't want this to ruin the short time we have together. "Can we not talk about this right now? I want to focus on us."

Igor pops his head out the door. "We're going to spend the day at the beach. You two enjoy yourselves."

Amelia and I stare at one another. No words are exchanged until they leave.

"I need you, *moya zirka*."

"You have me. You'll always have me." She takes my hands and leads me to our room. "I've missed you." Amelia slides her yoga pants off. Then she pulls her shirt over her head. She's not wearing a bra or panties.

"You were walking around bare under your clothes with another man in the house?" I growl.

"Igor?" She tilts her head. "Let me let you in on a little secret. He's gay." She smirks.

"I don't care," I say as I rip off my shirt and unbutton my jeans, pushing them and my boxers down in one move. "I don't want another man even accidentally getting a glance at what's mine."

"I love it when you get possessive."

"Do you now?" I advance toward her, grab her waist, and put her over my shoulder.

Amelia laughs and pretends to punch my back. "Put me down."

I slap her ass. "As you wish, my lady."

Gently, I toss her onto the bed. She pushes up on her elbows and watches me as I spread her legs and devour her pussy.

"God, I've missed you," I say between licks. Then, I add two fingers fucking her while my tongue attacks her clit.

"Viktor, it's too much," she pants.

"Come for me. I want to hear you scream my name."

I increase the intensity of my fingers and suck her clit. She calls my name as her body explodes. Then, she grabs at my arms, trying to pull me up.

"Do you need something, moya zirka?"

"I need you."

"Where?"

"Inside me. Please, Viktor."

"I love it when you beg for me." I line myself up with her opening and push myself inside in one forceful action. "Is that better?"

"Mhm. More, please."

"I'm not going to be gentle. But if it's too much, all you have to say is stop." I may be possessive, but I never want her to feel like she's a possession. She must always feel empowered and remember she has a voice that'll be heard and respected.

"Okay." Her voice is breathy.

My hips move in a punishing rhythm. "You. Are. Mine. Do you hear me, Amelia? Mine."

"Yes, Viktor." Her tiny hand cups my cheek. "I'm yours. I've always been yours. I'll always be yours. You'll never be alone again."

Amelia doesn't know how much power her words hold. They took root in my heart, binding me with her. There's no force on earth that can separate us.

I fuck her harder and deeper until the lines of where one of us begins, and ends are no longer clear. We're one as our bodies climax together.

Amelia

Viktor and I spent the day making up for lost time. As much as I want to spend every second we have alone, we also need to eat. We're sitting in the kitchen, deciding whether we'll cook or order take-out when Igor and Yury come back from the beach.

This is the first time I'm seeing Igor without my father around. He's usually uptight, like all the other men my father employs. I like this version of Igor much better.

"Did you kids have a good afternoon?" Igor asks, a knowing smile on his face.

"It was acceptable." Viktor shrugs.

I slap his arm, and we share a laugh. "Have you two eaten yet?" I ask as they join us at the table?

"No. We were going to see if you want to go out for dinner?"

Viktor and I look at each other before we answer in unison. "Sure."

Viktor calls Bay Front, our favorite go-to restaurant, and makes a reservation for an early dinner.

"So, what's the plan?" Igor gets right to the point.

"I have no choice but to return to Russia."

Every muscle in my body tenses while Viktor's speaking. "I don't want you to go."

"I don't want to either, but there's no other option."

"He's right. If he doesn't confront your father on his turf, there's no chance of resolving this."

"My father made it clear he isn't changing his mind. I don't see the point of you going."

"*Moya zirka*, it must be done."

"And when he still refuses?"

"I'll deal with that if it happens." Viktor takes my hand in his.

"Yury and I will stay with you while Viktor's gone."

I give him a small smile. I've gotten to know Igor better over the past few days, and although I'm glad they'll be here, I'm worried for Viktor.

"Let's not overfocus on that tonight. I have another twenty-four hours before my flight leaves."

Twenty-four hours. That's it? My next breath is hard to take. I can feel the panic clawing at me, seeking to drag me into its deep abyss. Fight it, Amelia. Don't let the fear win. Instead, I do what I'm taught and focus on the things around me. My hand in Viktor's. The men talking. Take it one breath at a time until the panic abates. I'm okay, and Viktor will be too.

We arrive at the restaurant a few minutes early. Every head turns as we pass the other diner's tables. I can only imagine what they're thinking. One younger girl with three much older and drop-dead gorgeous men. I hear some of the whispers and almost laugh out loud. Eat your heart out, ladies. These three are spoken for.

We're seated on the back patio that overlooks the bay. In my opinion, this is the best seat in the entire restaurant. It's the best time, too. The sun's just beginning to drop below the horizon. The sky is painted vivid shades of purples and pinks.

"I'll be right back." Viktor excuses himself from the table.

"Did Viktor tell you it's his birthday Sunday?" Igor asks.

"New Year's Day?"

"Yep."

"No, he didn't." Our server arrives at our table to take our drink orders. "We're here celebrating my boyfriend's birthday." The server takes note and promises an after-dinner surprise.

The food's delicious as always, and the company's even better. It's a nice reprieve from the stress of the past few days. The four of us get along so well. It's easy to forget who these men are and what they do when we're sharing these ordinary moments together.

While we talk, I learn that Igor and Yury have been together for nearly ten years. However, their relationship and Igor's sexuality have always been a secret.

"I'd like us to go public. I want to marry him. But Igor's worried we won't be accepted." Yury takes Igor's hand in his. "And that he'd lose his job," he says quietly.

Before this week, I would've said that's a crazy thought. But after seeing how my father treated Viktor when he found out about us, Igor's worries may be legitimate.

"You'll always have a safe place with us," I reassure them.

"Thank you, sweetie," Yury says with a smile. "We both appreciate that."

"How often do you see each other back home?"

"Not very much," Igor says sadly. "When Yury lived in St. Petersburg, we could see each other more. But, since he's moved back to Ukraine, it's much harder to sneak away."

"Why do you keep working for Max when that's the very thing keeping you apart?"

"Your father saved my life." A haunted look comes over Igor's face.

He's interrupted when several servers head our way with a

cake in hand and singing Happy Birthday. Viktor's eyes grow wide in surprise. I grab my phone to record the moment.

"How did you?" Viktor asks and then looks at Igor, who shrugs.

After we leave the restaurant, we go back home, where we spend the rest of the evening playing a highly competitive game of Monopoly. The game continued until three a.m. when Viktor was declared the winner.

"Can we go to bed now?" I yawn.

Viktor scoops me up from where I sit on the couch. "Goodnight, everyone."

"Don't worry," Igor calls. "We'll clean up the mess."

"Leave it. I'll get it in the morning," Viktor calls before closing the bedroom door behind us.

Viktor

THIS IS THE LAST TIME I'LL SEE AMELIA FOR A WHILE. I keep saying it'll be a few days, but in reality, I don't know how long it'll take to get through to Maxim. But right now, I don't want to think about that. I want to focus all of my attention on Amelia.

"Lie down," I say.

Amelia crawls onto the bed, and I straddle her. My hands start at her hips and slide her shirt up her body. She puts her arms out over her head as my hands continue their path, taking her shirt off. After tossing her shirt off to one side, I hold her arms above her head with one hand and lean down to kiss her.

Her lips are soft as they welcome mine and open, allowing my tongue access to her mouth. The kiss isn't hurried. It's languid and full of unspoken emotions. It tells the tale of impending separation and heartache.

I let go of her arms and pull my shirt over my head. I need to feel her. To memorize the feel of her body beneath mine. Amelia runs her hands down my chest and abdomen. She works to open the button on my jeans. I help her slide them and my boxers off and then help her shimmy out of her leggings.

She's on full display for me in her dark purple bra and panties.

"You're perfect." I make no effort to move. Instead, I take in every inch of her beauty. "I don't deserve you."

"Don't say stuff like that." Amelia puts her finger to my lips. "You, Viktor Dobrow, deserve all the love in the world."

Reverently, I slide her satin panties down her legs, then reach behind her to unclasp her bra. I toss it to the floor with the rest of our clothes. I lean down and take one of her pert nipples into my mouth. She mewls in pleasure. I take my time lavishing attention on her breast before moving to the other side and doing the same.

Amelia runs her hands up my back, pulling my face back to hers. Our mouths collide. This time, the kiss is filled with a sense of desperation. We both know time's running out.

"Please, Viktor. Make love to me." Amelia's plea is barely above a whisper.

I guide my erection inside her and begin moving slowly and gently. I don't want to rush this. Don't want to miss a single touch. This, tonight, needs to last until we're together again.

Our hands explore every inch of one another. Our bodies rock in perfect synch. Our hearts beat as one as we chase a shared climax. Her body begins to pulse around mine, triggering my orgasm. As we share this most intimate of moments, Amelia's tears pour down her face.

"Please don't cry, *moya zirka*," I beg between kisses.

"I don't want to let you go. I don't want us to be over."

"We're not over. We'll never be over."

Viktor

Quietly, I pack a bag while Amelia's still sleeping. My flight leaves tomorrow afternoon. Igor plans to stay with Amelia while Yury drives me to LAX.

I've been downplaying this trip. I don't want Amelia to worry any more than she already is. But I can't lie to myself. I'm not looking forward to this trip. Not only because I'll be apart from Amelia, but I'm sure what we saw from Maxim when he was here was nothing compared to what's going to happen when I get to St. Petersburg.

"Are you packing already?" Amelia asks.

"I am." I walk to the bed and sit next to her. "Did you sleep well?"

"I guess so." She sits up. "Are you sure—" Her sentence is interrupted by the ringing of her phone. "It's my father." Amelia accepts the call and puts it on speaker. "Hello?"

"I did not wake you, did I?" Maxim asks.

"No, I've been up for a little bit."

There's a long pause.

"Amelia, I do not like how we left things between us."

"Neither do I."

"I know you want me to give my blessing for you to have a relationship with Viktor. But I cannot."

"Why are you being so unreasonable? You know Viktor. You trust Viktor. So, how is he not a good choice of a man for me?"

"You are little more than a child. He is old enough to be your father."

"Age doesn't matter. I told you about my parents."

"You did, yes. But moya malen'kaya ptichka, please try to see this from where I am looking. I want you to meet a boy your age. Someone who is not involved in this business. With Viktor comes danger. Danger, I do not want you in."

"Aren't I in danger just by being your daughter?"

Maxim hesitates before answering, "Yes."

"Then I don't understand. How's being with Viktor any different?"

"He is actively working. He will have to be gone on jobs." Max pauses. "One day, he may not come back. You will be left alone."

Amelia looks at me with tears in her eyes. "I understand, and I accept that risk."

"I do not."

"Dad, I'm going to see him with or without your blessing."

"Viktor is due back here tomorrow. Since I know he is most likely listening to this conversation, let me make myself perfectly clear. If you and Viktor try to see one another after tomorrow, I will no longer be responsible for what happens to him."

"Please don't do this," Amelia begs.

"My decision is final."

"Goodbye, Dad." Amelia hangs up the phone. Her hands are trembling, and tears stream down her face.

"Don't go, Viktor. Please."

"I have to." I wipe the tears from her face. "I'll be back. I promise."

"No, Viktor, you won't. Dad's not going to let you come back."

"I have to face him."

"He's going to let the Albanians take you." She's getting more frantic by the second. "Don't go back there. We can run away together. Igor will help us."

I take her hand in mine. "What about your tour?"

"I don't care about the tour. The only thing I care about is you." She drops to her knees in front of me. "Please. Let's pack our things and go. Right now."

"*Moya zirka*, don't do this." She folds in on herself, falling deeper into a panic attack. I get on the floor with her. "Stay with me, Amelia. Don't let the fear win." But she no longer hears me. Instead, she's alone, lost in her panic.

There's a knock on my door. "Everything ok in there?" Igor calls.

"No."

The door cracks open. When Igor sees the state Amelia's in, he rushes into the room. "What's going on?"

"She's having a panic attack."

"What the hell do we do?"

"First, you need to calm down."

Igor goes to reach out to her.

"Don't touch her. You'll make it worse," I say as calmly as I can. "Amelia, baby, listen to me." Despite Igor's presence, I begin to sing quietly. She doesn't respond right away. I keep singing, praying I break through the walls she's erected.

Finally, her crying begins to subside. I put my arms out, and Amelia collapses against me. "It's okay, *moya zirka*. I've got you." I look up at Igor, who's watching over us with tears in his eyes. "Everything's going to be okay."

"I'll leave you two alone," he says quietly and leaves the room, closing the door softly behind him.

We stay on the floor until she feels more secure. Then, we take a long, hot shower together before joining Igor and Yury in the kitchen.

Amelia

Yury loves to cook, and he's really good at it. He makes sure the four of us sit down together for all our meals—like we're a real family. This morning's no different. He's cooked breakfast, and we sit down to eat, but things are not okay. Viktor's leaving for the airport tomorrow. Yet the guys talk as though nothing's wrong. I sit quietly, not really listening or eating. I'm just pushing the food around on my plate.

"Are you all going to keep pretending Viktor's not leaving?" I finally speak up.

"That's not what we're doing, Amelia. This is the life we're used to. Things like this happen. We take it one day at a time."

"Dad's not going to let Viktor come back." I look between the men. "Don't you all see that?"

"Amelia, I need you to trust me," Viktor says.

"I do trust you," I reply and set my fork down. " But I don't want you to go. I can't do this without you."

He takes my hand in his. "I'm going to call Alex and Natalie. Maybe they can come out and stay with you until I get back."

"Okay," I say softly.

Viktor pulls up Alex's contact and puts the phone on speaker.

"Hello?" Alex answers.

"It's me."

"Is everything okay?"

"We're in a bit of a rough spot right now."

"Lana called. She told us what happened."

"I have a flight back to Russia. I'm leaving today," Viktor explains. "Is there any chance the three of you can fly out here and stay until I'm back?"

"Natalie's in the other room with Rose. They just finished up a session. Hang on while I get her."

Yury and Igor clear the breakfast plates while we wait.

"You should try to eat." Yury encourages me.

"I'm really not hungry. I'm sorry."

He leans down and kisses my forehead. "Let me know when you get hungry, and I'll make whatever you want."

"Sorry about that," Alex says when he returns

Natalie tries to quiet Rose, who's chattering away in the background.

"I filled Natalie in on what's happening."

"Can you guys come out here?" Amelia asks.

"Of course. Alex's looking for a flight right now. How long do you think you'll be gone?"

"I'm hoping only a few days."

I can't sit here and listen to this. I don't know if everyone is putting on a brave face for my benefit or what. They can't really believe my father's going to let Viktor come back in a few days.

If Viktor leaves me tomorrow, he'll never come back.

I can't listen to the rest of the call, so I go out onto the balcony. It's a stormy day, and angry waves crash onto the shore. They look and sound like I feel.

"They got a flight at six this evening. They're going to fly into the Long Beach Airport," Viktor says as he joins me on the balcony. "Yury probably won't be back by then, so Igor will pick them up."

"Thank you." I wrap my arms around him. "I still wish you wouldn't go."

"The last thing I want to do is leave you, but I have to do this." Viktor sits down and pulls me onto his lap. "If I don't go back, Max will hunt us down. We'll always be on the run, looking over our shoulders. You deserve better than that."

"He's never going to change his mind."

"It's not going to be easy, but please trust me. I'll make this work for us."

I rest my head against his chest, listening to the steady beat of his heart. There are no more words left to say.

"It's time to leave," Yury says quietly from the doorway.

"I'll be right there."

I lift my head and gaze into Viktor's blue eyes. His lips meet mine for a passionate kiss. He pulls back and tucks a curl behind my ear. As much as I don't want to, I force myself to stand.

"I can't say goodbye."

"Then we won't say it."

With a final kiss, he turns and walks away from me. I wanted to be strong, but I can't. "Please don't go," I cry and try to go after him, but Igor grabs onto me.

Viktor stops with his hand on the doorknob. "I'll be back as soon as possible," he says without looking back.

Then, he walks out the door.

"Let me go." I struggle to get out of Igor's grasp. "I have to stop him."

"He has to go."

"No. I need him to stay." My body shakes from the depth of pain and fear I'm experiencing.

Amelia

IGOR SHOULD BE HERE WITH ALEX AND NATALIE ANY minute. I've picked up one of Viktor's habits, pacing back and forth while I wait for them to get here. It's been forever since I've seen them, and right now, I really need their support.

The sound of a car pulling into the driveway interrupts my cadence, and I rush to the window. "They're here."

I rush over to unlock the door and throw it open. Natalie's already on her way up the steps. "Oh my gosh, this house is amazing." She gushes.

"Hello to you, too," I joke.

"Hi, sweetheart." She gives him a hug. "It's been too long."

"It has. You look great." Natalie's a few months pregnant and is just starting to sport a tiny bump.

"Thank you." She runs her hand over her abdomen.

"Auntie Melia." Little arms wrap around my leg.

"Hello there, big girl. I've missed you," I say as I pick her up and pepper her face with kisses, making her giggle.

"How are you holding up?" Alex asks.

"Not well. I still wish he didn't go."

"I know, but this is something he has to do."

"I guess." I shrug. "Are you guys hungry? Yury made a bunch of appetizers."

"I sure am." Igor kisses my cheek on his way to the kitchen. "He'll be okay."

We make our way to the kitchen and pick on the light snacks that are artfully arranged on our serving platters. While we're eating, Yury comes back from dropping Viktor off. He joins us at the table.

Everyone's chatting away as if this is a typical night. The only thing I can focus on is that Viktor's on his way to what I'm sure isn't going to be a fun time. I smile and pretend I'm having a good time, but my mind and heart are on a plane heading to St. Petersburg.

It's not long before Rose starts to get cranky.

"It's been a really long day for her," Natalie says. "We're going to have to call it a night."

I show them to my old bedroom, where they'll be staying. Igor's already brought their luggage in and set up the portable playpen for Rose to sleep in.

Then, I head to our bedroom. It's cold and lonely here without Viktor. I'm not ready to sleep, so I take my cell, sit on our private balcony, and wait for a call to let me know Viktor's arrived safely.

Viktor

Leaving Amelia sobbing in Igor's arms nearly shattered me. Every fiber of my being screamed to turn back, to hold her, to promise her everything would be okay. But I couldn't. I had to force myself to walk away, to board the plane to St. Petersburg, even though it felt like I was tearing out my own heart.

Now, I'm halfway through the eighteen-hour flight, and sleep is impossible. Every time I close my eyes, I see Amelia's tear-streaked face and hear her desperate pleas for me to stay. The memory claws at me, relentless. Desperate for distraction, I try to focus on the conversation I'll have with Maxim. But it's no comfort. Every scenario I run through ends the same way—with me either dead or wishing I were.

Snow is beginning to fall as the plane touches down in Russia. I quickly grew used to the climate in California and didn't miss winter at all. Dimitri's supposed to be picking me up. I search for him but don't find him anywhere.

Me: I'm here. Where are you?

Dimitri: In the car waiting.

I make my way to the main doors and scan the area for the car. I spot him on the far side of the parking lot. Dimitri and I have been on shaky ground for a while. The situation in Grenada didn't help anything. The fact he sees me freezing my ass off as I trek through the parking lot and he doesn't even attempt to drive closer is all I need to let me know he's still pissed at me.

When I get to the car, I'm shivering. I didn't pack any winter gear when we moved to California. I'm paying for that now.

I open the passenger side door and climb into the black SUV. I've never been so thankful for heated seats. My hands are so cold, they're numb. I hold them close to the vent to warm them.

"Did you forget it's winter?"

"No. I don't have my winter things. I left them all here."

"Oh. That's too bad," he says with mock sympathy. He's enjoying seeing me suffer.

Dimitri pulls out of the parking spot, and we make our way to the main road.

"I never got a chance to thank you for bailing me out. I wouldn't have made it out of Grenada alive if you didn't show up."

He doesn't answer. Doesn't give me any hint that he's even listening.

"I know I screwed up."

"Screwed up? You took off without telling anyone where you were going."

I was in a bad place. I put not only my life but the lives of others in danger.

"We've been brothers for most of our lives. It would've been nice to at least know you were alive."

"I didn't think you'd care."

"Oh yeah. I forgot. I have no feelings."

"I needed some space to clear my head."

"You nearly got yourself and Jessica killed."

"I realize that." I close my eyes, knowing how lucky I am that Dimitri showed up when he did. "I thought going to visit *Babusya* would help. I had no idea she was sick," I say quietly. "Her death only made things worse. I didn't care if I lived or died."

"Did you ever think that other people might give a shit?"

"No." It's not a great answer, but it's the truth.

Dimitri doesn't respond again until he pulls into Max's garage.

"And now? Have you decided to live?"

"Yes." Although I'm not sure how long Maxim's going to let that happen. "I have a lot to live for."

"Amelia?"

"You know?"

"Everybody knows. Max was livid when he came home."

We get out of the car. "How is he now?"

"Still out for blood." Dimitri snickers. "By the way, he's waiting for you in his office. I'll put your bag in your room."

He walks away, and I'm left to face the boss alone.

Viktor

Dimitri makes a right and heads toward the guards' wing while I go straight to Maxim's office. Pyotr is on duty outside the office.

"Good to see you, Viktor."

"You too. I'm told the boss is waiting for me."

"He is. You can go in."

I've never been afraid to enter Maxim's office—until now.

"Dimitri said you wanted to see me right away."

"Sit," Maxim says without looking up.

Hesitantly, I walk to the leather chair across from his desk and take a seat.

"You are being reassigned. Starting today, you will be stationed here," Max explains. "You will report to Yevgeniy."

"That won't be necessary. I'm resigning."

"That is unacceptable." He stands and rounds the desk. "The assignment was not a request."

I stand, meeting him head-on. "The only reason I returned was to discuss my relationship with Amelia. I'm in love with your daughter. When I leave here, I'm going back to her."

The words are barely out of my mouth when Max's fist connects with my face.

"The hell you are," he yells. "Whatever you think you had with her is over. Do you understand me?"

"No, boss. It isn't." His fist connects with my face again. "What we have is real, and I'm not willing to walk away from her."

Max may be an older man, but he keeps himself in good physical shape. His fist connects with my face again, and blood spatters on the floor. I don't try to block or defend myself, knowing he needs an outlet for his anger.

"You will stay the fuck away from my daughter."

"I can't do that, boss." He can physically punish me however he wants, but I refuse to turn my back on Amelia.

"You do not have a choice. She is off-limits."

Fists rain down on me, relentless and punishing, each blow brutal. He lands one squarely against my torso, and a sharp crack reverberates through the room. Pain explodes in my chest, stealing the air from my lungs. My knees hit the floor, and I'm left gasping, unable to draw a single breath.

"I should have let the Albanians kill you. It is not too late. One phone call is all it will take.

"I'm sorry," I cough, trying to catch my breath. "Neither of us planned this."

"You are a grown man. She is an eighteen-year-old child."

"Amelia isn't a child. She's a grown woman who's free to make her own choices."

"I do not want to hear you speak her name," Max roars. "Stay the fuck away from my daughter."

"You're going to need some more time to accept that we're together. I understand that."

Another barrage of punches and kicks rains down on me. I curl into myself, trying to shield vital areas, but there's no true escape from the onslaught. Max's fury pours out with every strike, each blow a brutal reminder of the price I have to pay. I grit my teeth against the pain, knowing this is the only path forward.

The office door flies open and cracks off the wall.

"What the hell?" Dimitri yells. "Max, you're going to kill him."

"That is my plan." Maxim doesn't stop his assault on me.

"Boss, stop," Pyotr yells as he pulls Max away.

"Get the fuck off me." Max struggles to get out of his hold.

"You don't want to do this." Pyotr tries to reason with him.

"The fuck I do not," Max argues. "If you value your life, you will let me go."

Pyotr ignores Max's threats.

"Since when do we turn on our own men?" Dimitri faces off with his uncle.

"Since he touched my daughter."

"I get it. You're mad."

"Mad? Is that what you think, nephew?" Max's voice booms. "I am beyond mad."

"Okay, you're beyond mad. But Viktor's one of us. He's family."

"He is no longer family. He is dead to me."

His words hurt worse than any one of his physical strikes.

"Come on. Get up." Dimitri helps me from the floor. "Uncle, you don't mean that."

"Do not tell me what I mean or do not mean, Dimitri." Max points at me. "He touched something that did not belong to him."

"Amelia is not a piece of property," I snap back. "She made a choice."

"She is too young to know better." Max takes another swing at me, but Dimitri jumps in front of him.

"Boss, Amelia's an adult. She's old enough to make her own decisions—even if they're ones you disagree with."

"Are you taking his side?"

"I'm taking Amelia's side since she's not here to speak for herself," Dimitri says calmly. "I get it. You want to kill him. But what about Amelia? If you take away her voice. If you refuse to let her have a voice, you're no better than Moreno or any of the men who've hurt her."

Silence.

Dimitri struck a nerve.

"Get him out of my sight." Max storms out of his office. Pyotr follows behind him.

"Are you okay?" Dimitri turns to me.

"I'm pretty sure he broke at least one rib." Breathing is harder than it should be.

"Let's go." Dimitri helps me walk. "We'll have the doc take a look at you."

I lean on him for support. "You shouldn't have gotten in the middle of that."

"Should I have let him kill you?"

"He wouldn't have killed me."

"How about you just thank me for saving your ass again."

"Thank you for saving my ass again," I say mockingly.

"You owe me." Dimitri grins. "And I plan on cashing in on that debt."

Amelia

I'm lying on my bed when my phone buzzes next to me. Viktor's name lights up the screen, and I answer immediately.

"How are you?" I ask, my voice tight with worry.

He exhales, the sound weary. "Your father called me to his office as soon as I arrived," he begins, recounting everything that happened.

My stomach churns as he finishes. "Three fractured ribs? Viktor, that's not okay," I exclaim, sitting up.

"It is," he replies. "Max needed to vent his anger, and this was the only way."

"He didn't have to hurt you," I argue, my voice rising. "I hate him for this, Viktor. I really do."

"No, you don't," he counters gently. "You're angry and upset right now, but deep down, you know your father loves you."

I pace the length of my room, my free hand clenching into a fist. "That's not love," I snap. "Love doesn't do this to people."

"He was protecting you," Viktor says, his tone maddeningly calm. "In the only way he knows how. I don't blame him for it."

I stop in my tracks and glare at the floor as though he's standing there. "I don't know how you can forgive him so easily."

"I understand him," he says. "If I were in his position, I'd probably do the same thing."

His words hit me like a slap. "How much longer are you going to be gone?" I ask, desperate to change the subject. It's been two days, but it already feels like an eternity.

"I'm not sure," he admits, his voice softer now. "Hopefully, not much longer. Dimitri just came in—I need to handle something. Can I call you later?"

I swallow hard, the ache in my chest growing. "Yes," I murmur reluctantly.

"I love you, *moya zirka*."

"And I love you," I reply, my voice trembling.

We hang up, and I hold the phone against my chest. I can't believe my father physically attacked him. I'm furious and debate calling him to tell him exactly what I'm thinking. The only thing holding me back is Viktor. I fear my father would retaliate by hurting Viktor more.

Instead, I decide to ask Natalie if she'd intervene.

It's just the three of us here right now. Alex gave Igor and Yury a few unofficial days off. They went to a nearby hotel to ring in the new year alone. I find Natalie sitting on the sofa, a movie on pause. Alex is on the phone out on the balcony. It looks like they're having some downtime while Rose takes her afternoon nap.

"What's wrong?"

"Everything," I say and sit on the ottoman across from her.

"What's going on?" Alex asks as he comes back into the room.

"My father broke three of Viktor's ribs."

"Oh my God." Natalie brings her hand to her mouth. "Is he okay?"

"He said he's fine." I sigh. "Dad told Viktor he's dead to him. I think that hurt more than the broken ribs." Alex and Natalie exchange a worried glance. "Natalie, I need your help. Dad will listen to you if you talk to him."

"I don't know—"

"Please, Natalie."

"What do you think, Alex?" We both stare at him expectantly.

"Give me a little time to figure something out," Alex says. "Meanwhile, we have a New Year to celebrate tonight."

"I don't feel like celebrating."

"I didn't ask," Alex smirks. "Go take a shower or whatever you need to do to get ready for a party." He tilts the ottoman, forcing me to get up.

"What's wrong with your husband?"

"He likes to be in control." Natalie winks.

"You two can celebrate. I'll keep Rose tonight."

"Nope. We're all celebrating together," Alex insists.

I roll my eyes at him. "Whatever you say, boss," I say in my best sarcastic voice.

"That's better. Now go." Alex points down the hall.

There's nothing for me to celebrate. I was planning a quiet evening in my room where I could feel sorry for myself. I guess that's not going to happen now.

Alex

"YOU REALIZE SHE'S NOT IN A PARTYING MOOD?" Natalie asks, her brow furrowed in concern.

"She will be," Alex says confidently, a hint of a smirk playing on his lips. "Dimitri called. He just put Viktor on Max's jet a few minutes ago. If all goes well, he'll be here just before midnight."

Natalie's eyes widen. "Max changed his mind?"

"No," I interject, lowering myself onto the couch beside her. "Max is still determined to keep them apart. But Dimitri was worried about Viktor's safety if he stayed there. So, he went behind Max's back and got Viktor on a plane home."

Natalie's expression shifts from surprise to unease. "Oh. What's going to happen to Dimitri when Max finds out?"

"He'll be fine," I reassure her, picking up my phone. "I have an idea."

Her gaze sharpens. "What kind of idea?"

I don't answer; instead, I tap the call icon. After a few rings,

Max's deep voice filters through the line. "Alexander. To what do I owe this?"

"Max," I say, keeping my tone light. "I didn't wake you, did I?"

"No," he replies, his voice heavy with exhaustion. "I have not been sleeping much lately. Is everything well there?"

"Yes," I say casually. "The girls are getting ready for tonight. Meanwhile, I'm trying to tie up some loose ends at Jelena's Hope NYC before the New Year."

There's a pause before Max speaks again, his voice softening. "How is Amelia? I am sure she has heard what occurred here."

"She did," I admit. "She's upset, as you might imagine."

Max sighs audibly, the weight of his guilt palpable. "I do not know what came over me. The thought of Viktor with my little girl... I could not control the rage I felt."

"Amelia isn't a little girl anymore," I remind him, keeping my tone even.

"That is what everyone keeps saying," Max says gruffly, "but I do not see it."

If I want my plan to work, I can't risk antagonizing him. I shift gears, opting for a softer approach. "I get it," I say. "I have a little girl too."

Finally, a hint of approval creeps into Max's voice. "Finally, a man with some sense."

"The reason for my call," I say, steering the conversation in a new direction, "is about Jelena's Hope. We've outgrown our residential units. We had to turn away the last two calls we received."

"We are going through the same growing pains here," Max notes, his tone thoughtful.

"Would you be able to meet me in New York to look at some new properties? I'd like to move on this quickly."

"How is the end of next week?" he offers.

"That would be perfect. Thanks, Max."

As I hang up, I feel a sense of relief wash over me. Getting Maxim on board was the biggest hurdle—now I need to pull the rest of this together.

Natalie looks at me skeptically. "Are you planning on bringing them both to New York?"

· · ·

"I am," I reply, my jaw tightening slightly.

"Do you really think that's a good idea?"

I shrug, the weight of uncertainty settling over me. "I don't know. But I have to try something. If we can get them on neutral ground, maybe we can make some progress—without the violence."

Natalie arches an eyebrow. "I sure hope you know what you're doing."

"So do I," I admit with a faint smile.

Amelia

I'VE BEEN TRYING TO REACH VIKTOR FOR HOURS, BUT my calls keep going straight to voicemail, and my texts remain unread. Frustration twists in my chest, but I refuse to speak to my father. Instead, I scroll through my contacts and call Lana.

"Good morning," Lana answers, her tone light. "Or should I say good evening?"

"Sorry for calling so early," I say quickly. "I've been trying to reach Viktor, but he's not answering his phone."

There's a pause before she responds. "I'm not sure where he is," she admits. "If I see him, I'll tell him to call you."

"Thanks." I hesitate, my voice faltering. "Lana, was he okay the last time you saw him?"

She exhales audibly. "He looked a little roughed up, but he'll live."

My heart clenches. "What got into Dad?"

Lana lets out a bitter laugh. "You do know who our father is, right?"

"Yes," I say, my voice quieter now. "But I didn't think he'd hurt one of his own men."

"Dad will stop at nothing if he believes it's to keep us safe," she replies matter-of-factly.

I shake my head, anger bubbling beneath my worry. "I'm not in danger with Viktor. I don't understand it."

"He still sees you as his little girl," Lana explains, her voice softening. "And Viktor is Dad's employee. He knew the boundaries and didn't respect them."

"The boundaries?" I ask sharply. "Don't I get a say in these so-called boundaries?"

"In Dad's eyes? No."

"Can you talk to him?" I plead. "Try to make him understand?"

Her tone shifts, turning guarded. "We're not really speaking to each other right now."

"Lana, what's going on with you?" I press gently. "I know something's up."

"I'm just trying to figure out what's next for me," she says vaguely.

She's not telling me everything. But I know if I push too hard, she'll shut me out. "Well, if you ever decide you want to talk, I'm here. I'm a good listener."

"Thanks, Melia," she says, her tone warming slightly. "I have to run. Happy New Year."

"I'll try," I murmur before the call disconnects.

I toss the phone onto my bed and sigh, running a hand through my damp hair. At Alex's insistence, I'd showered, but if he's hoping for a dress-up event, he'll be disappointed. Sweatpants and a T-shirt are as fancy as I'm getting tonight.

After tying my hair into a ponytail, I slip my phone into my pocket and head to the living room.

"It's about time you joined us," Alex greets me with a wide grin. "I had some food delivered."

I glance toward the kitchen counter, where an impressive spread of appetizers and finger foods is laid out. "That's enough food for an army. Are we expecting company?"

"I am eating for two," Natalie teases, rubbing her growing belly.

"Auntie Melia! Want some?" Rose toddles over, holding out her half-eaten peanut butter and jelly sandwich.

"Thank you, princess." I kneel to her level and pretend to take a big bite. "Your turn."

Giggling, she takes another bite before scampering off to her daddy, who scoops her onto his lap.

Natalie passes by, a plate in her hand, and gives me a pointed look. "That'll be Viktor and your baby one day."

"Not me," I say quickly. "I don't want kids."

"You'll change your mind."

Her words settle over me like a heavy cloud. Realizing I'm not in the right frame of mind to be around everyone, I head toward the door. "I'm going down to the beach for a little while."

"Want some company?" Alex asks, his grin fading slightly.

"No, thanks," I reply softly. "I just need some time alone. I won't go far."

Alex's expression turns serious. "Keep your phone with you," he says firmly.

"I will," I promise, stepping outside into the warm night air.

With the moonlight as my guide, I walk along the water's edge. The old year is quickly coming to a close, while the new year and all its promises are at the cusp of being born. The tranquility of the beach allows me the opportunity for reflection.

Life guarantees one thing: change. But the ocean, the constant I've come to love, remains steadfast. No matter the chaos that unfolds, the waves remain unaffected. They roll in, crashing against the shore in their steady, rhythmic dance. One after another. Day after day. Predictable. Safe. Calming.

It's a stark contrast to the storm raging inside me. Just days ago, my life felt perfect—more perfect than I ever dared to dream.

Then, in the blink of an eye, everything crumbled. Facades shattered. People revealed their true colors. I went from feeling protected in the arms of the man I love to standing alone, vulnerable, and exposed.

The ache in my chest is overwhelming, a suffocating weight I can't seem to escape. The ocean soothes me in a way nothing else can, but even its steady rhythm isn't enough to quiet the pain in my heart.

Opening my music app, I select my favorite playlist. Music plays softly as I lie down on the cool sand. The sky is full of millions of twinkling stars that transcend time and space. Somewhere up there are two stars that can never be separated—unlike Viktor and me.

I don't realize how long I've been lying here until I get a text alert.

Natalie: It's almost midnight. Will you come ring in the New Year with us?

Me: I'll be right there.

I try calling Viktor once more, but there's still no answer. Standing up, I wipe the sand off my clothes and start back toward the house.

Viktor

"Thanks for picking me up," I say to Igor and Yury. "Looks like we'll make it just in time."

I don't know how Dimitri pulled it off, but Max's jet was fueled and ready to fly me back to California. The universe must have been cheering me on because not only did we have the help of a tailwind, but Dimitri also arranged for us to land at the Long Beach Airport.

"Does Max know you're here?" Igor asks.

"I'm sure he does by now. Dimitri was going to speak to him after the jet was safely out of Russian airspace," I explain.

Right on cue, Igor's phone rings.

Yury checks it since Igor's behind the wheel. "It's Maxim."

Igor glances at me in the rearview mirror. "Answer it. But put it on speaker, please."

"Hello?" Igor answers, his tone carefully neutral.

"My nephew tells me my jet has landed in California with Viktor on board," Max says, his voice sharp and authoritative.

"That's what I've been told. I'm on my way to pick him up now," Igor replies, keeping his tone steady.

"Where is my daughter?"

"She's at home," Igor responds quickly, already anticipating the next question. "The doors are locked, and the security system is armed. I won't be gone long," he reassures him.

"I am trusting you to keep him away from Amelia."

"If I may speak freely, boss," Igor ventures carefully, "I think this is a good call—an olive branch if you will. Amelia's a sweet girl, but she's uncomfortable being alone with me. Having Viktor around will help ease some of her nerves."

There's a pause before he speaks again, his tone colder this time. "He is not to be alone with her."

"I understand, boss," Igor says, his words laced with dutiful respect. He's walking a fine line now, fully aware of the risks. "When will her new team arrive?"

"I am hoping it will be soon," Max admits, a rare note of frustration slipping through. "Unfortunately, it is taking more time than I would prefer to assemble a qualified team."

"Okay, no problem."

"I am trusting you to keep my little girl safe," Maxim says firmly, his protectiveness unmistakable.

"Amelia's a capable young woman," Igor replies with quiet sincerity, "but I'll guard her with my life, sir."

The call ends, and Igor exhales a relieved sigh.

"Thank you for doing this," I say.

"It's for a good cause," Igor says with a small smile. "You both deserve to be happy."

With it being close to midnight, there's not much traffic. Even still, the ride feels like it's taking forever. Finally, we're pulling up to the house. I rush inside and find Alex, Natalie, and Rose watching Times Square's New Year's Eve festivities.

"You made it." Natalie gives me a quick hug.

"Barely." I look around. "Where's Amelia?"

"She's on the beach," Alex says, "We've been keeping an eye on her."

I step onto the balcony and spot her lying on the sand. My beautiful girl.

"She's been lost without you," Natalie says as she comes to stand next to me.

"Are you sure I'm doing the right thing?"

"Viktor, you have so much love to give. I know because, for a few months, I was the recipient of that love. I'm ashamed to admit this, but After Alex came back, I wanted both yours and Alex's love," she admits. "It took a long time for me to see that it was unfair to everyone. Especially you." She looks up at me.

"You deserve to have a woman look at you and see their whole world. Someone who'll love you with the same all-encompassing love you give. Amelia is that woman. You're everything to her."

"I was afraid of how you'd feel about her and me. That you'd disapprove because of our age difference or that you'd think the feelings I had for you weren't real because I moved on."

"I'm not going to lie. I was shocked." She chuckles. "But I never questioned your feelings for her or me." Natalie touches my arm. "What you and I shared was beautiful and very complicated."

"That's putting it mildly."

"Circumstances beyond our control threw us together. I know you loved me, and I loved you. I always will. Love doesn't go away. But what you and I had wasn't the same all-encompassing love Alex and I share—what you and Amelia share."

"When she looks at me, she sees only me. Wants only me."

"That's exactly how it's supposed to be. As hard as I tried, I wouldn't have been able to give you that. In life or death, Alex and I will always be connected."

"I knew that."

"And yet you were willing to sacrifice what you deserved to be with me."

"I made a promise to Alex."

"And you honored that." Natalie looks out into the darkness. "I see the way you look at Amelia and the way she looks at you. Your heart recognized its soulmate."

"Even though I'm so much older than her?"

"Age is irrelevant. Your hearts and souls are connected. You were made for each other."

"Thank you, Natalie." I hug her. "I think I'm beginning to understand how lucky I am."

"It's about time." Natalie smiles.

"Hey, you two." Alex joins us on the deck. "There's only fifteen minutes until midnight. Amelia needs to come back for her New Year's surprise."

"I'll text her now." Natalie's fingers fly across her screen. It's only seconds before she gets a reply. "She's on her way."

"Let's ring in the New Year, baby girl," Alex says, and we walk into the house together.

"I'm going to wait in our room. I don't want her to know I'm here until midnight."

Amelia

"Igor. Yury. What are you guys doing here?" I'm surprised to see them. I thought they were ringing in the New Year alone.

"We wanted to spend the holiday with friends," Yury says.

There's less than five minutes until the ball drops. Natalie passes champagne flutes out to everyone.

I look around the room. Rose is passed out on the couch. Igor and Yury are together. Natalie's wrapped in Alex's embrace. But I'm alone. The man I wish was by my side is on the other side of the world.

The ball slowly starts to fall, and everyone counts aloud. "Five, four, three, two, one."

"Happy New Year, *moya zirka*."

Everything disappears as I spin around and find Viktor a few steps behind me, a champagne flute in his hand and a huge grin on his face.

"Viktor? Are you really here?"

He takes a step toward me. "I am."

I close the distance between us and throw my arms around him, spilling champagne in the process. His breath catches.

"I'm sorry." I try to back away. "I forgot about your ribs."

"You're not going anywhere." He holds me tight with one arm.

"Your face." She gently touches the bandage over my eye. "Did you need stitches?"

"Yes, but don't worry about it." He holds up his glass. "Here's to a happy and prosperous new year."

We clink glasses, and then our lips meet for a kiss.

"Happy Birthday," I whisper between kisses. "I wasn't able to get you anything."

"You're all I want."

"You already have me."

"And I plan on having you all night," he growls in my ear, making me squirm.

Alex clears his throat, "Did you two forget you're not alone?"

Viktor kisses me once more before we exchange New Year's toasts with everyone. I don't know what I did to deserve these wonderful friends—my chosen family. But I'm so thankful for them.

"Look at the time." Viktor pretends to check his non-existent watch. "It's time for us to go to bed."

"Smooth, Dobrow," Igor jokes.

I want to crawl under a piece of furniture and hide from embarrassment.

"Sleep tight." Alex laughs.

Viktor takes my hand and leads me out of the living room. As we walk away, I hear Yury say, "Well, it's past our bedtime, too."

"I really wish the rooms were soundproof," I mumble as we go into our room.

Viktor

Once we're in our room and the door's locked, I waste no time removing my shirt. My movements are stiff because of the pain.

Amelia gasps when she sees my chest. "I thought your face was bad. What did he do to you?"

I didn't stop to think about what her reaction would be. My chest is covered in bruises, and my ribs are taped tight.

"I'll be fine."

She steps closer and places her tiny hand on my chest.

"Does it hurt?"

"Only when I breathe."

"You need to lie down and rest."

"No, I need to be with you."

"I don't think so." Amelia puts her hands on her waist.

"It's my birthday wish." I smile.

She pauses as though she's considering my appeal. Then, she reaches out and opens my jeans. She pulls them down, followed by my boxers. I'm already hard for her.

"We can do this on one condition."

"I like bossy Amelia," I chuckle. "What's your condition?"

"You need to be on the bottom so you don't put stress on your ribs."

"That's a condition I can agree to."

She steps out of my way so I can lie down. I appreciate the sacrifice she's making tonight. Amelia's often insecure about being on top, so the significance of what she's doing is not lost on me.

"I think my birthday boy deserves a little show."

Carefully, I put my hands behind my head. Every movement is painful, but I try not to show that on my face.

Amelia takes out her phone and puts on music. She sways her hips to the seductive song that plays. As she does, she hooks her fingers in the waistband of her sweatpants and slowly slides them down her legs. When they're off, she tosses them to the side. She's bare underneath—something that usually infuriates me, but right now, I don't care. I'm entranced by this sexy, brave woman in front of me.

When she turns to face me, she's biting her lower lip. A move that gives away her insecurities.

"You don't have to do this," I remind her.

"I want to. But I don't feel very sexy doing it."

"Amelia Solonik, you are very sexy."

A smile spreads across her face as she crawls over me. If I'm not careful, I'll come before she touches me. Amelia sits back on her knees and pulls her shirt off. Her bra follows. She maneuvers her body between my legs until her mouth is centimeters from my cock. Then, she glances up at me through her thick lashes.

Her next move seems to go in slow motion. Without breaking eye contact, she drags her tongue from the base to the tip of my cock. My eyes roll back in pleasure as her tongue circles the sensitive tip before teasing my slit. Amelia looks up and licks her lips.

"You taste delicious, Mr. Dobrow." She runs her tongue across my tip once more.

"If you keep doing that, I'm not going to last."

"No?" she teases. "So, if I do this." She opens her lips and lowers her head, taking me all the way in before sliding back up slowly.

"Amelia," I growl.

"Yes?" Without warning, she takes me in her mouth again. She glides her mouth along my length while her other hand massages my balls.

"You need to stop."

She ignores me and continues her sensual movements.

"I can't hold back much longer," I grit out. "I'm going to come in your mouth if you don't stop." And I don't want to do that.

Amelia told me how she was forced to take men in her mouth. She described the helplessness of being unable to breathe as they forced their length down her throat. She's expressed fear that I wouldn't want her if she wouldn't do this for me. I reassured her that I would never ask or expect her to do anything she was uncomfortable with and that she could never be a disappointment to me.

She looks up at me. Her brown eyes dance with delight as she opens her mouth and takes me in again. My hips buck up of their own accord. She takes all of me—everything I have to give her. With a final thrust, I come in her mouth. Amelia doesn't falter as she swallows everything I have to give. When my cock stops throbbing, she sits back on her heels, a satisfied look on her face.

I don't say it aloud, but I'm so proud of Amelia. My brave girl's just conquered one of her fears. Taken back something that was stolen from her and made it her own.

"You're going to be the death of me. Get up here." She crawls up my body and situates herself over my still-hard dick. I take her by the waist and guide her down my length. "I missed you, *moya zirka*."

"Promise me that you'll never leave again."

As much as I want to make that promise, I can't. "If I leave, I'll always come back to you."

Amelia nods. She understands what my job is and what assurances I can and can't give her.

Without warning, she starts moving. My world is thrown off its axis by the sheer pleasure of being inside her.

"Touch yourself."

Amelia slides her hand down her front and between her legs. Her head falls back with a moan.

"That's it, *moya zirka*," I encourage her. "Fuck, you're amazing." Despite the stabbing pain in my chest, another orgasm is building. "Are you ready to come for me?"

"Yes. I'm—" Her sentence is interrupted by the orgasm that rips through her.

My hips thrust wildly. Once. Twice. "Fuck. Amelia." Blackness creeps into the corners of my vision from the force of the orgasm mixed with the pain in my chest. I try to hang onto consciousness. Despite my efforts, everything goes dark and silent as I lose the battle.

Amelia

"Viktor." I gently shake his shoulder, but he doesn't respond. "Viktor, wake up. You're scaring me." I knew it was too soon. I shouldn't have let him talk me into this. What do I do now?

I dig through the pile of clothes on the floor for my sweatpants and T-shirt and get dressed quickly. Before I leave the room, I pull the covers over him. Even though I don't want to disturb anyone else, I have to. Viktor still isn't waking up.

I knock on the bedroom door. "Igor," I call, not too loudly. I don't want to wake up the whole house.

It takes a minute before he answers the door. When he does, he's wearing only a pair of shorts. "What's up?"

"I'm sorry for bothering you. Viktor passed out, and I can't wake him up."

"Shit." He rushes down the hall and into our room. "Viktor." He shakes him more aggressively than I did.

I stand back, frightened by my unresponsive boyfriend.

"What happened?" Yury asks when he gets to our room.

"Um. Well, we were—"

My sentence is interrupted when Viktor begins to come to. I rush over to the bed.

"Is everything okay in here?" Alex appears in the doorway.

Yury fills him in while Igor and I tend to Viktor.

"Welcome back," Igor says with a smirk.

"What happened?"

"You passed out after you—"

"Stop," Viktor interrupts.

"You're lucky you didn't injure yourself any further," Igor says. "You have three broken ribs. You need to be resting, not fucking."

"Watch your mouth." Viktor glances my way before sliding himself to a sitting position with a groan. "I'm fine. You can all go back to bed."

"I'm serious. You need to take it easy." Igor looks at me. "I don't care what he says. The answer's no."

"Got it. I'm sorry for bothering everyone."

The men exit the room, leaving Viktor and me alone.

"You shouldn't have gone to Igor."

"You wouldn't wake up." I rest my head on his shoulder. "I was scared and didn't know what else to do. Are you sure you're okay?"

"I'll live."

"We aren't doing that again until I'm certain you're healed."

I don't have the strength to argue with her. The exhaustion from my injuries and the long flight are hitting me hard. "I'll let you win this one."

Amelia climbs out of bed.

"Where are you going?"

"Stay there. I'll be right back." She disappears into our bathroom.

It's not like I have much of a choice. I don't think I could follow her if I tried. When she returns, she has a wet washcloth and a towel in her hands. With great tenderness, she washes my body and then helps me slip on a pair of pajama pants.

"Do you need anything else?"

"You. Next to me."

Amelia climbs into bed and pulls the blanket over us.

I was only gone a few nights, but I'd grown used to her next to me. One night without Amelia is too many.

Tonight, I fall asleep with my world in my arms.

Amelia

AMELIA

It was so much fun having everyone here this week. For a little while, I didn't think about everything with my father. Instead, we were able to focus on spending quality time with Alex, Natalie, and Rose.

Viktor's so good with Rose. He's still having difficulty with movements, but somehow, he's managed to get on the floor with her to have a tea party. He's even wearing her princess tiara.

"I hate that you guys are leaving today."

"Me too," Natalie says. "It doesn't feel like we had enough time, but we have to get back to Jelena's Hope NYC."

While Viktor was sipping tea with Rose, Natalie filled me in on Alex's plan to get Viktor and Max together in New York next week. I'm scared that Dad's going to flip. That he's going to hurt Viktor again or worse. Natalie assured me that there would be enough security to keep any more violence from happening. I'm not totally on board, but I don't see we have any other choice.

"Princess Viktor," Natalie jokes.

"What?" he asks, pretending to take a sip from a little pink teacup.

Rose lets out a belly laugh.

"How about you and Amelia come out to visit us for a few days next week?" she asks. "Rose, do you want Friker and Auntie Melia to come to our house?"

I have to give it to her. Natalie's good. She knows Viktor can't say no to Rose.

"Friker, can you come see me at my house?" Rose jumps onto his lap. "Pwease?"

"What do you think, Auntie Melia?" he asks.

"I'd love that."

Viktor grabs Rose and holds her in the air. "I guess we're going to New York City, then."

Viktor and I drive to Long Beach Airport for Alex and Natalie's flight.

"We'll see you two in a few days," she says. "Try not to worry. We'll figure this out."

"I hope you're right."

Natalie gives me a reassuring smile before walking over to Viktor, who's holding Rose and chatting with Alex.

"We're going to need to take her with us." Natalie reaches out, but Rose turns away and wraps her little arms around Viktor's neck.

"Printessa, you need to go with your mama. I'll see you very soon." He tries to pry Rose's hands from his neck, but she whimpers.

My heart aches watching this scene unfold. Even though Viktor hasn't spent much time with her since he left, she's still very much bonded with him.

"Rose, we have to go home so you can get your toys ready to play with Friker," Natalie says. After a moment of indecision,

Rose lets go, and Viktor passes her to Natalie. She rests her head on her mama's shoulder while big tears fall. "Don't cry." Natalie soothes her daughter.

The boarding call for their flight plays over the speakers.

"That's us," Alex says. "We'll see you soon." He and Viktor exchange a quick hug. Then, he turns to me. "Hang in there, okay?"

"I will." We hug each other goodbye.

Viktor and I hold hands while we watch them go through security, and they disappear from our sight.

Amelia

Alex and Natalie flew out a few days ago, and last night, Yury flew back to Ukraine. We went from a full house to just the three of us. The quiet won't last for long. Tomorrow, Viktor, Igor, and I are flying out to New York, where I'm afraid sparks will fly.

I've finished packing and am going outside to collect the day's mail while the guys are in the house discussing the new security team that's currently in St. Petersburg on trial with my father's men. If they get the final approval, he'll be sending them here sometime next month.

I open the mailbox and pull out the stack of mail. Most of it's junk, but one envelope catches my eye. It's from Mateo. I sit on the step and carefully open the envelope.

Dear Amelia,

I know I'm probably the last person you want to hear from, but I'm writing anyway. By now, Sparrow has probably told you what happened and where I am. I want you to know that I've been sober for three weeks. It's not much, but it's a start. I see my therapist every day, and we're working through my issues. Part of that work is making amends to the people I've hurt. You are one of those people.

The last day I saw you, you shared some of your story with me. I never got the chance to tell you mine. I'm adopted, too.

My biological mom was an addict. I never knew who my father was. After she overdosed, the Harts adopted me. They're good people —they don't deserve the shit I've put them through. I've never felt like I really belonged anywhere.

Summer was the perfect daughter—smart, accomplished, and always doing the right thing. And me? I'm the kid from the wrong side of the tracks, always screwing up. Sparrow was the only person I ever felt I could trust.

Until I met you. You only saw me. And by some stroke of luck, you liked me.

Amelia, you're so easy to love. You're good, kind, and everything I'm not. For a while, my world felt right, or at least I could pretend it was.

But I was so messed up—drugs, alcohol, all of it. I couldn't see straight. I wanted a future with you, but deep down, I knew you were right not to want me. I was as much of a screwup as my bio mom. The only difference was that no one knew what I was doing— or so I thought.

I messed up. I hurt the only people who cared about me. Everything that happened is my fault, and I accept that.

I'm sorry.

Those two words don't feel like enough, but they're all I have right now. I can't promise I'll never mess up again. Honestly, I can guarantee I'll screw something up at some point.

I accept that you're with Viktor. He's a lucky man. I won't lie— I'm jealous. But I know he'll protect your heart.

I plan to do everything I can to earn your trust and friendship back—if you'll let me. I don't expect an answer right away. I know this will take time.

I want to be better—for the tour, yes, but more importantly, for myself.

I've come to realize there are people who care about me in ways I didn't fully see before. That's something else I need to work through.

I can't have phone calls or visitors, except for family, for another two weeks. But when I can, I hope you'll be one of them.

Sincerely,

Matteo

I wipe the tears from my cheeks. I didn't expect this, but I'm glad to hear Matteo's getting the help he needs. He's a good guy. My phone dings with a text.

Sparrow: Did you get a letter from Matteo too?

Me: I did. It sounds like he's doing a lot of soul-searching.

Sparrow: It does.

Sparrow: He knows.

Me: He knows what?

Sparrow: How I feel about him. Once he was three weeks sober, he was allowed to start having contact with his family. His dad asked that he also be allowed to talk to me since we've been like brothers.

Me: That must've been a difficult conversation.

Sparrow: It was. I didn't know if I should tell him or not, but I decided there wouldn't be a better time.

Me: What did he say?

Sparrow: He wasn't as shocked as I thought he'd be. He didn't close the door on it completely.

Me: That's a good thing, right?

Sparrow: We'll see.

"There you are," Viktor says as he comes to sit next to me.

Me: I have to go. We're flying to New York City tomorrow.

Sparrow: Have a great trip.

"Why are you crying?"

I show Viktor the letter from Matteo. He's as surprised as I am. But we both agree it's a good sign.

Matteo has a long road ahead of him, but he seems to be working in the right direction.

Amelia

Viktor's alarm blares in the silence of the morning. Viktor sits up and throws off the covers. I roll over and put my pillow over my head, trying to ignore it.

"Let's go, sleepyhead." Viktor takes my pillow. "We have a plane to catch today."

"Can't I sleep just a little longer?"

"Nope," he says, far too awake for me. "We have enough time to take a shower, eat, and get to the airport."

"Fine." I sit up and swing my legs over the side of the bed. "As long as I can have coffee."

"That can be arranged."

After a hot shower, Viktor and Igor pack the car, and then we're off. We stop to grab a late breakfast and a coffee at the drive-thru. My stomach is twisted in knots, making it hard to enjoy the coffee I was craving.

I'm terrified we're going to have a repeat of whatever went on between them in Russia. Viktor refuses to discuss it with me, but he's wearing the evidence on his body. The stitches are out, and the bruises are starting to fade, but his ribs are still healing.

As much as I want to get there, I want to turn around and go home just the same.

The flight goes by way too quickly, and we find ourselves in a rental car on the way to Alex and Natalie's.

Me: What time are my parents supposed to get here?

Natalie: About two hours.

Me: I'm so nervous I might throw up.

Natalie: Try to relax. There will not be any fighting. I promise.

I wish I was as confident.

"Is everything okay?" Viktor asks. "You don't look so good."

"I'm just a little nauseous from the car ride."

"You don't usually get carsick." Viktor looks concerned.

"It's probably because I didn't really eat. I'm sure I'll be fine once I have some food." I give him a reassuring smile.

Viktor turns into the underground parking. For better or worse, we're here. We have a few hours to get settled before the fireworks begin.

Viktor

AMELIA'S VERY PALE. SHE SAYS SHE'S OKAY, BUT I'M NOT buying her story. I can tell when she's nervous. We're not alone, so I don't push her to talk.

"You two go on up," Igor says. "I'll grab the bags."

"You sure?"

Igor nods and goes to the trunk while Amelia and I make our way to the elevator. I take her tiny hand in mine. It's trembling. When the elevator doors close, I turn her to face me.

"What's wrong? And don't tell me it's that you're nauseous from not eating."

"I'm feeling overwhelmed, and I'm trying to deal with it."

"I'm here." I put my arm around her. "You can lean on me."

"Thank you," she says quietly and tucks herself against me.

The elevator doors open, and Rose comes barreling at us.

"Friker. Auntie Melia," she squeals.

I step out of the elevator and squat down to her level to catch her. She wraps her arms around my neck as I stand up with her.

"My little *printessa*." I kiss her chubby cheek. "I told you I'd come to your house."

"Can we have a tea party?"

"We need to let Friker and Auntie Melia get settled in first, honey," Natalie says as she catches up to her rambunctious toddler. "Did you have a good flight?"

"We did," Amelia answers and gives Natalie a hug.

"Are you okay?"

"Just a bit nervous."

"We're going to have a great visit," Natalie says reassuringly. "Come on in and make yourselves at home. Are you hungry?"

"Amelia isn't feeling well." I pretend to go along with her story for now. "She says it's because she hasn't eaten." After I say the words, I experience a flashback. When this happened with Natalie, she was pregnant. Could Amelia be pregnant?

"Auntie Melia." Rose reaches her arms out, and I pass her over. "Do you want my *wunch*?"

"Thank you, princess. If I eat your lunch, your belly will be hungry." Amelia tickles Rose's tummy, making her laugh. "How about we go with mommy, and I can get my own lunch?"

"Okay." She gives Amelia a big smile.

That has to be it. Once we're alone, I'll bring it up. A smile spreads across my face at the thought—I'm going to be a father. With that realization, I follow the girls into the kitchen.

We've barely taken our seats when the elevator chimes, announcing someone's arrival.

I glance toward the sound, my curiosity piqued, but the sight that greets me stops me in my tracks. Stepping out of the elevator is Igor, followed closely by Pyotr, Irina, and Maxim.

"You're early," Natalie says as she hurries to greet them.

"Did you know about this?" I ask Amelia quietly.

She nods, a guilty look on her face. Suddenly, everything makes sense. What the hell was I thinking? Amelia takes her birth control religiously. She's not pregnant. She was nervous because she knew Maxim was coming.

Alex enters the room, followed by Timur and Sasha. He freezes when he sees everyone.

"Max and Irina got in early," Natalie says with a tight smile.

"I see that."

"What is *he* doing here?" Maxim asks, disdain dripping from his every word.

"This was my idea," Alex says, stepping between Max and us. "Viktor didn't know anything about it."

"Then, you have much explaining to do, Alexander."

Natalie moves to stand next to Alex. "There's going to be some ground rules to this visit." She puts her hands on her hips. "There will be no yelling or fighting. Rose is here, and she loves each one of you. I don't want her scared or confused seeing everyone she loves arguing."

"Then you should take her out," Max snips.

"This is her house. That isn't going to happen." Alex stands his ground. "What will happen is we're going to sit and discuss this like rational adults." He looks between Maxim and me. "There's been enough hurtful words said and violence unleashed."

"Irina, we are going home." Max turns to walk out.

"No, Maxim. We are not." Irina's voice doesn't waver.

Maxim looks like he's going to explode. It isn't like Irina to ever go against her husband's orders.

She touches his arm. "Maxim, this has gone on long enough. Our daughter loves both you and Viktor. She's stuck in the middle, and it's hurting her."

Max looks at Amelia, who now has tears in her eyes. I take her hand in mine and stroke it gently with my thumb. The room is bathed in uncomfortable silence. The men on both sides stand at the ready for whatever comes next, but no one moves or makes a sound.

"I was just about to take Rose to the park. Would you go for a walk with us, Max?" Natalie asks.

Max doesn't answer. His icy stare is locked on me.

"Rose, ask *Dedushka* if he'll come and push you on the swing."

"*Dedushka*," Rose says and goes to Max, taking his large hand. "Will you *pway* with me at the swings?"

His body visibly relaxes. "How can I say no to *moya vnuchka*?" Max lifts her into his arms. "But *he* better be gone before we get back."

No one moves while Natalie still bundles Rose up in her pale pink snowsuit, an adorable pink hat, and matching mittens.

"I think we're all ready to go."

We watch as Natalie opens the stroller and Max buckles Rose in. Then, the three of them leave for the park with Timur in tow.

"What the hell are you trying to do?" I ask Alex once they've left. "Maxim already made his point loud and clear. And I'm really not up for a round two."

"That's why I arranged this," Alex says patiently. "Threats and violence are not going to fix this. You and Maxim are better than that." He looks at Irina. "And I believe Amelia deserves this to be solved peacefully."

"I agree with you, Alexander," Irina says. "But I sure hope you know what you're doing." She motions between Amelia and me. "Maxim hasn't been able to reconcile this."

"Are you against us too?" Amelia asks nervously.

"It's taken a little bit to wrap my head around it." She smiles. "But I've known Viktor for many years. I trust him with our lives and your life. You couldn't have chosen a better man to fall in love with."

"Why can't Dad see that, too?"

"Because neither of you was honest with him. He feels betrayed."

"Why does he keep carrying on about the age difference then?"

"Your age difference bothers him, but it's also the easier thing for him to be mad at. He's a proud man and doesn't admit his hurt easily."

"I understand that. We were trying to figure out how and when to tell him." I take Amelia's hand in mind. "I love your daughter. I would never do anything to hurt her."

"I know. And hopefully, we can get Maxim to see that, too."

Natalie

It's chilly outside, but that's okay. We try to visit the park at least once a week, especially on a mild day. Rose's need to run and play doesn't go away just because it's winter.

Maxim pushes Rose's stroller as we walk down the sidewalk. Anger is rolling off him in waves, so I don't force conversation. I glance behind us to make sure Timur isn't lagging too far behind. The look he gives me doesn't help my confidence right now.

"Did you know your husband planned this little get-together?" Max asks.

"I did."

"And you went along with it?" He looks at me with a raised eyebrow.

"I did, yes."

We walk the last block in silence. But when the park comes into view, Rose gets very excited.

"*Dedushka* swings. *Pozhaluysta?*" she asks.

"Her Russian is coming along very well."

"She has such an easy time switching back and forth." I smile proudly. "Timur, Katia, and the kids have been a huge help. They usually only speak Russian to her. She catches on so naturally."

"It is easier when they are young." Max unbuckles Rose and

sets her on the ground, and she runs to her favorite swing. When Max and I catch up, he puts her in the swing and fastens the safety harness. Then, he pushes her gently. "I suppose you are planning to lecture me about Viktor and Amelia."

"I wasn't planning on a lecture. But I was hoping we could talk about it."

"There is nothing to talk about, Natalia." He pushes Rose a little higher, making her giggle. "He will return to Russia once Amelia's new security team is in place."

"I agree that she needs a new security team."

"I knew you were more sensible than that husband of yours."

"You didn't let me finish," I say, earning a disapproving look from Max. "Viktor will always protect her with his life. That'll never change. With them together, though, Viktor may be distracted. It's safer, more sensible, to have someone who is only there for her security needs."

"I think you have misunderstood. Viktor will be leaving."

"Can I *pway* in the sand, mommy?"

"Of course." Max takes Rose out of the swing, and she runs over to the sandbox. I grab the sand toys I keep in her stroller and put them next to her. "Tell Mommy if you get too cold, okay?"

Rose nods and goes right to work shoveling sand into her bucket. Max and I sit on a nearby bench.

"May I speak freely?"

"Of course, Natalia."

"Do you remember how my parents hated Alex?"

"That is something hard to forget."

"They tried everything to keep us apart. And Max, that hurt. It almost completely ruined our relationship." Even though they get along now, those memories still hurt. "Alex and I were forced to sneak around and lie to the people we cared about most."

"That was a different situation. Your parents are very small-minded."

I don't respond. I simply stare at him. His words aren't

untrue, but right now, Max fits into that definition, too. It takes several minutes before I see the recognition in his eyes.

"You think I am being small-minded?"

"I do. It may not be for the same reasons as my parents, but you're doing the same thing to Amelia that my parents did to me. You're forbidding her to be with the man her heart chose to love. If you don't fix this now, you'll alienate your daughter."

"But his age, Natalia. Now, he is thirty-three to her eighteen."

"She's almost nineteen, but I understand your concern. However, you need to remember Amelia has not lived a typical life. She was forced to grow up far earlier than she should've. She's experienced horrific things and has come out the other side a strong and confident young woman."

"They did not come to me." Max looks at me, tears in his eyes. "I am her father. He should have come to me first."

Now, I realize what the heart of the matter is. It's less about anger and more about hurt—something there's too much of right now.

"I can't imagine the shock of walking in and seeing them together."

"She was in his arms. They were—." Max stops, the sadness replaced by a mask of anger once again. "I cannot talk about it."

"They never intended to hurt you."

"Viktor betrayed my trust. And still, he has not apologized or taken responsibility."

"Have you given him the chance?" Max goes to speak, but I hold up my hand to stop him. "He went to Russia intending to make things right. But from what I understand, he wasn't given a chance to speak. You beat him like he was one of the criminals you go after." I put my hand over his. "That's not the Maxim I know."

He nods but says nothing.

"I spent nearly a year with Viktor. He showed me nothing but love and tenderness even though I was unable to give him anything in return."

"He lives a dangerous life, Natalia."

"Did you worry about Rose and me being with him?"

"Of course not. He loved you and would never let anything —" Max stops mid-sentence.

"Viktor loves your daughter." I look over at Rose. "When Alex came back, it nearly destroyed Viktor. In a matter of a few hours, he went from having a family to being alone. The day he said his goodbye to Rose nearly broke me." A tear slips down my face. "At the time, if I could've chosen both Alex and Viktor, I would have."

"You can. Polyamory is real," Max offers with a smile.

"It is, but it's not for me. Alex is my soulmate. And as much as I cared about Viktor—loved Viktor, my heart always belonged to Alex. Viktor knew when I looked at him and kissed him, it was always Alex I imagined in his place." That's still difficult to admit aloud.

"Viktor was willing to accept being my second choice. I'll forever be grateful for every day we spent together. But he deserves to be number one in someone's life. When Amelia looks at him, she's not wishing he was someone else. Viktor is her heart."

"Mama. I'm cold," Rose calls as she climbs out of the sand-box. I wipe the sand off her snowsuit while Max gathers her toys.

"Let's get you in your stroller. When we get home, I'll make you some hot chocolate, okay?"

"Yummy." Rose claps her mittened hands.

"Why did they not come to me sooner?"

"You can be a bit intimidating." I smile. "They weren't purposely hiding it from you. It was all new. They were trying to make sense of their feelings for each other before they could tell anyone else."

"They told you?"

"Not at first."

While we walk, I explain to Max how Amelia was talking to me about someone she met who she was interested in but who wasn't interested in her. And how I assumed it was a boy at school.

"The night she called me and told me she was in love with Viktor, I almost fell over." I laugh, remembering the conversation. "But once the shock wore off, I knew her heart was safe. Not only that, but Viktor would finally get the love he deserves."

"Natalia, I am afraid. I do not want my daughter to be hurt if he decides she is not what he wants. Or worse. If he is killed doing a job I send him on."

"I understand. No parent wants to see their child's heart hurt. But something tells me she is his forever." I slip my arm through his as we're walking. "And if the unthinkable ever happens, we'll all be there to help her through. But this division and fighting are what's hurting her now. She only wants your love and support. They both need that from you."

Maxim's silent again for a few minutes. "Your words make sense," he says, finally.

"Does that mean you'll give them your blessing?"

Max stops walking. "They both owe a debt of gratitude to you, Natalia." He kisses my forehead. "I will give them my blessing as long as Viktor continues to respect my daughter."

I let out a big breath. Part of me was terrified I wouldn't be able to get through to him, and we'd have a repeat of what happened between them in Russia.

I'm glad we're back at our building because the air is turning chillier by the minute.

"Thank you, *Dedushka*." I stand on my tiptoes to kiss his cheek.

The elevator opens, and we step in.

"But you are not to tell them I have conceded." Max gives me a wicked grin, and we share a laugh.

"As long as no punches are thrown."

"There will be no violence, but I would like to see them squirm just a while longer." Max looks around the front of the stroller. "It appears our conversation has bored *moya vnuchka* right to sleep."

"I might keep you around. It's getting more and more difficult to get her to nap."

"I remember those days. They were very tiring."

Alex is waiting in the foyer when the elevator arrives. Timur must've told him we were on our way.

"Rose is asleep? It's a miracle." He chuckles and looks between Maxim and me, but I give no hint of how things went. "I'll take her and put her in her crib," he says hesitantly.

Max and I join everyone in the living room. Amelia looks at me, and I shrug. I feel bad not letting them know everything's okay, but it's important that Max is able to do this on his own.

Maxim

I did not intend to give in, but Natalia's words made too much sense. I remember well the devastation she experienced when her family would not accept her and Alexander. Yet, I have done the same thing to my daughter.

I never intended to hurt her. I hoped if I said no, Amelia would back down and find someone else. But she has not. Natalia is correct. This between Amelia and Viktor is not just a fleeting thing.

The age difference is concerning. But I must remember Amelia has not had a normal upbringing. Her childhood was stolen from her, and she was forced to grow up at a very young age. At eighteen, she is more mature than most young ladies.

Her history also explains why she is attracted to someone like Viktor. He is a good man—a kind man. He has fought against evil for his entire adult life. It only makes sense that Amelia is drawn to him. Her heart knows it is safe with Viktor.

I have turned a blind eye to what was happening. Refused to hear the truth in their words.

The room has been silent since we walked in. I sit next to my wife. "Do not stop talking on my account. Please continue." Everyone's eyes are wide. They are not sure what to make of me right now. Alex returns to the room and sits next to Natalie. My men all stand at the ready. They are waiting to intervene at any given second.

"I apologize for bringing you both here under false pretense," Alex says.

I hold my hand up. "Please, let me speak first."

Alex sits back, allowing me to address the room.

"Amelia, I know things have been strained between us the past few weeks. I take full responsibility for that." I look at Viktor. "I apologize for my behavior when you were at my home. Reacting out of anger and using violence was unacceptable."

"I accept your apology." Viktor visibly relaxes.

"Amelia, I must apologize to you as well. I will never forget your fear of me when you first came to us. I worked hard to prove to you that what I do for a job would never cross into our home and family. In a matter of a few minutes, I destroyed that trust."

Tears pool in her eyes. I get up and go over to her. I lower myself to her level and take her hands in mine. "I am so very sorry for breaking my word to you. Because of what I did, you see me as a monster. If I could go back in time, I would. I never again wanted to see that fear in your eyes when you looked at me. But I deserve it."

I lower my head and try to get my emotions under control. It is no use. Tears are already falling. "How do I fix this? How do I get my daughter back?"

"I forgive you," she says, her voice cracking with emotion. "You did scare me, and I have lost some of the trust I gave you. But it's not gone for good. Every day is a new chance to wipe the slate clean and move forward." She squeezes my hands. "I love you, Dad. Even when I was angry and thought I hated you, I still loved you."

"I do not deserve your forgiveness." Those are not just words meant to sugarcoat this situation. They are my true feelings. I have acted like the monster she once believed I was. I have shown her that I can be just as scary as the men who took her, yet she still loves me.

"Don't say that. You made a mistake. I hope this is a turning point and you're ready to accept Viktor and me as a couple?"

"It is still not easy for me to see you with Viktor. And it is not because I do not trust Viktor. On the contrary, I trust him with your life." Expressing my emotions is not easy, but it is the only way right now. "I am hurt that you hid this from me."

"And I apologize for that. We were planning on talking to you. We had to figure it out for ourselves before explaining it to you."

"I understand that now." I pause. "The age difference and Viktor's job are also a concern. Being in his life will put you in danger."

"Before I agreed to the adoption, you told me about your life. You wanted to make sure I fully understood what I was agreeing to. You are the one who told me I'm in danger by being Amelia Solonik. Yet, I still chose to be your daughter. I just had to get used to a different life. One in which I trust you to keep me safe." She pauses and wipes the tears from her face. "I've accepted the potential consequences of being your daughter, and I accept the same being with Viktor. I trust both of you to keep me physically safe. I trust Viktor to keep my heart safe."

I look at Viktor and speak directly to him. "Today, I have realized my actions are hurting Amelia. I have been a hypocrite, accusing you of hurting her when I was the one doing the damage. I am ashamed of my behavior."

"I understand your concerns, boss. Like Amelia said, we were planning on talking to you about the change in our relationship. We weren't expecting you to show up at the house. I'm sorry that's how you found out. That was never our intention."

"I know that now."

"Maxim, I love your daughter. She's entrusted her heart to me, and I treasure that. I will do everything in my power to keep her safe.

Looking at them together right now, I see the love between them. "You have my blessing to be together."

Amelia lunges off the sofa, nearly knocking me over, and wraps her arms around me. "Thank you, Dad. You have no idea how much this means to me."

I hold my daughter. This young woman who was chosen for us and who chose us. "You are precious to me, Amelia. I wish you only love and happiness."

Amelia

I PULL BACK SO I CAN SEE HIS FACE. "YOU AND MOM have given me the world. You've reminded me what it means to be loved unconditionally. I will always love my birth parents, but I'm so grateful that fate brought me to you when I needed you the most. And you chose me to be your daughter." She softens her voice. "And I'm thankful you're finally accepting Viktor and me."

I go to my mom and hug her. "I love you very much."

"And I you, *moya malen'kaya ptichka*," Mom says and kisses my cheeks. "It's sometimes difficult as a parent to accept that our child is no longer a child. No longer dependent on us for everything. That she's transitioned into a beautiful and capable young woman. It can make a parent scared to be no longer needed."

"Growing up and falling in love doesn't mean you lose me. I'll always need you and Dad." I look at Viktor. "The only thing that's changed is now I have one more person who loves me."

"It has been difficult being your parent," Dad says. "Not because you are difficult, quite the opposite. You have been easygoing and never challenged us." He takes his seat next to mom.

"I have always felt that we missed out on so much of your life. That somehow, we needed to make up for that time—for all the wrong that was done against you. I have been so focused on correcting the past that I failed to see you growing up and moving forward. I want to hold on so tightly, but moya malen'kaya ptichka, it is your time to spread your wings and fly."

Dad's eyes are a mix of sadness and pride. Knowing that sharing his feelings is not comfortable for him makes this all the more special. I knew he loved me, but until right now, I didn't understand the depth of his love.

"Thank you, Dad. I will make you proud of me." I walk back to Viktor and take my seat next to him.

"Amelia, I am already proud of you."

I can't speak because I'm crying once again. Viktor holds me close.

The silence is broken by Alex's laughter. All heads turn his way. "I know this was my idea, but I was scared to death it would backfire and we'd have a disaster on our hands." His comment makes everyone laugh.

Rose's soft talking comes through the baby monitor. "She's up just in time," Natalie says.

"May I get her?" Viktor asks.

Viktor adores Rose. He's been head over heels for that little girl from the day she was born. He still talks about the first year of her life, when he was her father. His eyes hold a mix of pride, joy, and pain.

"Of course."

"What's this I hear about you not returning to school?" Alex asks when Viktor leaves the room.

"Wow. Good news travels fast." I chuckle. "Our group was offered a contract to go on tour with Zapped Euforia. The tour will start before the semester is over."

"Can't you arrange something with your professors to at least finish out your first year?"

"If it was just for the tour dates, I'm sure I could do that. But we're going to have rehearsals, press events, and so much other stuff. I wouldn't be able to give my full attention to either one," I explain. "So, I chose the band."

I glance at Dad, whose body is stiff with tension once again.

"I know it isn't the choice most of you would've preferred I made," I say and look at my father. "There have been too many things in my life that I didn't have a say in. This decision is mine, and it's one I feel good about. I hope you'll all support me."

"Of course we will," Natalie says. "I'm starving. Let's order some dinner, and you can tell us all about it."

Viktor

I'm hit with an onslaught of memories as I walk the familiar hallway to Rose's nursery. I used to look forward to being the one to get her when she woke from a nap. We'd sit in the rocker and cuddle while I whispered all my dreams and hopes for her future.

When I open her door, Rose sits in her crib, talking to her teddy bear.

"Did you have a good nap, *printessa*?"

"Friker," she exclaims, dropping the teddy bear in exchange for standing up and reaching her arms out to me.

Ignoring the pain in my chest, I lift her from the crib, and just like when she was little, Rose rests her head on my shoulder. Instinct takes over, and I sit in the rocking chair. She stays cuddled against me while I rub her back gently.

"Friker misses you very much."

"Me too. Are you staying with me again?"

"No. Auntie Melia and I are just visiting."

"Oh." She sticks her bottom lip out in a pout.

"Don't be sad, *printessa*. We can still talk on the video, and you can come to visit us again."

"I *wike* you here." She rubs my bald head with her little hand. "Mama shows me TV of Friker and baby Rose."

"You're still baby Rose, silly girl."

"No. I big girl Rose."

"Oh, I see." I chuckle. "My baby Rose is all gone." I pretend to pout.

"Friker is silly." Rose giggles.

Movement catches my eye. Amelia's standing in the doorway watching.

"You can come in."

"I didn't want to interrupt."

"Auntie Melia." Rose wiggles from my lap, and I set her down. She runs over to Amelia. "Can we *pway* tea party?"

"I think we need to have dinner first."

Rose rubs her tummy. "I hungry."

"Me too." Amelia grins. "Let's go potty, and then we'll go eat."

Rose takes Amelia's hand. The sight of them together fuels a yearning deep inside. I never thought about having children until Rose. When everything fell apart, I thought that dream was gone forever. Seeing Amelia and Rose gives me renewed hope. I can see Amelia and me with our own little girl one day.

I'm still sitting in the rocking chair long after Amelia and Rose leave the room.

"Viktor." Maxim's deep voice startles me.

"Yeah, boss?" I jump to my feet and groan from the sudden movement.

"I wanted to speak to you alone." He closes the door behind him.

"Okay." Worry builds once again. I know what he said earlier, but I'm still apprehensive. Is this when he asks me to leave quietly?

"I do not feel my public apology was sufficient."

"It was more than sufficient. We're good now."

"No. I am not good. When my nephew brought you to me

many years ago, you were not healed from the loss of your parents. I took you in not only as an employee but as family. I grew to love you like a son." Maxim pauses. "I have practiced self-control in all aspects of my life until the day I hurt you. I am ashamed of my behavior as a boss, a Dominant, and a man."

"Max—"

"Please, let me finish. I neglected to see Amelia as an adult. I still viewed her as the frightened young girl who came to live with us." I see the pain in Max's eyes as he recalls those days. "Those first weeks were some of the hardest in my life. Not since my Jelena was taken have I felt utterly useless. Nearly every night, she would partially wake terrified from a nightmare. Tears covered her face as she screamed and fought an invisible enemy—relived the hell she had been forced to live. Amelia was inconsolable.

Some say I do not have a heart, but I know they are wrong. Because each night, my heart was ripped from my chest watching the pure terror Amelia experienced. Those memories will never fade. They not only overshadowed her healing but also blinded me to her growing self-confidence and maturity. To the fact that she is no longer a little girl. She is a woman who is free to make her own choices—to fall in love."

"I know how much you love her and how much she loves you." I'm forced to sit from the pain in my ribs. "You need to know that we weren't trying to deceive you."

He holds up his hand, stopping me.

"Amelia does not trust easily. It makes perfect sense that her heart found yours. You have much love to give, and you deserve to be loved in return." Max takes a deep breath. "Your age difference also clouded my thoughts. I was unable to see past a number. I failed to recognize two hearts that were made for each other."

"Boss, I tried to fight it. To push her away. Love was the last thing I was looking for."

"But love found you. My little girl's heart is safe with you. I know you will treat her with the love and respect she deserves. And I am certain she will return that love to you."

"I never thought I'd get over losing Natalie. When we were together, I knew that even though Alex was gone, he was still very much there. He was all she saw—all she wanted. I was content to be the runner-up. After Alex came back, and I know this makes me a horrible person, I wished he didn't. I wanted to keep Natalie and Rose."

"Viktor, that only makes you human."

I stand back up. My breath catches from the pain, and I wrap my arm around my ribs. "But when Natalie told me she was pregnant again, something inside me changed. I realized it was time to stop pretending and dreaming of the what-ifs. To stop torturing myself. I had to let her go."

"You will always have a special bond with her," Max interrupts. "Love never fully goes away."

"You're right. I will. Natalie and I have discussed it. And more importantly, Amelia and I discussed it. Grigor was instrumental in teaching me how to honor those feelings and then how to put them away so I could move forward." I smile and shake my head. "Never did I imagine Amelia would be part of my moving forward. She took me by complete surprise."

"She is quite the force sometimes." Maxim chuckles.

"That she is. Boss, I'm sorry for not coming to you right away. God." I run my hand over my head. "My world was turned upside down."

I explain about the night Mateo came to the house drunk and how Amelia had a panic attack.

"Then, she kissed me. I pushed her away. Told her there was no way there could ever be anything between us."

"Stop. The boy came to the house drunk, looking for Amelia? I thought you checked him out."

"I did. Like I said, on paper, everything was good. Mateo's not a bad kid. He had a rough past and lost his way. Right after Thanksgiving, he attempted suicide."

"Does Amelia know this?"

"She does. She got a letter from him the other day. He's three weeks sober and making amends with the people he hurt. The letter meant a lot to her. Although she's not been allowed to speak to him, she's relieved knowing he's beginning to find his way." I return to the story, picking up when she kissed me. "The more we tried to stay apart, the more we were drawn together. I didn't know what to think except that you'd kill me." I laugh and then grab my ribs and groan from the pain.

"Nothing has ever felt so right. Something that scared us both because we didn't know how to tell you and Irina. But I guess fate did that for us."

"Yes, it certainly did." Max leans against Rose's changing table. "Amelia is still young. She may change her mind about this in a few months. Are you willing to go through another loss?"

"If it means having the chance to love her and the possibility of having a forever with her. Yes."

"I only ask one thing."

"Okay?"

"Do not rush her to marry and have children. Allow her time to grow up and to experience more of life before she becomes a wife and mother."

"I won't push her into anything she's not ready for. You have my word."

I reach my hand out to shake Maxim's, but he pulls me in for a hug instead. He pats me on the back and then realizes his mistake. "I am sorry. I did not think."

"It's all good. I'm happy we've fixed this between us."

"As am I, son."

Amelia

OUR TIME IN NEW YORK CITY WENT BY TOO QUICKLY. We would've loved to stay longer, but I was due back in California to start our rehearsal schedule.

We've already had several interviews and have had to field too many prying questions on Mateo's whereabouts. I wish people would drop it. He's struggling enough. He doesn't deserve to have his name dragged through the mud. I didn't know, but Mateo also has Type 1 Diabetes. So the group's official statement is Mateo suffered a medical emergency due to a pre-existing condition and is in the hospital for stabilizing treatment. Our hope is that if we don't make a big deal about it, the extreme curiosity will fade.

Today's rehearsal is at an actual recording studio. We're recording our first demo song that will be going out to local radio stations. There's a guy here who's using recordings from previous concerts to mix Mateo's voice into the songs.

"Sorry I'm late," Sparrow says as he bursts into the room out of breath. "I was a little tied up with something."

Sparrow's been attending video therapy sessions with Mateo. His therapist knew the significant role Sparrow played in Mateo's life and asked him to be involved in some of their sessions. Sparrow's revelation about his feelings for Mateo has only strengthened the decision to have him involved. The guys are trying to explore what, if anything, it means to Mateo. Other than me, no one else in the group knows about it.

"Something of the female variety?" Tristan jokes.

"Yeah, something like that." Sparrow comes over and gives me a quick hug. Although we've seen each other a few times, we haven't really had the chance to talk since I got back from New York. He doesn't know everything that happened. "How are you holding up?"

"Much better. We'll talk later."

"Sounds good." He turns to the guys. "Let's get to work."

It took about a million tries to get a clean copy of our single "Dangerous Vibes." Nerves played a significant role in all our screw-ups.

"Do you two mind if we record your duet?" Nick, our new agent, asks.

"I'm fine with it if you are," Sparrow says.

I look to Viktor for his approval. "It's up to you."

"Sure. Let's do it."

After we signed the contract for the tour, we started working on doing more of our own music instead of cover songs. The "Just Give Me a Reason" duet has been replaced with "Written in the Stars." It's a beautiful ballad Sparrow wrote about star-crossed lovers who stumble through the night, missing one another—missing a piece of their heart. Until their worlds finally collide.

While we sing, Viktor stands outside the window of the sound booth. His gaze never wavers from mine while I sing the magical lyrics, my soul being laid bare at his feet. I don't know how Sparrow did it, but somehow, he reached into both our hearts and pulled out the most intimate and private of emotions. It's a powerful song that I'm sure will become a fan favorite.

"Great job today, everyone," Nick praises us. "We'll work on the edits and mixes. I'll give you a call when they're done."

Tristan and Quincy hang by Nick and pepper him with questions. They're both very interested in the inner workings of how everything comes together.

"How's everything going with Mateo?" I ask Sparrow quietly.

"He's a little over thirty days sober."

"That's awesome. Can you tell Mateo how proud I am?"

"I will."

"Is everything else between you two okay?"

"It's complicated." Sparrow holds the door to the studio open, allowing me to go through first.

Viktor follows behind us. "I'll get the car. Take your time here."

Sparrow and I sit on the bench in the hallway.

"Mateo knows how I feel about him and that I've felt that way for a long time. He's not totally turned off by it."

"That's a good thing, right?"

"Kinda." Sparrow rests his head back on the wall. "Mateo's attracted to girls but said that a part of him is also interested in me as more than a friend. But he's not ready to act on anything."

"Keep being there for him. That's all you can do."

"Enough about me," Sparrow says, changing the subject. "How was your trip to New York?"

"Viktor and my father were surprised, to say the least. When Dad walked in and they saw each other, I was terrified. But somehow, Natalie was able to get through to Dad. He ended up apologizing and giving us his blessing." I smile, still shocked at the way everything worked out.

"I'm so happy for you." Sparrow puts his arm around me, and I rest my head on his shoulder.

"You'll get your happy ending too. I'm sure of it."

"We'll see."

"Look at these two lovebirds," Tristan jokes as he and Quincy come down the hall. "Where's Viktor? Does he know you two are so cozy together?"

"Viktor doesn't mind sharing me with Sparrow." I give him a quick peck on the cheek and stand.

"Will he share you with us too?" Tristan waggles his eyebrows.

"No chance. Let's go, Sparrow." I grab his hand. "Viktor might be okay with sharing, but I'm not." Sparrow and I share a laugh as we walk toward the doors.

Just as he promised, Viktor has the Audi pulled out front. He's leaning against the car, wearing dark sunglasses, his arms crossed over his chest. My heart rate picks up, and my stomach flip-flops when I see him.

"We didn't know you loaned Amelia out." Quincy's laughing so hard he barely gets the words out.

Viktor lifts his sunglasses. His blue eyes zone in on Quincy. "What the hell are you talking about?"

I rush over and put my hands on his chest. "I let them know you share me with Sparrow." I smile sweetly.

His body relaxes under my touch. "Oh, that. Yeah. Sparrow and I have a private arrangement." The corner of his mouth turns up slightly. "You need a ride, Sparrow?"

"I have the car today. I'm good." He hugs me and plants a kiss on my cheek. "I'll call you later."

Quincy and Tristan elbow each other, laughing. I roll my eyes at them.

"I'll see you two next week."

"See ya, Mel," Quincy says.

"You know I was just kidding, right? I hope I didn't offend you," Tristan says in a rare moment of seriousness.

"It's all good with me. It's him you have to worry about." I point at Viktor and walk to my side of the car, leaving Tristan face-to-face with Viktor.

"Yeah, well. I'm heading out. See ya around, Vik."

Viktor gets in the car and turns to face me. "Sharing you is completely out of the question. You are mine, Amelia."

Viktor

This girl better not be getting any ideas that I'm willing to share her. I want to kill anyone who dares to look at her. The thought of them touching her makes me want to do it with my bare hands.

"Relax," she giggles. "They saw me sitting with my head on Sparrow's shoulder and were giving him a hard time."

"You're lucky."

"You're the lucky one. You get me all to yourself."

"You're damn right I do." I put my hand on her leg and slide it up to the top of her thigh, teasing her.

"I like it when you go all caveman on me."

"You do?" I glance at her with a raised eyebrow.

"I think it's pretty hot."

"It doesn't scare you?" I've been hesitant to let Amelia see how possessive I feel. Knowing her history, I didn't want to trigger her or make her feel like she was nothing more than a possession to me.

"I know who you are," she explains. "You're not *them*. Your possessiveness isn't about manipulation or coercion."

"What the hell?" My attention is drawn away from our

conversation when I turn onto our street and see two unfamiliar cars in our driveway.

"Who is it?"

"I don't know." I pull the car over a few houses away and come up with a quick plan. "You're going to get in the driver's seat and keep the doors locked. I want your phone out. If I don't give you the all-clear in five minutes, you're going to drive to the police station and call your dad."

"I don't have my license yet." Amelia's been behind the wheel a few times, but she isn't comfortable driving and hasn't wanted to take her driver's license test.

"I don't care. We'll deal with the consequences later. My only concern is your safety."

Damn it. Right now, I wish Max hadn't taken Igor back to St. Petersburg. I haven't forgotten the lesson about not doing things on my own, yet here we are. I'm about to not only walk into an unknown situation without backup, but I'm also leaving Amelia alone with the hope she stays safe.

I force myself to get out of the car and wait for Amelia to come to the driver's side.

"Why can't I come with you?"

"I will not put you at risk." I grab her by the back of the neck and pull her in for a kiss. "Get in the car and lock the doors. If anyone approaches the car, you will not hesitate. You will drive away. Okay?"

"Viktor—"

"I won't be focused if I have to worry about you. Promise me you'll drive away."

"I promise."

I watch her get into the car and lock the doors. She follows my instructions and shows me her phone. I reward her with a smile before turning and walking toward the house. Am I doing the right thing? Should I have stayed with her? Should I have made her drive away? I have to stop second-guessing my decisions and focus my attention on whoever is in our house.

Once I get to the sidewalk leading up to our front door, I take the gun from the waistband of my pants. I'm not sure what I'll find when I get to the house, but I know I'll be ready.

Quietly, I walk up the steps. The door's open, and people are inside talking. It's clear there's more than one person, but I'm not sure how many. Standing out of sight, I shoot a quick text to Dimitri.

Me: I need you to access the cameras in the house. Someone's in there.

Dimitri: On it.

Seconds that feel like hours tick by before I get his response.

Dimitri: Have you checked your email lately?

Me: What the hell does that have to do with anything?

Dimitri: Boss sent you an email last week letting you know that Amelia's new security team would be arriving today.

I open the email program, and sure enough, there's an email sitting there. He should've known I don't regularly check my inbox. That's why he usually texts.

Me: I see it now.

Dimitri: Should be a team of three. One female. Two males.

Me: Thanks.

Sliding the gun back into my waistband, I make my way back down the sidewalk to the car. Amelia unlocks the doors, and I get in the passenger seat.

"What's going on?"

"It's the new security team. Pull the car up to the house."

"Dad didn't tell you they were coming?" Amelia asks as she parks behind the cars in our driveway.

"He emailed," I reply and hold up my phone.

She laughs. "Like you ever check your email."

"I guess I'm going to have to start."

I hold the door for Amelia, allowing her to walk in first. The three people sitting at our table jump up when they hear us come in.

"Viktor?" The female asks.

"Yes." I know Maxim approved these people, but my guard's still up.

"I'm Indigo. These are my partners, Chase and Bode." She looks next to me. "And you must be Amelia. It's a pleasure to meet you." Indigo offers her hand to Amelia.

"How did you get into our house?"

"Your father had us programmed into the ID system."

"It was nice of him to tell us," Amelia mumbles.

We've already gotten off to a rather uncomfortable start, and I'm about to make it worse. "Have a seat. We're going to go over the boundaries and how this will all work."

"With all due respect, sir. Mr. Solonik has already briefed us on our assignment."

"It's me you'll be reporting to day-to-day, correct?"

"Yes, sir."

"Good." I pull out Amelia's chair and look pointedly at the new team. "Now, take a seat."

"We were told Ms. Solonik will be going on tour?" Chase asks.

"That's correct. The tour kicks off in May, but we'll be moving to Los Angeles in late April."

"How long is the tour?" Bode asks.

"The last show is in August," Amelia answers.

"You must be excited." Indigo smiles.

"Excited and nervous."

"I can't wait to hear you."

"While we're at home, we do not want our privacy interrupted." Viktor directs the conversation back to the guidelines. "The house has a security system, and I'm here. Your presence is not required."

Bode sits up straighter. "That isn't what Mr. Solinik—"

"As I previously said, Mr. Solonik is not here. I am."

"Yes, sir."

"Where will they sleep?" Amelia asks quietly.

That's a detail I haven't figured out. This house is luxurious, but it's not set up to have extra people living with us. Having Igor here was different. Amelia and I both knew him and were comfortable having him around. He also had Yury, so they were off on their own for much of the time. I need to come up with a solution quick.

Amelia

Viktor doesn't waste time letting these new people know who the boss is. Indigo isn't intimidated by him. I think I'm going to like her. In contrast, the two men sit with wide-eyed stares while Viktor barks orders at them. Their fear works for me. Dad screened them, so I know they're okay, but they're also men. I don't know them, and I don't trust them—trust must be earned.

I'm a bit shocked at how quickly Viktor went from the tender man I know to this intimidating man who's all business. I know he's experienced and good at his job, but I've never witnessed this side of him. If I didn't know him, I'd be scared too. Instead, I'm able to sit back and relax, knowing Viktor's got it under control. He details the distance they must remain from me, especially the men. And places they're forbidden to follow me.

While he's giving his instructions, I realize the one thing that hasn't been discussed is our sleeping arrangements. The three bedrooms are all next to each other, and I'm not comfortable knowing there will be other men that close.

"Where will they sleep?" I ask quietly.

For a brief second, Viktor looks at me like a deer caught in the headlights, but he quickly regains his composure.

"Indigo, you will have the first bedroom on the right. It's Amelia's old room. Chase and Bode, you'll sleep downstairs. Tomorrow we'll rearrange the game room. There's already a pull-out sofa in place. We can bring the furniture from the guest room down. That should work." Viktor turns his attention to me. "Are you comfortable with those arrangements?"

"I am. Thank you."

"The overnight shift will be on a rotation. I believe Mr. Solonik provided you with that schedule." The newcomers nod. "I see no reason to alter that. Where it's not necessary while we're here, it's something we will put into practice, so we all have a chance to get used to it and work out any kinks."

I think we've done enough business talk for tonight. My stomach agrees, which is evident by how loud it growls. "Is anyone hungry?" I ask.

"Do you want to order out?"

"I'd like to cook. Is that okay?" I'm not the world's best chef, but I'm trying.

"If you'd like to." Viktor smiles appreciatively.

I look to our new housemates. "Do you have any allergies or anything you really don't like?"

"Nope. Not picky at all," Chase says, and the others agree.

"Okay then." I head into our walk-in pantry with the intention of finding something manageable for me to cook.

Instead, my over-reactive nervous system decides to make an appearance. Thoughts rapidly fire in my head. They said they weren't picky, but were they only trying to be polite? What if they hate everything I make?

The familiar waves of panic start to seep into my consciousness. I reach out and touch some of the boxes and cans on the shelf. My eyes want to close, but I resist recognizing I need to stay in the moment—stay grounded. I refuse to let fear win. After taking a few controlled breaths, my heart rate slowly returns to normal. I'm proud of myself. I've managed to avoid a full-blown panic attack. Even just a few months ago, that was something I wouldn't have been able to accomplish on my own.

"Did you get lost in here?" Viktor asks from the doorway.

"I needed a minute."

"Are you okay?" He steps closer.

"I am now. But I don't know what to make."

Viktor scans the shelves. "We have breaded chicken in the fridge." He grabs a box of pasta. "How about that chicken parmesan and pasta you made a few weeks ago?"

Sparrow's dad's a chef and has been teaching Sparrow how to cook since he was little. Now Sparrow's passing those lessons on to me. He was over a few weeks ago, and we made this meal together.

"I'm pretty sure I can do that."

Viktor grabs a few boxes of cut pasta, and I grab some cans of sauce.

"Can I help?" he asks.

"No, thank you." I want to prove I can do this on my own. That I can do something to care for Viktor. "Why don't you go entertain our new guests." I look over at the table where the new arrivals sit.

"I'll bring them out on the balcony." He leans down and gives me a quick kiss. "If you need help, just give a yell."

Viktor escorts our guests, or whatever I'm supposed to call them, outside. Then, I busy myself in the kitchen. I have to text Sparrow a few times, but overall, I think I did okay. While the food's in the oven, Sparrow and I chat back and forth.

Sparrow: Did Nick text you the pics of the tour buses?

Me: I saw a text from him, but I haven't had a chance to look at it yet. We had some unexpected visitors.

Sparrow: Is everything okay?

Me: Yeah. It's my new security team. It's weird having three new people around.

Sparrow: Having people follow you everywhere must get annoying.

Me: Most of the time, it's okay. It's harder when it's new people. How's Mateo?

I'd rather not dissect the intricacies of being Maxim Solonik's daughter. Sparrow never pries, but I know he's curious about exactly what my Dad does back in Russia. And why it requires me to have so much personal security. It's not something I really like talking about, though.

Sparrow: Next week, he'll be sober for sixty days. He's getting discharged, then.

Me: That's awesome. I'm sure you're super excited.

Sparrow: Part of me is. The other part is terrified. We haven't seen each other since I told him, and he's still unsure how he feels. I'm afraid it's going to be awkward and that I screwed up our friendship.

Me: I'm sure that's not true.

The fire alarm blares over my head, and I nearly fall off my chair. I spin around and see the smoke pouring from the oven. How did I not notice it sooner?

Viktor's already at my side, pulling the oven door open. I grab the hot pads, pull the tray out, and set it on the stovetop. Once the smoke clears, I see the blackened chicken.

"I ruined it." I toss the hot pads onto the counter.

While Indigo's on the phone with the security company, giving them the passcode and letting them know it was a false alarm, one of the other guys manually turns the alarm off. I flop on the kitchen chair, embarrassed.

"Are you okay?" Viktor gets down to my level. "Are you hurt?"

"Only my pride." I can't believe I screwed up dinner. "I was texting Sparrow. I must've forgotten to set the timer."

"It's okay. We can order something."

"I know, but that's not the point." I wave my hand at the still-smoking tray. "I wanted to prove that I can cook and care for you."

"*Moya zirka*, there's no doubt in my mind that you can care for me. Whether or not you can cook doesn't matter."

"It does to me." I look into his sparkling blue eyes. "What kind of woman can't cook dinner for her man?"

"We will cook together. I don't ever expect you to do everything. Cooking, cleaning, and raising our children. They're responsibilities we'll share."

Raising our children? Viktor's never mentioned children before. The thought scares me. I don't have time to focus on it because Viktor's taking my hand and pulling me to my feet.

"Come on. Let's take our new guests out for a meal."

Amelia

When I wake up, I spot an envelope on Viktor's pillow. I open it and pull out the notecard.

Moya zirka,

Happy Valentine's Day. I had to go out and do something. Indigo's in charge while I'm gone. Take some time to pamper yourself. You'll find a red dress and heels in the closet. Be dressed and ready for six. I'll be there to pick you up.

I bring the note to my chest. What's he planning? Reaching over to the nightstand, I grab my phone.

Me: Do I get any hints?

Viktor: Good morning to you, too.

Me: It's actually good afternoon. But you didn't answer my question. Do I get a hint?

Viktor: We're not leaving the state.

Amelia: Haha. You're so funny.

Viktor: Go eat and have a relaxing afternoon. I'll see you later. Love you.

Amelia: I love you, too.

Indigo and I spend the afternoon on the balcony, getting to know one another. She's in her mid-thirties and is ex-military. She served with Michael, which is how Dad found her. Apparently, he reached out to Michael, hoping to find well-trained and trust-worthy people.

"How do you like living in California? It must be a big change from St. Petersburg?" Indigo asks.

"It was a difficult transition. I'm glad Viktor was here, or I don't think I would've lasted a week."

"He seems like a nice guy."

"He is." I smile. "But don't tell anyone else. I don't want it to ruin his tough guy reputation." Indigo and I share a laugh. She's quickly becoming a friend.

The past few weeks have been interesting. At first, it felt like we were always in each other's way—that we were tripping over each other. I was uncomfortable having three virtual strangers in our house. I called Dad more than once, begging him to change his mind, but he refused.

I tried pleading my point with Viktor, but I didn't get anywhere there either. Viktor wants to be able to focus on us as a couple. He said he couldn't do that and act as my primary security. That being in a relationship can compromise his abilities. And how he'd never forgive himself if harm came to be because he refused to expand my security team.

It's been a bit of trial and error, but we've finally worked it all out and have found a comfortable rhythm. Hopefully, that will carry over to our living arrangements while I'm on tour.

The dress Viktor bought for me is stunning. It's a deep red form-fitting dress that sits off my shoulders and stops several inches above my knees. Using the full-length mirror, I check out myself from different angles, admiring how the dress accentuates my curves.

It's almost six, so I slide my heels on and make my way out to the living room. Viktor should be here any minute.

"You look gorgeous," Indigo says when I enter the room.

"Viktor picked it out." I smile and give her a twirl.

"That man is sure head over heels for you." She grabs the small gift bag from the table.

"Thank you for keeping it for me."

The door opening interrupts us. Viktor strides in, wearing a black suit and a tie that matches my dress. In his hands is a bouquet of red roses. His eyes are locked on me as he crosses the room.

"I'll leave you two alone. Enjoy your evening." Indigo makes a quick exit.

"You look stunning, *moya zirka*." He kisses me. "These are for you."

I take the bouquet from his outstretched hand. "They're beautiful."

"They don't hold a candle to you."

"Give me a minute to put these in water."

"Leave them on the counter. Indigo will take care of them. We have someplace to be."

"Wait. I have something for you." I hand him the bag.

He takes out the small box inside and gives me a quizzical look. "What is it?"

"Open it."

He tosses the bag onto the couch and opens the box. There's silence while Viktor reads the paper inside.

"You bought a star?" He looks up.

"I'm sorry if you think it's a dumb gift."

Viktor takes another step, closing the distance between us. "There's nothing dumb about it."

"If you look under that paper, I bought two stars next to one another. They're named after us.

"*Moya zirka*, this is the most perfect gift anyone's ever given me."

I wrap my arms around his neck and pull him to me. Our lips meet for a passionate kiss that ends far too soon.

"If we don't leave now, we're going to be late."

"Or we could just change plans?"

"Nope. Let's go." He takes my hand and leads me out to our car.

Viktor

Amelia's quiet in the car. I know she's trying to figure out where we're going. Fortunately, it's not too far, so she won't have to wonder for long. Amelia sits up when I make the final turn into the parking lot.

"Are we having dinner on the Queen Mary?" Amelia asks, her eyes sparkling with excitement.

"We are. And we're spending the night on board."

"I don't know what to say."

"This is the last time we'll get to be alone for a while. I want to make the most of it."

We get out of the car, and I grab the bags I packed this morning while she was still sleeping. It doesn't take long to check in and arrange for our bags to be delivered to our room. With her hand in mine, we make our way to the restaurant.

I reserved a table by the windows overlooking the bay. We've grown to love being by the water and will miss it while she's touring, so I'm taking every opportunity to enjoy the views while we can. Over the next two hours, we share a decadent meal and each other's company.

"Do you want dessert?"

"Not anything they have here." Amelia bites her lip.

"We need to go now."

The security team does their best to stay out of our way, but we still don't have the privacy we used to. If we're anywhere other than our bedroom, there's always a chance someone can walk in. I miss it being just Amelia and me.

The walk to our room is excruciating. Amelia doesn't realize how sexy she looks in that little red dress. We're barely inside the door when I lose what little self-control I have.

I kick the door closed behind us as my mouth attacks hers. Amelia's already sliding off my suit jacket. Reaching behind her, I open the zipper on her dress. I step back and watch as she allows the fabric to slide off. It lands in a puddle at her feet.

Amelia stands before me in a strapless red lace bra and matching panties.

"Once again, you're very overdressed, Mr. Dobrow."

"I think we should remedy that." While I unbutton my shirt, Amelia starts to take off her heels. "No. They stay. Get on the bed."

I think I see uncertainty in her eyes for a brief second, but it quickly disappears. Amelia turns around and walks to the bed. She gets on all fours and crawls to the center of the bed, pausing to look over her shoulder. "Like this?" she asks with a flirtatious smile.

"Just like that. Now lay down and spread your legs. I want to see if you're wet for me." With her legs open, I see the wet spot on her panties. She's enjoying this as much as I am. "Touch yourself."

Amelia slides her hand down the center of her breasts, inching it down her abdomen. She stops when she reaches her panties. Teasing me, she puts a finger under the elastic of the waistband and then pulls it out.

With my shirt hanging open, I walk to the bed and lean over, placing my hands on each side. She arches her back, and the lace of her bra rubs against my bare chest.

"Are you trying to tease me?" I ask in a low, deep voice.

"Maybe." She bats her eyelashes.

I reach between us and tear the delicate panties from her body. "These won't be a problem now."

I push off the bed and watch as she teases her wet folds with her finger before it disappears inside her entrance. She moans in pleasure while she fucks herself with her finger.

Without taking my eyes off her, I finish undressing and toss my clothes to the side. My cock's hard and ready to sink into her body. Amelia watches as I stroke my length.

"Do you like watching me, Amelia?"

"Yes." Her voice is breathy. "Very much."

"Make yourself come for me."

Her fingers alternate between circling her clit and pumping in and out of her body. She doesn't take her eyes off me as I continue touching myself. As she climbs closer and closer to her orgasm, her breathing becomes more rapid, and mewls of pleasure escape her lips. She's a goddess lying before me, uninhibited and unashamed of her sexuality.

"That's it, *moya zirka*. You're almost there," I encourage.

She circles her clit once more. Her back arches from the bed, and her hand stills as pleasure flows through her body.

"Fuck, Amelia. You're so damn gorgeous." I'm in awe. "I love when you come for me."

"I need you, now."

Amelia's plea barely leaves her lips before I'm on top of her sliding my cock into her wet center. Being sheathed inside her is like coming home. Her body was made for mine.

I pull the cups of her bra down, allowing her breasts to spill out. Leaning down, I take one of her hardened nipples into my mouth, suckling and teasing her. Leaning closer, I whisper, "I want to take you hard and fast, okay?"

She nods.

"Nodding your head doesn't work." I still my movements waiting for her to answer.

"Harder, please. I want to feel every inch of you."

I nip at her earlobe. "Your wish is my command." I grab her hips to steady her body while I thrust deep inside her.

Amelia's body begins to squeeze my cock as her orgasm takes over. I thrust two more times, and then I follow her over the edge. I still, allowing myself to spill into her body.

"Happy Valentine's Day," she whispers.

"It's the first of many more to come, *moya zirka*."

Amelia

VALENTINE'S DAY WAS THE LAST DAY OF WHAT I NOW consider my *normal* life. Since then, everything has been on hyper speed.

Mateo was discharged two weeks ago. Sparrow brought him over a few days after he was discharged. He looked good—healthy. And more importantly, he seemed content.

As far as his relationship with Sparrow—it's complicated. They're still exploring what, if anything, is between them. Neither is in a rush to make any decisions, but it's obvious something's shifted. They aren't outwardly affectionate with one another. I don't know how to describe it. They seem comfortable being near each other. I'm rooting for them and hope they can make a relationship work.

Our rehearsal schedule has been getting more intense. It's great having Mateo back. It feels like the band is whole again. We also have an official new name. None of us wanted to rename the group without Mateo. Some of the vendors weren't happy, but it was a battle we were willing to fight. Once he was discharged, finding a new name was the first thing on the list. Death Rat is no more. We are officially—Beautiful Division.

Mr. Hart handled the legal end, and Nick worked his magic

on the merchandise. Yesterday, we received a shipment of samples. It's surreal knowing fans can buy T-shirts, hats, hoodies, CDs, bandanas, and a bunch of other things with our pictures and names on them.

Speaking of concerts, tickets have already gone on sale. Some of the packages include a meet and greet with us. And they're selling out. I can't believe this is even my life.

"How's the packing coming along?" Viktor asks as he walks into our room and sits on the bed.

"I think I'm just about done." I look around. "I can't believe we're leaving tomorrow."

Our tour buses are ready and waiting for us in Los Angeles. We're driving up early to check them out and ensure they're exactly as we ordered. As long as all is well, we'll be moving into them.

The next few weeks, we'll be traveling from L.A. and Hollywood to do some radio and television spots. We're booked pretty solid until the tour kicks off in L.A. the first weekend in May.

"Are you having second thoughts?" Viktor sits on the bed next to me.

"Not second thoughts, no." I sit next to him. "We've made so many memories here. It's bittersweet leaving."

"Once we have a better idea of what life's going to look like, we can discuss buying our own house."

"Our own house?"

"That is if you want to spend your forever with me."

"I couldn't imagine not waking up next to you every day." I climb over his lap, straddling him. "I don't want to think about my life without you in it."

He pulls me close to him and kisses me. It's unhurried but so full of emotion that it brings tears to my eyes.

I never imagined falling in love and never with a man like Viktor. But now that we're together, I'm never letting him go.

Amelia

We arrive at the campground in Universal Theme Park, which will be our home for the next few weeks. Four buses are waiting for us. Nick points out who's going to each one. Quincy and Tristan head off to check out their new digs. Mateo and Sparrow are up next. Then, Viktor and I. Lastly, my security team.

"Ready to check out our new mobile home?" Viktor jokes.

"I guess." I'm not super excited about this, but when I step inside, everything changes. "Can you believe how incredible this is?" I ask Viktor excitedly. "Living on a bus didn't sound appealing, but this is beyond anything I imagined."

"I think we'll be pretty comfortable on here." Viktor sits on the couch across from a fireplace. He hits a button, and a television screen rises from the mantle area. "Not bad." He smiles.

We continue the tour. There's a full kitchen complete with granite countertops. Past the kitchen is a hallway. Behind a door on the side, I find a washer and dryer. The door across from the laundry leads to the bathroom.

"The shower looks big enough for two."

"I can't wait to try it out." Viktor grins.

The last room is the bedroom. I didn't think it was possible, but we have a king-size bed. On each side is a night table with a small lamp.

"I think this room is going to be my favorite," Viktor says when we enter the bedroom. He lays down on the bed. "Come here. Let's see how it works."

I crawl onto the bed beside him. It's surprisingly comfortable, and I don't want to get up. I'm so tired already that I could fall asleep right now. Unfortunately, I have rehearsal in a half hour, so there's no time to rest.

It's only been a week, and already, my head's spinning from traveling back and forth from L.A. to Hollywood. We've done several morning talk shows, one late-night show, and some national radio broadcasts. Each time we show up at a studio, there's a line of fans outside wanting selfies and autographs. It's overwhelming and is giving my security team a run for their money.

Viktor's continually reminding me I'm not required to say yes to anything I'm not comfortable with. But I don't like saying no to people who've waited for hours to see us. So, I try to spend just a few seconds with as many people as possible.

"This is nothing compared to what you'll experience on tour," Nick says. "There will be meet and greets before each concert, and fans will always try to sneak into the tour bus area."

"I need specs on each venue so we can arrange for Amelia's security," Viktor interrupts.

"The venues will have plenty of security." Nick attempts to reassure him.

I already know that answer isn't going to work, but I sit back and watch the scene play out.

"Amelia has her own security." Viktor sits up straighter. "How soon can I expect to have the information?"

"I'll email you by the end of the day." Thankfully, Nick doesn't try to argue with Viktor.

Knowing fans are anticipating seeing us helps with our excitement level during rehearsals. Today's session is one of the best we've had so far. Having Mateo back makes the group feel whole again. Mateo and Tristan split the lead vocals between them. It's a whole new look and feel for us, but I think it's great.

"You guys are on fire," Griffin, the lead singer from Zapped Euforia, says.

"Hey, Grif. I didn't see you there. You like the new setup?"

"I think it works great." He puts his arm over Tristan's shoulder. "We don't have to hear this one all the time." He laughs. "You guys really have it all. There's Mr. Plays to the crowd here." He points to Mateo. "And Mr. Broody Musician over there." He points to Sparrow. "Then you have the girl who will break all the guys' hearts." He flashes me his mega-watt smile that drives all the girls crazy.

I glance at Viktor, who's sitting in a folding chair next to our stage. His focus is zoned in on Griffin.

"There's only one heart I'm interested in." I walk over to Viktor and sit on his lap. "Are we done for today?"

"You guys sound great and look super comfortable on the stage," Nick says from the back of the room. "I think you're ready."

"Hell, yeah, we're ready," Tristan calls.

"I'm giving you guys the rest of the week off. Rest up because this will be the last downtime you'll have until the end of the tour."

Viktor

As soon as the email from Nick arrives in my inbox, I send it off to Dimitri. He'll test each venue's security systems and will get the details of the tour bus areas. It's a relief knowing Dimitri's handling the details. That leaves me free to spend some quality time with Amelia before the tour kicks off. Part of that quality time includes a surprise party for her birthday.

Between her schedule and Maxim's, coordinating this surprise party hasn't been easy. It took a bit of doing, but I finally received a text a few hours ago confirming Max, Irina, and Lana have arrived safely and are staying at a local hotel. Unfortunately, Alex and Natalie couldn't fly out. She's too far along in her pregnancy for traveling.

Amelia's official birthday isn't until next week, but I wanted to have it early since we'll already be on the road. She thinks we're just going out to dinner.

"You look stunning," I say when she comes out of the bedroom wearing a satin emerald green skater dress.

"Do you like it?" She spins, and the skirt of the dress floats around her.

I get up from where I'm sitting on the couch and pull her to me. "You're beautiful no matter what you wear."

"Thank you." She smiles as she takes in my outfit of black dress pants and a white button-down shirt. "You don't look so bad yourself."

"Are you ready to go?"

"I am."

When we get out of the car, she looks around. "No security detail tonight?"

"I gave them the night off." She doesn't need to know they've gone ahead and are already at the venue.

"Perfect," she says and slides into the car.

While we drive across town, we talk about the upcoming concert.

"I'm so nervous," she explains. "We've never played to audiences like this."

The tour has stops at stadiums across the U.S. The first concert is at Dodgers Stadium here in L.A. The venue holds over fifty thousand people, which is small compared to some of the venues they'll play.

"Everyone's going to love your music," I reassure her. "And I'll be front and center for each show."

"You have no idea how much that means to me."

I make the turn into the venue's parking lot. One of the guys in Zapped Euforia told me about this place. I've only seen pictures of it, but at first glance, it isn't going to disappoint.

Amelia looks out the window and then back at me. "What is this place?"

"It's called Spellbound. I was told it's a great place to eat."

"It looks like something straight out of a fairy tale."

Offering my hand, I help her out of the car. We walk toward a stone cottage, which is the main building. Inside is decorated with rustic hand-carved furniture set up around a fireplace. It feels more like we've entered someone's home rather than a party venue.

We're met by an older couple. "I presume you are Mr. Dobrow?" the man asks.

"I am."

"It's nice to finally meet you in person. I'm Oliver, and this is my wife, Josephine."

"This is my lovely girlfriend, Amelia."

"Our birthday girl," Josephine says with a smile.

Amelia looks at me, a bit confused.

"I know your birthday isn't until next week, but since we'll already be on the road, I thought we'd celebrate early."

"You amaze me." Amelia slips her hand into mine.

"If you'll follow us," Oliver says.

He leads us to the back of the cottage and through a set of French doors. I thought the inside was gorgeous, but the outside puts the place over the top.

Several stone cottages are spread out around the inner courtyard. Trees and flowers give the place a natural feel. More hand-carved tables and chairs are set out on inlaid bricks. Each table is draped in white linens with live flower centerpieces. Twinkling lights are strung around the area, and lanterns hang from various branches. The sound of flowing water draws my attention to the far side of the courtyard, where there's a large pond with a waterfall.

"Your restaurant is magical," Amelia says as she looks around.

"Ah, the magic is just beginning," Oliver says and walks away.

He stops outside one of the other cottages and opens the doors. Then, he steps aside, allowing our guests to begin filtering into the courtyard.

"Viktor," Amelia says, bringing her hands to cover her mouth. "How did you do this?"

<h1 style="text-align:center;font-style:italic">Amelia</h1>

NOT ONLY AM I STANDING IN THE MOST ENCHANTING garden I've ever laid eyes on, but everyone I know and love is here.

"Happy Birthday, *moya malen'kaya ptichka*," my father says and kisses me on both cheeks in a traditional greeting.

Mom hugs me. "You didn't think we'd miss your birthday, did you?"

"I didn't know we were celebrating my birthday tonight." I look at Viktor, who's standing off to the side, grinning from ear to ear.

Quincy, Tristan, Mateo, and Sparrow are here, as are the guys from Zapped Euforia. Movement in the shadows catches my eye, and for a brief second, I panic until the figure steps out.

"Lana," I squeal and run over to my sister, wrapping my arms around her. "I can't believe you're here."

"Mr. tall and broody over there can be pretty persuasive." She smiles and leans in close. "I think he's got it bad for you."

We both laugh.

"I'm so glad you're here." I turn around and address everyone. "I'm so glad you're all here."

After the initial shock passes, we're seated for the meal to be served.

I grab Viktor's hand under the table. "You didn't have to go through all this."

"*Moya zirka*, there's nothing I won't do for you."

Dinner's nothing short of exquisite. We're served a mix of American and Russian dishes—my favorites of both. It's nice to be able to relax and enjoy everyone's company.

"Are you and your guests ready for cake?" Josephine asks Viktor.

"We are."

Josephine signals to Oliver, who's standing where the servers have been coming in and out. He nods and opens them. Two servers carefully exit, carrying my cake.

"Oh, my word," I exclaim. "It's a piano."

The cake, which is more like a piece of art, is a grand piano. The servers set it carefully on a display table. Everyone gathers around, snapping pictures. After I get my photos, I step out of the way and return to our table. Viktor watches me for a moment before coming over.

"Are you okay?"

"I'm so overwhelmed. This is more than I could've ever asked for."

"I intend to make all your dreams come true." He wraps his arms around me and holds me close.

"You're every one of my dreams come true." I bring my hand to his cheek.

"It's time to sing to the birthday girl," Mateo interrupts us.

"We'll be right over." Viktor places a soft kiss on my lips.

The party's finally winding down, which is good because I'm exhausted. The only people left are my family and us.

"How long are you in town for?"

"We're staying for your first concert," Mom says. "We go home the next day."

"Really?"

"We would not miss it," Dad adds with a proud smile.

When we left New York, I was happy that Dad and Viktor made up and gave us his blessing. However, Dad rarely mentions our relationship, and I find myself filtering what I say. Making up so there's peace and really being happy for us are two different things.

However, tonight Dad's acknowledged we're a couple several times. I overheard him talking to Foster, the drummer from Zapped. Dad was telling him how, at first, he wasn't sure of us as a couple, but now he couldn't be any more pleased. This is the first time we've all been together, and things feel normal. I couldn't be any happier.

Amelia

"I'M GOING TO THROW UP." I PACE BACK AND FORTH backstage. "I can't do this."

"Listen to me, Mel." Mateo puts his hands on my shoulders. "This is just like any other show."

"Except that there are fifty thousand people out there." I point toward the stage. "And the most we've ever played to is a couple hundred."

"Alright, so that's a little different." Mateo smiles. "But other than that, it's exactly the same. We can perform these songs in our sleep."

"Maybe I should've asked Viktor to stay."

Viktor was backstage for the pre-show meet and greets. Then I sent him to take his seat with my family. At first, he put up some resistance, but I reminded him he was not part of my official security team anymore. Eventually, he gave in.

"Everything okay over here?" Indigo asks.

"Mel's freaking out a bit."

"What can I do to help?" she asks, concern etched on her face.

"I need to get some fresh air. Can we go outside for a few minutes?"

"We go on in fifteen," Mateo adds.

"I'll be there." Indigo leads me out the backdoor. I slide down the wall and sit on the ground. "I can't do this, Indi."

She squats down to my eye level. "I didn't think you were the type to give up so easily."

"This is too much. I don't know what I was thinking."

"I suppose it was something about how much you enjoy music and performing."

"That's pretty close." I pull my knees to my chest. "But I didn't think about stadiums full of people."

"What scares you most about it?"

"What if I screw up?"

"You might, but you'll keep going."

"What if everyone hates us?"

"I've been backstage all night. I highly doubt that's going to happen." She pauses and searches my face. "What if you don't screw up? What if everyone loves you, and you grow your fan base? What if you're the headliner on the next tour?"

Indi's always calm under pressure, and she gives excellent advice. This isn't the first time she's taken my negative what-ifs and turned them into positives.

"Those are all good points."

"Let's take a few deep breaths."

I inhale and exhale slowly until I feel centered. Then, I get myself up to my feet. Indigo follows me.

"You've earned your place here. Hold your head high and go kick ass."

I don't know what I imagined fifty thousand people to be like, but whatever I thought didn't cover it. The energy in the stadium is palpable while everyone sings along to our most popular songs. It's beyond my wildest dreams.

We've played almost our entire set. There's only one song left.

As Sparrow and I take center stage to sing "Written in the Stars," the audience goes silent. Sparrow opens the song on his acoustic guitar. As soon as he starts playing, cell phone flashlights turn on all around the stadium. Looking out across the audience, it looks like thousands of stars twinkling. Tears spring in my eyes.

I look down to the front row, and like everyone else, Viktor's on his feet. His gaze is locked on me. I smile and mouth the words *I love you.*

When we finish the song, the audience erupts in applause. Mateo, Quincy, and Tristan join us at the front of the stage for our bows. We exchange hugs with each other. The tour photographer takes pictures of us with the audience as our background.

At this moment, my life feels complete. My family is here supporting me. I am in love with a wonderful man. And I have the career of my dreams.

Viktor

We've been on the road for a little over a month. Today, we're somewhere in North Carolina. Things are so fast-paced the towns blend together. That's where Nick comes in. He makes sure we all know where we are from one day to the next.

It's all worth it, though. Amelia's positively radiant. She shines like the star I already knew she was. I'll travel anywhere. Live anywhere. As long as we're together.

Today's her first day off since the tour started. Last night, we shut our phones off so we could sleep in. When I wake up, Amelia's still sound asleep next to me, her leg thrown over mine. Carefully, I reach over to my night table and grab my phone, powering it on.

As soon as everything's loaded, I see several text messages from Alex. I know Natalie's due any time now, so I hurry to read them.

Alex: Are you still awake?

Five minutes later.

Alex: I'm guessing not. It's almost 2 am. Natalie's water broke. We're heading to the hospital.

I stop reading and shake Amelia gently.

"Amelia. Wake up."

She groans.

"You need to get up. Natalie's water broke."

"It did?" Her eyes pop open. "Did she have the baby?"

"I don't know. I didn't want to keep reading without you."

She pushes up on her elbow to read my screen with me.

Alex: I don't know how you did this with her. She's in so much pain, and she's refusing pain meds.

A half-hour later.

Alex: It's a boy. I have a son. Michael Alexander Montgomery.

Alex: He's so small. 5lbs. 3oz. and 16 inches. But he's perfect and healthy.

The following texts contain pictures of the baby. The sweetest one is of Rose holding her new little brother.

"Oh my gosh. He's adorable," Amelia gushes. "Can we try calling them?"

I hit Alex's contact, and the phone rings.

"Hello?" he answers.

"Congratulations and Happy Birthday." Amelia and I say in unison.

"Thank you."

"I hope we didn't disturb you."

"You didn't. Misha just brought Rose home. You're on speaker now."

"Congratulations, Nat. Michael's gorgeous."

"I can't believe he's here. I wish you two were here, too."

"I wish I knew where we were," Amelia says and giggles. "All this traveling gets confusing."

"I'm sorry I didn't get your texts earlier. We had our phones off so we could get some sleep."

"It's all good," Alex says. "It wasn't last night, but it is now."

"Natalie was stubborn and refused pain meds again?" I chuckle.

"It was awful, but she was amazing."

I stay silent for a moment, remembering just how helpless it felt watching her suffer, knowing there was relief at the press of a button. Relief, she refused. Seeing that precious baby at the end was worth it all, though.

The sound of a baby crying interrupts our conversation.

"We'll let you two go. It sounds like you have your hands full."

"We can't wait to see you guys," Natalie says.

"Did you get the tickets?" Amelia asks.

"We did," Alex answers.

The crying gets louder.

"We'll talk to you both soon."

We say our goodbyes and disconnect the call. Amelia taps my screen, bringing pictures of the baby back up.

"Just look at him," she coos. "He's so tiny and perfect."

"He is." I watch as she flips through the pictures again. "I can't wait until we have babies of our own."

Her finger freezes mid-motion, and she looks up at me. "What do you mean?"

"I can't wait to see you pregnant with our baby." I push a stray curl behind her ear. "A little boy or girl with your red hair."

Amelia sits up and turns to face me. "I don't want children."

"Not yet, of course. But someday."

"No, Viktor." She shakes her head slowly. "I don't want children at all."

She doesn't ever want to have children. Her words are like a punch to my gut, knocking the air out of me.

"Maybe you'll see things differently in a few years."

"I've known since the first night Seth snuck into my bedroom that I didn't want to be a mother. Being taken by Moreno only solidified my decision."

"Your life is different now. I'd never allow anyone to hurt you or our baby."

"I believe you mean every word, but even you can't control everything. There are no guarantees in life."

"Can we agree to table this discussion for another time?" I have to hold onto hope that she'll eventually change her mind.

"No. My answer isn't going to change."

I never thought being a father was in the cards for me. A man like me doesn't get to have a wife and kids—a happily ever after. But then I experienced Natalie giving birth to Rose, and I got the chance to raise her. Even for just a short time, and that changed everything.

After getting a taste of being a father, I knew I wanted that again. This time with a woman who was mine—who I'd spend my forever with.

"Amelia." I reach out to her, but she backs away.

"I need to get some air." She jumps out of bed and hurries out of the room.

I don't follow her. We both need a few minutes to gather our thoughts before we talk again.

Amelia

I'M GLAD I SLEPT IN SHORTS AND A T-SHIRT LAST NIGHT because I'm able to get out of the bus quickly. My sandals are by the door. I slide my feet into them and go outside. Wherever we are today, the sun is shining brightly.

Chase is standing outside my bus. "Where are you going?" he asks.

"For a walk." I don't stop to chat.

"Ms. Solonik," he calls, but I don't turn around. "Amelia, wait."

I need a few minutes alone. I hurry to get away from him, but the buses are parked in a fenced-in area. It usually doesn't bother me, but today, I feel like a caged animal.

"Ms. Solonik, you can't wander off like this," Chase says when he catches up to me.

I spin around and nearly explode. "I'm locked in a fenced-in area. It's not like I can actually go anywhere. Go away, please."

"I apologize." Chase turns and hurries away.

He doesn't go as far as I would like, but at least he gives me some space.

"What's going on?" Sparrow pops his head out of his bus.

"I'm sorry. I hope I didn't wake you."

"We're up." He steps out and closes the door behind him. "I heard you yelling. Is everything okay?"

"No." Tears spring from my eyes.

"Hey." Sparrow walks over and puts his arms around me. "I've got you. You're okay."

His words are soothing, and his arms are comforting. He allows me to cry without pushing me to talk until I'm ready. Once the tears stop, he leads me to a spot behind his bus where there are some picnic tables set up.

"Are you ready to talk about it?" Sparrow asks as we sit down.

"Viktor wants a baby," I say bluntly.

"Now?" he asks, his brow furrowing.

"No. Sometime in the future," I reply with a shrug.

"That's reasonable," Sparrow says cautiously, trying to gauge my reaction.

"I don't want one."

"You're only nineteen," he says, his voice soft but insistent. "You'll change your mind eventually."

I shake my head, my voice firm. "I've seen how evil this world can be. I won't ever change my mind."

Sparrow leans forward, his expression a mix of concern and diplomacy. "I don't think it's something you need to decide on today. Give it some time."

"Yeah, you're probably right. Thanks for the talk," I mumble, standing up abruptly and turning to leave.

"Mel, wait," Sparrow calls after me, his voice filled with concern.

But I wave him off without looking back and keep walking.

When I get back to the bus, Viktor is up, standing at the small counter, making lunch for us.

"You're right on time," he says with a smile, but it doesn't reach his eyes.

We sit at our tiny table and eat in silence. I hate this tension between us, but I don't know how to fix it. I can't give him false hope, and I also can't agree to something I don't want.

When we finish eating, I silently gather our plates and put them in the dishwasher. My chest tightens as dread seeps in—I know what I have to do.

"I think we need some time apart," I say quietly.

"What?" Viktor stands up so fast his chair scrapes against the floor. "Let's pretend I never said anything."

"We can't do that," I reply, shaking my head.

"We can do anything we want." Viktor walks over to me, his voice desperate. "Having children isn't important."

Even as he says it, I see the sadness in his eyes. It's a lie he's telling himself—and me.

"That's not true," I whisper.

"It is. It was a stupid thought," he says, his voice cracking. He reaches out to me, but I step back, raising my hands to stop him.

"Your thoughts and desires aren't stupid," I say, my voice firm despite the ache in my chest. "And I won't let you give up on something you want."

"I want you, Amelia," Viktor says, his voice breaking.

"But you also want to be a father," I reply softly. "If you stay and I won't give you that, you'll resent me—resent us. I won't let you do that."

"Amelia, please," he whispers, his desperation cutting through me like a knife.

"I'm going to get dressed and meet the guys outside," I say, my voice cracking. "I have to be at a band meeting in a few minutes. I'll stay with Sparrow and Mateo until you can find a flight home."

"*Moya zirka*," Viktor pleads, his voice raw. "Please don't do this."

"I have to," I whisper, tears threatening to spill.

I hurry to our bedroom, close the door behind me, and lock it. Only then do I let the sobs escape.

I get dressed and pull my hair into a ponytail. I couldn't care less what I look like right now. When I'm ready, I take a deep breath and open the door. I'm both relieved and saddened to find the bus empty. Holding back tears, I start walking to the stage door at the back of the stadium. Chase learned from earlier and gives me enough space but still follows behind me.

When I get inside, I hear voices coming from down the hall. I get to the room and see I'm the last to arrive.

"You look like hell," Quincy says.

Sparrow and Mateo make space between them on the sofa. I sit between them, and Sparrow puts his arm around me. I rest my head on his shoulder.

"What's wrong?" Tristan asks.

"Mel and Viktor had a disagreement," Sparrow answers for me. "Let's get started."

I don't know what Nick talked about because I couldn't focus on anything other than my heart breaking. The last thing I want to do is be apart from Viktor, but I can't let him give up on a dream just because I don't share it. He deserves better than that.

"Enjoy the rest of your day off," Nick says, ending the meeting.

Quincy, Tristan, and Nick walk out together, leaving me alone with Mateo and Sparrow.

"What happened?" Mateo asks. "Did he hurt you?"

"No. He'd never do anything like that." I wipe my face. "We had a big difference in opinions on our future."

Mateo's phone dings. When he checks it, a smile lights up his face.

"Are you two okay here? I need to take care of something."

"Go on. We're good." Sparrow says.

"You still good to find somewhere to stay tonight?"

"Yep."

I look between them, knowing I'm missing something, but no one stops to explain.

"Awesome. I'll see you two later." Mateo hurries from the room.

When the door closes, I look at Sparrow. "Care to tell me what that was about?"

"Mateo met someone."

"I thought you two were—"

"We are. This is a girl."

"A girl?" I'm confused.

"Mateo's bi. He met a girl a few cities back. They've been talking, and he invited her to spend time with him."

"How do you feel about that?"

"I'm not sure right now. It's all really new." He shrugs slightly. "Back to you. Are you sure time apart is what's best for you and Viktor?"

"No. But it's what has to happen. I can't ask him to give up on something as big as wanting children. That's not fair." I swipe at the tears that are once again falling. "But that doesn't mean it doesn't hurt."

"I'm so sorry, Mel. I know how much you love him."

"Do you need a place to stay tonight?"

"I do."

"Why don't you stay with me? I'm going to be alone."

"You sure?"

I nod.

My heart's shattering into a million pieces. I don't know how to do this. How do I go on when a part of my soul is missing?

Viktor

WHY DID I SAY ANYTHING ABOUT A BABY? I SHOULD'VE kept my mouth shut. Look at the mess I've made. My world has been thrown off its axis. Amelia asked me to leave. I don't want that, but I swore I'd always respect her wishes and not push her into anything she didn't want.

Before she comes out of the bedroom, I walk out of our bus. I have to stop and talk to her team and then try to find a flight out of here. Where to? I don't know.

Chase's standing by the bus when I go outside.

"I'm not going to be here today. Please keep an extra eye on her."

"Sure thing."

I head over to the team's bus and knock on the door. Indigo answers. "This is a surprise."

"Can I come in?"

"Sure." She steps aside. "Is everything okay?"

"No," I say as I sink down on the sofa.

"Can I get you a coffee?"

"No thanks." I drop my head into my hands. "I'll be heading out today. I need to make sure you're capable of handling Amelia's security without me."

"We are." Indigo sits next to me. "May I ask what's wrong?"

I sit up. "Amelia and I are taking a break to figure some things out." That's the most I can admit to right now. To say we're over for good would break me.

"I'm sorry to hear that. I won't push you to talk, but I'm a good listener if you need one."

"I want children. She doesn't." It's as simple and as complicated as that.

"She's young. I understand why she's not ready for them right now."

"Amelia's had a rough life. She doesn't want children, ever," I reply. "She asked me to leave. I can't push her to let me stay. I need to know that your team will keep her security tight."

"You have my word. We'll keep her safe."

"Can I stay here while I make arrangements for a hotel?"

"Stay as long as you need."

"I'll be out of here as soon as I can." I can't be this close to Amelia and not be able to go to her.

"I'm going to take a shower. Make yourself comfortable."

Indigo walks to the back of the bus, and I pull my phone out to book a hotel room. I'll figure out where I'm going from there. The venue offers a driver if we need to leave the area, so I shoot a text asking them to have a car ready.

Amelia has a band meeting soon, so I watch for her to leave the bus. Once she's out of sight, I make my way over and grab my bag. I thought I was done packing and leaving. The emotions are familiar and are accompanied by a tremendous feeling of loss. One I hoped to never feel again.

A text alerts me that my ride's outside waiting for me.

Before I leave, I write a note.

Moya zirka,

I don't know how to walk away from you. How to turn my back on us. You're everything to me, Amelia. My life is empty, meaningless, without you. I'll do anything to change this. I love you.

~Viktor

I set the note on the table and take a final look around before I walk out the door.

The night drags on as I sit in the hotel room alone. Somehow, no matter what I do, I always find myself alone.

Me: Is it okay if I stay at the lake for a while?

Alex: Sure. What's going on?

Me: Amelia and I are taking some time apart.

Alex: Do you want to talk about it?

Me: No.

Alex: When you do, I'm here.

I book the next available flight to Missouri and arrange for a rental car to be ready when I get there. Hopefully, spending some time at the lake will give me the clarity I need to figure this shit out—to get my girl back.

Amelia

Sparrow and I are sitting on the couch watching some sappy romance movie. Why? I have no idea because it's not helping either of us to feel any better. My phone rings, interrupting our pity party.

"It's my sister."

"I'll pause this."

I take a deep breath and connect the call. "Hey, Lana. What's up?"

"Mom told me Viktor called to let Dad know he has some business to attend to. That he's going to be gone for a while."

"Mhm."

"Want to tell me the truth?"

"We had a disagreement." I swallow over the lump in my throat. "I asked him to leave."

"What could possibly be that bad that you made him leave?"

"Babies." The line goes silent. I wait a few minutes and then check to make sure the call's still connected. "You there?"

"I am," she says. "You want a baby, and he doesn't?"

"It's the other way around."

"He knows you're young. What the hell is he asking you to have a baby for?"

"He didn't. He said in the future. But I don't want kids—ever."

"And he couldn't get past that?"

"I can't ask him to give up something that important. That's not fair."

"That's not for you to decide."

"Was whatever the reason why you left Brandon something for you to decide?"

Even after all this time, Lana still hasn't opened up about why she left Brandon. And as much as she denies it, she's still in love with him.

"What happened was out of both of our control," she says quietly. "Don't make the same mistake I did. Don't let this come between you two."

"It already has."

Lana encourages me to reconsider. That if Viktor's willing to stay together despite wanting kids, I should go with that. But I can't. I refuse to be selfish and ask him to stay with me when I'm unwilling to give him the children he wants.

I've watched him with Rose. He's tender and patient. He's content. I should've seen this coming. I guess I just ignored the warning signs. But having children isn't a dream one simply gets over. I'd never be able to live with myself for keeping this from him.

After we hang up, I rest my head back on the couch and let out a big breath.

"Mel, maybe you should call Viktor," Sparrow says softly, his expression cautious as he tests the waters.

"Why?" I ask, lifting my head slightly.

"I think maybe you two should talk more before you give up," he suggests.

"There's nothing to talk about," I say, shaking my head as I sit up straighter and force myself to meet his eyes. "Do you mind if we save the rest of this for another night? I'm tired, and we have a long day ahead of us tomorrow."

"That's fine," Sparrow replies, though the concern in his voice lingers.

I stand up and head toward the bedroom, but when I glance back, I realize Sparrow hasn't moved. He's still sitting on the couch, his hands resting on his knees.

"Aren't you coming to bed?" I ask, pausing in the doorway.

"I'm going to sleep on the couch," he says, his voice casual, though his posture is rigid.

"You aren't going to be comfortable out here," I protest, crossing my arms. "It's not a pull-out."

"I'll be fine," Sparrow insists, leaning back into the cushions as if to prove his point.

"There's no reason you can't share the bed with me." I step closer and grab his hands, tugging him gently to his feet. "I don't think I'm in any danger with you. Wrong body parts, remember?" I add with a chuckle, trying to lighten the mood.

"You're so funny," Sparrow says with a grin, though his eyes briefly flicker with hesitation.

"There's no reason for either of us to be alone," I say, my voice soft but firm.

"You sure?" he asks, his tone serious, as if giving me one last chance to change my mind.

"I'm sure," I reply with a small smile, squeezing his hands before leading him toward the bedroom.

Other than Viktor, Sparrow's the only other man I trust enough to fall asleep when I'm alone with him. "I'm positive."

I thought having company would help me feel less alone, but I was wrong. I feel Viktor's loss so strongly tonight. Unwanted tears begin to fall. I try to stay quiet, so I don't disturb Sparrow. But he's already sliding his arm under me, pulling me close.

"It'll be okay," he says and kisses my head.

I cry myself to sleep.

Amelia

Over the past few weeks, we've made our way up the east coast. Tonight, we're playing Madison Square Garden. I'm excited because Alex and Natalie will be here any minute. Timur and his wife Katia are accompanying them to keep the kids on the bus while we're at the concert.

I peek my head out the door for the millionth time, but there's still no sign of them. Closing the door, I resume my pacing. Time seems to be going backward.

"Relax, Mel," Sparrow says. "They'll be here."

"It's getting late, and I haven't seen them in forever," I murmur, glancing toward the road. A car's horn blares, drawing my attention. My heart leaps. "They're here."

I throw open the bus door and sprint outside. Natalie steps out of the car first, and I rush over, wrapping her in a tight hug.

"Thank you so much for coming," I whisper, my voice thick with relief.

She squeezes me back. "We wouldn't have missed this for anything."

"Hey, kid," Alex says as he pulls me into a quick hug. "How are you holding up?"

I exhale shakily. "It's been hard. Have you heard from Viktor?"

Alex's expression turns serious. "We talk every day."

"Is he okay?" I ask, my voice dropping to a tentative whisper.

He hesitates, then sighs. "To be honest, no."

"Auntie Melia!" Rose's voice breaks the tension as she bounds toward me.

I crouch to scoop her up, spinning her in a playful circle. "Hey, big girl. I've missed my favorite niece."

She giggles and points excitedly toward the car. "I'm a big sister now. See?"

I follow her gaze as Natalie turns around, cradling a tiny bundle in her arms. She approaches, her face glowing.

"Auntie Melia," she says softly. "Meet your nephew, Michael."

My breath catches as I peek at the baby. "He's so small."

Natalie laughs, pulling the cotton hat off his head to reveal a fluff of unruly hair. "Look at this."

"Oh my gosh." I laugh, reaching out to gently touch the tufts.

"That's one reason I keep a hat on him," she admits with a giggle. "His hair's always wild."

I can't help but grin. "He's absolutely perfect." Hugging Rose closer, I glance toward the bus. "Come on inside and get settled. I have to be at the stadium for a meet-and-greet soon."

Bode steps forward to open the bus door, and Alex helps Natalie climb the steps with Michael. Timur takes Rose and carries her inside. Katia trails behind and pulls me into a firm embrace.

Her voice is low but concerned. "You don't look well. Your usual sparkle is missing."

"It's been difficult."

"I know you and Viktor aren't together right now," she says gently, searching my face. "I don't know what happened, but I urge you to work it out."

"I wish it were that easy," I reply, my tone tinged with exhaustion.

Katia's eyes soften. "Sweet girl, relationships require compromise on both sides. When the love you share is real, like I know yours and Viktor's is, you can't let anything stand in your way. You both need to fight for it."

I shake my head. "This is a big issue. There's no compromise."

"There's always room for compromise," she insists before stepping onto the bus.

I take a deep breath and follow her inside. Sparrow's already showing everyone around.

"We'll leave you all to settle in," Sparrow says, reaching for my hand. "Amelia and I need to be backstage in less than five minutes."

Alex waves us off with a reassuring smile. "Don't worry about us. I think we've got it handled."

"I'll send someone to get you closer to showtime," I promise before Sparrow and I exit the bus.

In comparison to some of our other venues, Madison Square Garden is small, only holding about twenty thousand fans, but their enthusiasm was over the top. Despite my depressed mood, I think it was probably one of our best concerts this summer. We finish our songs, take our bows, and exit the stage. One more concert in the books.

Although I've loved being on tour, I'm glad it will wrap up in a few weeks. I'm exhausted emotionally and physically. I'm looking forward to some time off to rest and regroup. I'm about to push the door open to leave the stadium when Sparrow calls me.

"Mel, wait a second."

. . .

I turn back. "What's up?"

He shifts his weight awkwardly, rubbing the back of his neck. "I'm not going to be staying on your bus tonight."

"You're more than welcome to. Alex and Natalie are heading home."

Sparrow hesitates, his tone nervous as he explains, "Mateo asked me to spend some time with Aspen and him."

I study him for a moment. "How do you feel about that?"

He shrugs, looking down at his shoes. "I'm not sure yet. There's a lot... but I want to give it a chance."

Placing a reassuring hand on his arm, I soften my tone. "If anything changes and you need a place to stay, just come over."

"Thanks," he murmurs, leaning in to press a quick kiss to my cheek before walking away.

When I open the door to the bus, Alex, Natalie, Bode, and Indigo are waiting outside. Natalie immediately lets out an excited squeal.

. . .

"You were amazing," she gushes, her eyes sparkling. "I can't believe this is your life now. You're a rock star."

I laugh softly, brushing off her enthusiasm. "It's still just me."

"Just you? Don't sell yourself short," Alex interjects. "Look at everything you've accomplished. You should be proud of yourself."

"I just happened to be in the right place at the right time."

Inside, the bus is quiet. Timur and Katia must have already put the kids to bed. I hesitate, glancing at Natalie and Alex. "I hate for you guys to have to wake them. Why don't you stay here tonight? I can sleep on the couch, and Timur and Katia can move to Indigo's bus. They've got an extra bed."

"Are you sure?" she asks, her voice cautious. "We don't want to inconvenience you."

"I'm positive," I insist. "Honestly, it's kinda selfish. I want to spend more time with you guys before we leave tomorrow."

Natalie glances back at Alex, who gives a slight nod of approval. "It's a yes, then."

"Thank you," I say sincerely. Opening the door, I call Bode over. "Can you bring Timur and Katia to Indigo's bus? Let them know they'll be staying there tonight."

"Yes, Ms. Solonik," Bode replies dutifully.

"It's just Amelia," I remind him with a playful smile, the habit starting to wear on me. "For the millionth time."

He chuckles sheepishly. "Sorry, Amelia. It's hard to get used to."

"It's all good," I reply, offering a smile before heading back inside.

Timur and Katia say their goodnights and follow Bode to Indigo's bus. I sink onto the couch with a deep sigh, the weight of the day pressing down on me. Natalie sits beside me, her warmth a comfort. Across from us, Alex grabs a snack and settles at the table.

"How many more shows do you have?" Natalie asks, tucking a strand of hair behind her ear.

"Six," I answer, my tone weary.

"What's your plan after the tour?" Alex asks.

"I'm not sure," I admit, pausing to take a sip from my water bottle. "Viktor and I were still trying to decide what we wanted to do. Now, I need to figure that out on my own."

Natalie reaches over, giving my hand a comforting squeeze as I continue, "I was wondering if maybe I could stay at the lake for a little while to sort things out?"

"You're welcome to stay as long as you want," Alex responds without hesitation, his tone full of reassurance.

"Thank you."

Michael's cries echo through the baby monitor, breaking the moment.

"The baby beckons," Natalie says with a tired but affectionate sigh as she starts to stand.

"Can I get him?" I ask quickly, already getting to my feet.

"Absolutely. But he'll probably need a diaper change."

"I can handle that," I reply, my voice lightening. I hurry off, thankful for the distraction. I walk into my bedroom and find a sleeping Rose in the center of my bed. Michael's in his travel bassinet. I don't want to wake Rose, so I keep the lights dim and then reach down to lift the baby.

"Hi there, precious boy." I kiss his soft cheek. "I'm your Auntie Melia."

He stops crying and watches me closely.

I grab his diaper bag from the closet. "How about we change your diaper, and then we'll go to your mama?"

I'm amazed at how tiny but perfect his features are. Both of his feet fit into the palm of one hand. I successfully get his diaper changed without waking Rose. Then, I snap his sleeper back up and cradle him close to me. Carefully, I sit on the edge of the bed. "I know we're just meeting, but I already love you very much." His tiny hand grabs onto one of my fingers while he coos at me.

Looking at this tiny bundle, I understand Viktor's desire to have a child of his own. It's not that I'm unaffected or hate children. On the contrary, I adore them. They're innocent and curious. A miraculous representation of the love between two people. It's those same reasons that make me not want them.

I've seen the worst this world has to offer. Moreno didn't only take adults. I witnessed what Moreno and the sick men he entertained liked to do to children. The little lives that were tortured before mercy was shown, and they were put out of their misery.

Moreno might be gone, but there are many more just like him. My father works hard to stop as many trafficking rings as possible, but they'll never be entirely eradicated. How can I justify bringing a baby into this world knowing that?

Holding Michael, I can't help but daydream about him being mine and Viktor's. Would he have my red hair and Viktor's blue eyes? Would he be a she—a little girl who would steal her daddy's heart?

Just because I didn't have anyone looking out for me doesn't mean it would be the same for a child we'd have. As long as Viktor and I are alive, he'd never let anything happen to them. And if the worst happened and we were taken away too soon, my family would be there to protect our child. The past wouldn't have a chance to repeat itself.

What about the evil that's out there? Viktor's only human. He can't be everywhere and see every possible danger. Is that a risk I'm willing to take?

"I don't know what to do. I wish I had the answers." Michael wiggles and pushes his bottom lip out in a pout. "Is your belly hungry?" I kiss his tiny nose. "Let's get you to your mama so you don't wake up your sissy."

Amelia

EVEN THOUGH I KNEW I'D SEE ALEX AND NATALIE again in a few weeks, saying goodbye to them was hard. I cried as they drove away, knowing this time I was really going to be alone.

Things seem to be working out between Mateo, Aspen, and Sparrow. He hasn't given too many details, but he also hasn't returned to being my roommate. The three of them spend their free time together. I'm happy for him, but I'm sad for me. The past few weeks have been incredibly lonely.

I'd hoped time would heal the ache in my heart. Instead, I think it's only gotten worse. Viktor texts me daily to tell me he loves me and that he'll wait forever. That not having children isn't a deal breaker for him. I've picked up the phone countless times to call or text him back but didn't go through with it.

Once I got past my pride and brought it up to Ania, she helped me talk through the whole subject of children rationally. She advised me not to make future decisions based on past trauma.

We've had some tough sessions. Ania encouraged me to respect Viktor's decisions, whatever they may be. That he gets to decide what he can or cannot live with, not me. Not respecting

Viktor's opinion and taking away his voice, his right to choose, was exactly what was done to me. And it's wrong.

After our sessions, I spent a lot of time alone with my thoughts. I took everything I'd always thought and all the things Ania and I discussed and made a decision. But I haven't talked to Viktor yet.

Ania encouraged me to reach out and talk to him. But I can't. I'm embarrassed. I behaved like a spoiled child and sent him away the first time we didn't agree on something instead of being an adult and talking through it.

"What do you think?" I turn away from the mirror and show Sparrow the new tattoo on my upper back.

His eyes widen as he leans in for a closer look. "Did it hurt

"Not really," I reply casually, a small smile tugging at my lips.

"It's beautiful," he says, admiration evident in his voice as he studies the intricate design.

I glance over my shoulder at him, my smile broadening. "I love it," I say with quiet conviction, the excitement evident in my voice.

Getting this tattoo was something I'd been planning for several months—before Viktor and I broke up. The problem was we were on tour and didn't stay in one place long enough to do much of anything. I knew our last show would be in Kansas City and that we'd be arriving a few days early.

A few months ago, I found a local tattoo shop and scheduled

an appointment. The plan was to get this one before tonight's show. It was supposed to be a surprise for Viktor. My heart sinks at that thought.

I haven't heard from him since we left New York. I guess he got sick of hoping and waiting for me to respond to his messages. I waited too long to come to my senses. I can't blame him for finally realizing what I said was true—he deserves to have every one of his dreams come true.

"Send him a text, Mel," Sparrow encourages me. "It's never too late."

"I was a jerk and never responded to his texts begging me to talk to him. I fear it's too late now."

"Love doesn't just go away."

"Tell me about it. You don't think my heart's still breaking?"

I've been paralyzed by fear and embarrassment. Because of that, I might've lost the best thing that's ever happened to me.

Viktor

"YOU NEED TO GIVE HER SPACE," GRIGOR SAYS FIRMLY, his tone steady but empathetic. "Amelia's had a traumatic past. The things she's gone through are things most people can't even begin to comprehend. And that's not a bad thing—it just means she's carrying a heavy burden."

I run a hand through my hair, frustration bubbling to the surface. "I don't want her to think I deserted her."

"She asked you to leave. To give her space, right?"

"Yes."

"And she hasn't responded to any of your attempts to contact her?" he presses, his tone more pointed now.

"No," I admit, the word coming out as little more than a whisper.

"Then," he continues gently, "I think you need to respect the boundaries she's put in place. Leave the ball in her court. If she wants to contact you, she will. And if not..." He hesitates for a moment, his voice dropping to a softer tone. "You'll have to face that it's over."

The words hit me like a blow to the chest, and I swallow hard, fighting the urge to argue. I can only nod, the weight of his advice settling heavily on my shoulders.

I know what Grigor's saying is the right thing to do, so I stopped texting her. That doesn't mean I haven't picked my phone up and typed them out. I've done that more times than I can count. Each text begging her to call me. But I didn't send them.

Instead, I took my therapist's advice and backed off. Amelia's boundaries must be respected. I also decided to use this time to honestly consider Amelia's point of view. I didn't want to admit it, but she had a valid point. I couldn't just pretend I didn't want children. I needed to take time to really consider if not being a father is something I can live with. When she first brought it up and asked me to leave, I reacted. But she was right. I needed to think it through.

The other night, I pulled up her playlist and listened to the songs. "Just Give Me a Reason" came on. I've heard her sing that song a million times, but this was the first time I really listened to the words.

If I didn't know better, I would've sworn the song was written about us—for us. Two people who've each experienced the worst of what the world has to offer. They have battle wounds and think they're damaged beyond repair. But then they meet each other. Their souls connect and heal every fractured part of their hearts. I put it on repeat and listened to it until I memorized every word.

Although I've enjoyed my quiet solace at the lake, I'm equally as happy that Alex and Natalie flew in two weeks ago. Natalie wanted to make sure the kids had happy memories of summers spent at Finn Lake. It also allows Charlotte and Stanley to spend time with their grandkids. They try to spend as much time as they can at their cottage over the summer.

I've been able to spend a lot of time with their family, too.

Which is where I am right now. Alex and Natalie needed some groceries, so I offered to sit with the kids. When Rose was a baby, I had our routine down to a science. But this whole two-kid thing is serious business. Meeting the needs of two little ones is certainly not for the faint of heart. Rose is well-behaved, but she's a busy toddler. She's curious about everything. And Michael, he's an infant. He can do no wrong, but it's an immediate need when he's hungry or his diaper requires changing. It's been a very long hour. I'm sitting on the floor watching Rose do a little wooden puzzle while I give Michael a bottle when I hear their car pull in.

"Mama. Daddy." Rose runs to the door.

I can't get up as fast as I'd like while balancing a baby. By that time, Rose is already turning the handle to open the door. I'm at a distinct disadvantage.

Natalie's the first one in. Rose wraps herself around Natalie's leg. As soon as Michael sees his Mama, he decides the bottle is no longer acceptable—his cries alert everyone to that fact. Natalie sets the bags she's carrying down and takes the baby.

"Thank you so much for watching them," Natalie says as she tries to make her way to the couch with one child in her arms, the other hanging onto her leg.

"Come here, Rose." I attempt to extricate her from her mother's leg. "Let's let mama walk."

"I'm used to it." Natalie shakes her head.

"I'll go help Alex with the bags." I turn to go to the door. "Thanks for letting me watch them."

"I should be the one thanking you. It was a treat to go out alone."

"I'm glad I could help."

I leave her to feed her baby and head outside, where Alex is unpacking the groceries from the trunk.

"You're still in one piece. That's a good sign."

"They're good kids. I love spending time with them."

Alex stops what he's doing and looks at me. "It sounds like there's a but coming."

I lean against the car. "You and Natalie and the kids are my family. Over the past few weeks, I've realized that the part of me that loves children is fulfilled when I spend time with Rose and Michael."

"Ah, we're talking about Amelia."

"We are."

"What are you thinking?"

"With them in my life, I don't think I'd ever feel like I gave something up."

After everything that happened between Natalie and me the year Alex was gone, I was afraid our friendship was ruined. Before I left, he told me he forgave me, but I assumed those were just words to send me off.

It took me too long to understand he honestly wasn't angry at me. He didn't blame me for anything that happened between Natalie and me. Hell, I still don't understand it. All I know is I'm thankful for his friendship and support. Especially now.

"I've been doing a lot of soul-searching since I've been here. I didn't want to believe Amelia was right. That the best thing for us was time apart."

"I'm not following," Alex says.

"Amelia was right when she said I couldn't pretend I never brought up wanting kids. And I couldn't just write off wanting them in the future. Having this time apart allowed me to weigh the possibilities for my future. Gave me the clarity I needed to make a decision I'm comfortable with."

"I guess I'm glad we were able to help." Alex chuckles.

"I'll help you get these in." I reach into the trunk and grab the last few bags. "Then I have to go. I have an important errand to run."

Amelia

"Can you believe this is it? The last show?" Tristan asks.

"It's been one hell of a ride," Quincy adds. "What's everyone's plans for after?"

"I need to take a few weeks off. There are some important things I have to do. After that, I don't know."

"Just the group I was looking for," Nick says as he strolls into the green room. "We need to chat before things get going here tonight."

"What's up?" Matteo asks.

"We received an offer from Crimson Flame Music to record a full album in preparation for a tour next year with Beautiful Division as the headliner."

The room is quiet while we let Nick's words sink in.

"A recording deal and a tour?" I'm sure I misheard him.

"I forgot another small detail. Beautiful Division has also been nominated for a Grammy in the Best New Artist category, and they'd like you to play at the awards ceremony." Nick grins.

"Nominated for a Grammy?" Sparrow asks in disbelief.

Nick nods.

Once the reality of what he said hits, the celebrating starts.

Never in a million years would I have imagined my life taking this turn. If it's a dream, I never want to wake up.

"Mr. Hart has the contracts. He's going through them now. We'll meet in a few weeks to go over the details. But guys and girl," Nick smiles. "I couldn't be more proud of you and more excited for your future."

We stay tucked away in the green room, talking excitedly about what's coming for us. Sparrow has been writing songs, so we already have some new music to record. Our celebration comes to an end when the pre-concert meet and greet starts.

After all the pictures and autographs are done, there are only a few minutes left until we take the stage. I pull my phone out to text Natalie.

Me: Are you guys here yet?

Natalie: We are. Front row center stage.

Me: Perfect.

Then, I do something I've been terrified to do.

Me: Can we talk?

It only takes a second for me to see he read the message. The little bubbles pop up on the screen, indicating he's texting back.

Viktor: Sure.

Me: I'm about to go on stage. Can I call you after the concert?

Viktor: I'll be waiting.

"Mel, it's go time," Sparrow says as he walks past me, heading for the stage.

"I'm right behind you."

The stage is shrouded in darkness as I take my place behind the keyboard. The familiar recording announcing Beautiful Division plays through the sound system, and the crowd goes crazy. We start playing our first song just as the lights come up.

It's become a habit for me to search the audience even though I know Viktor won't be there. I spot Alex and Natalie, but it's what's next to them, rather who's next to them, that shocks me most. My parents and Lana are here too.

I don't know if it's possible to smile even bigger than I already was. Knowing they're all here to support me and celebrate the last show is more than I could've asked for. The only thing that would make it even more perfect is if Viktor was here.

Viktor

Yesterday, I went to the local animal shelter. I walked the concrete aisles looking at all the dogs waiting for their forever home, not sure what I was looking for. I trusted fate would step in and show me which dog was the right one.

I stopped at a few kennels, and although the dogs were cute, I didn't feel a connection. I was about to give up hope when I came to the last cage. A golden brown pup was huddled in the corner, clearly terrified.

"What's the story on this one?" I ask the shelter worker who's accompanying me.

"This little girl's about four months old. One of our volunteers found her abandoned on the side of the road. She was only about eight weeks old and cold and dehydrated," she explains. "It was touch and go for a good while. But she's a fighter."

"How could someone do that to an innocent animal?"

"You'd be surprised at the things we see."

Unfortunately, I probably wouldn't. I've been witness to the evils of society against their own species. I can only imagine the unconscionable acts committed against animals.

"She's spayed and has her vaccines. All the tests we've run

show she's healthy. But as you can see, she's terrified. We've had people interested in her, but her trust issues scare them away."

"Can I meet her?"

"You can try, but you probably won't have much success."

"Do you have treats?"

"I'll be right back." She disappears for a few minutes and returns with a baggie containing several small treats.

"Thanks."

She pulls out her keys and unlocks the door, allowing me to enter the dog's space. "I'm going to close this so she doesn't try to escape. Take as much time as you want. I'll be in here cleaning up."

Once the puppy and I are alone, I sit down slowly, keeping my back against the wall and leaving enough space between us so she doesn't feel threatened.

I sit quietly, allowing her to get used to my presence in her space. She doesn't move from her huddled spot in the corner.

"I'm told you've had a rough start in life," I murmur. "I don't blame you for being scared of people."

Her ears move as I whisper to her, so I know she's listening.

"I know how scary trusting people can be." I take a small piece of treat out of the bag and gently toss it over to her. She looks between me and the treat several times. "It's okay. That's for you."

Although hesitant, she lowers her head, sniffs the treat, and then picks it up.

"That's a good girl," I quietly praise the puppy. "I know another girl. Her name's Amelia. You remind me of her when she and I first met." I take another piece of treat, this time tossing it so it lands a few steps away from her. "She had bad things done to her and was scared too."

The puppy stares at the treat. She wants it but isn't sure if she should move from her safe corner.

"It's okay. I won't hurt you."

The puppy doesn't move. I'm sure she's trying to decide if it's worth risking her safety to grab the treat. Eventually, she ventures forward and grabs the treat but quickly returns to her corner.

I continue to whisper to her and give her treats. Each time, she inches out, grabs the treat, and hurries away.

"I'd like to bring you home with me. You'd be safe. No one would hurt you ever again." She tilts her head as if trying to understand what I'm telling her. "How about you try coming a little closer?" I put a treat on the ground within my reach.

The puppy cautiously inches toward the treat. This time, when she takes it, she doesn't go back.

"That's a good girl," I say quietly. "Do you think you and I can try to get to know one another? Maybe become friends?" I hold out an open palm with a piece of treat in it.

Even though she's trembling, the puppy takes the treat from me.

"Very good, Nadiya," I say softly. "Nadiya means hope. You give me hope for the future." She wags her tail for a fraction of a second. I smile at her and offer another treat from my hand. "You like your new name, don't you, sweet girl?"

She takes the treat from my hand. Then, her barriers fall away, and she hops onto my lap. Her tail's wagging a mile a minute as she licks my face.

"I don't know how you did it," the shelter worker says with a big smile.

I stand up with the pup in my arms. "I'd like to adopt her."

I was able to get cleared to bring Nadiya home early this morning. Before I left the shelter, I also made a sizeable donation. If it were up to me, I would've taken every animal there and given it a home, but that's not realistic. The next best thing I could do was ensure there were enough funds to provide high-quality care.

On the way home, we stopped at the pet store to purchase food, bowls, a leash and collar, a bed, and more toys than one puppy could ever want. The shelter's getting a large delivery of supplies along with a note letting them know whenever they need more, to place an order, and the cost will be covered.

It took much longer than I thought, which is why I'm late getting to the concert. Who knew a puppy would take more work than a human child?

"She's adorable." Indigo gushes over the puppy that's slathering her in kisses.

Looking at her now, you wouldn't believe she's the same pup who was cowering in a corner less than twenty-four hours ago.

"Are you sure you're okay with watching her? She's not housebroken yet."

"Go. Nadiya and I'll be just fine. Won't we, little girl?" Indigo ignores me while she showers Nadiya with love.

Knowing my new little girl's in good hands, I head over to the concert venue, hoping that my plan is not about to backfire on me.

Amelia

We're in the middle of "Written in the Stars" when Sparrow quickly motions for me to look backstage. I glance over my shoulder and nearly lose my place. Viktor's standing there. I look back to Sparrow, who shrugs as if he's as surprised as I am by his presence.

My hands tremble through the rest of the song. Every emotion I've buried for the past few weeks bubbles to the surface. By the end of the song, tears are streaming down my face.

The rest of the guys join us at the front of the stage to take our final bow. Sparrow thanks the crowd for their support and tells them to be sure to follow us on social media for all our updates.

After we exchange hugs and the photographer finishes her on-stage pictures, we make our exit.

Viktor's striking blue eyes meet mine, drawing me to him.

"You're here." My voice wavers as I step closer, struggling to believe he's standing in front of me.

"I am," Viktor replies simply, his tone steady but his eyes betraying a depth of emotion.

"We need to talk," I say softly, glancing away to collect myself.

"Yes, we do." His voice is calm, but there's an intensity behind it that makes my heart race.

Without another word, Viktor places his hand on the small of my back and guides me through the crowd that's milling around backstage. The weight of our unspoken words hangs heavy in the air as we walk to my bus in silence. When we arrive, I freeze in surprise—Indigo is inside, sitting on the floor with a small, wiggling puppy.

As soon as the puppy sees Viktor, it abandons Indigo and sprints toward him, its tiny tail wagging furiously.

"Did you miss me, Nadiya?" Viktor asks as he kneels to stroke her head.

"She did fantastic," Indigo chimes in, getting to her feet. "I'll be outside if you need me."

Viktor straightens and gives her a curt nod. "Can you ensure we have privacy?"

"Will do, sir," Indigo replies before slipping out the door.

Turning back to me, Viktor gestures toward the couch. "Let's sit. We have a lot to talk about."

We settle on the couch, the little puppy curling up near Viktor's feet. She's utterly enamored with him, and it's clear the feeling is mutual.

I take a deep breath, the words I've rehearsed threatening to spill out. "Viktor, I—"

"Let me go first, please," he interrupts gently, his voice low but firm.

I nod, clasping my hands tightly in my lap.

"The past few weeks have been hell without you," he begins, his gaze locking with mine. "But you were right to ask me to leave. I needed the time and space to think about my future." He pauses to shoo the puppy away from his shoelaces, handing her a chew toy instead. "I didn't know where to go, so I asked Alex if I could stay at the lake."

The puppy, bored with the toy, bounces over to me and places her tiny paws on my leg. I scoop her up, cradling her in my arms.

"Is it a boy or a girl?" I ask softly, running a hand over her silky fur.

"She's a little girl—Nadiya," Viktor says, a proud smile touching his lips. "Her name means hope."

"She's precious." I stroke her gently, my heart warming as her tiny eyes flutter closed.

Viktor watches us for a moment before continuing. "While I was at the lake, I gave my future a lot of thought. About what my life might look like—with children and without. I also spent time with Alex, Natalie, and the kids. And I realized something important." He pauses, his voice catching. "My future is empty without you. Having children or not—that's not what matters most to me."

"But I've seen you with Rose," I whisper, the words tumbling out. "I've seen the longing in your eyes."

"I do love Rose and Michael with all my heart," he admits, his voice tender. "And they'll always be part of our lives. We can shower all the love we have to give on them—and on Nadiya."

I glance down, realizing the puppy has fallen asleep in my arms. "She's had a rough life, hasn't she?"

Viktor nods, his expression darkening slightly. "She was abandoned as a young pup, left for dead. When I went to the shelter, I found her cowering in a corner. The worker told me that, despite being a puppy, her fear kept her from getting adopted. She refused to connect with anyone—until yesterday." He reaches over to gently pet her head. "I saw her fear and knew I had to stay as long as it took to earn her trust."

Tears prick at my eyes. "How could anyone do that to an animal?"

"She needed someone to see her," Viktor says, his gaze never leaving the puppy. "I went there to find a dog for us. I know how much animal welfare means to you."

I smile at the thought. We've symbolically adopted animals at every zoo and aquarium we've visited. This feels like the next step.

"We both have painful pasts," Viktor continues. "And if we

never have children of our own, I'm okay with that. There are other ways we can show love and make a difference. Starting with Nadiya. We'll give her a life full of love and safety."

"Stop, please," I whisper, cutting him off.

The hopeful look in his eyes vanishes instantly. "Amelia?" he asks cautiously.

I carefully set the sleeping puppy on the floor, then stand and pull off my T-shirt. Viktor's gaze never wavers from me as I turn around to reveal the tattoo on my shoulder.

"I got this done a few days ago," I say quietly.

He rises from the couch and steps closer, his fingers tracing the delicate lines of the tattoo. The image is a watercolor Nightingale made of music notes.

"It's a mix of the both of us," I explain, my voice breaking. "You're my Nightingale."

"And you're my melody," he murmurs, his voice thick with emotion as he leans forward, his lips brushing my shoulder where the ink marks our bond.

"I did a lot of soul-searching while we were apart, too." I look up at him. "I'm scared to bring a child into this world because of my past. But I realized if I let trauma dictate my future, all those evil people would win. I don't want to have a baby right now, but I don't want to close the door on ever having children."

"I don't want you to say that because you feel you have to. We have Nadiya, and there are plenty more animals who've had traumatic pasts. We can change a lot of lives."

"And I'm for adopting as many as we can care for. But if one day we decide we want to add a baby to the mix, I'm okay with that too." I reach out and take his hand. "When I looked at my future, there was also nothing without you."

Viktor pulls me against him. "I love you, Amelia."

"I love you more, Viktor." I stand on my tiptoes, my lips meeting his.

There's nothing gentle about our kiss. We pour all of our

emotions into it. Viktor lifts me, and I wrap my legs around his waist. He starts walking back toward our bedroom.

"You will not keep me from my daughter." My father's voice booms from outside the bus, startling Nadiya awake. She runs behind Viktor.

"Sir, she's asked for privacy," Indigo argues.

"If you do not move, you will find yourself out of a job," he yells.

The bus door flies open as I scramble to grab my shirt. It's too late, though. Dad's already on the bus. I hold the shirt up, trying to cover myself.

"Amelia. Viktor." Dad looks between us, his eyes wide with shock. "I did not know you were here."

Indigo rushes in behind him. "I tried to stop him, sir."

"It's okay, Indi." Viktor gives her a kind smile.

I manage to step behind Viktor and use his large frame as a cover to put my shirt on. Once I'm presentable, I stand next to Viktor.

With the situation a bit calmer, Nadiya peeks her head from behind Viktor's leg before deciding it's safe. She runs over to my father, rubbing herself up against his legs. Dad's not a huge animal lover, evidenced by the dissatisfied look on his face at the mess Nadiya's making of his black suit pants.

"What is that?" Dad asks, pointing at the dog.

"This is our new little girl, Nadiya," Viktor introduces the dog proudly.

"Why?"

Viktor and I look at each other and laugh. "I've always wanted a dog, and now I have one." I stoop down and tap my leg. Nadiya runs back to me. "In her young life, she's only known abandonment and loss. Viktor and I are going to show her that not all people are bad." She licks my face, and Dad scrunches his nose. "We're her family now, and we'll give her all the love a puppy could ever need."

"I am guessing this means you two have made up?"

"We have." Viktor puts his arm around me. "And we made you a dedushka." Viktor grins.

As hard as Dad tries to keep a straight face, he loses the battle and begins to laugh. When Nadiya runs to him this time, my father leans down and pats her on the head.

"Ty schastlivyy malen'kiy shchenok."

"She is lucky and very loved."

Viktor

THE REST OF AMELIA'S FAMILY, ALONG WITH ALEX AND Natalie, pile onto the bus. I was hoping for some alone time to reconnect with my girl, but that'll have to wait. Everyone's hungry, so we order pizza and celebrate the end of the tour. It's well after midnight before everyone starts to leave.

"I'm going to walk them out. I'll be right back," I say, grabbing my jacket.

"I'll wait here," Amelia murmurs, stifling a yawn as she sinks deeper into the couch.

As I step outside with Irina and Max, Irina looks over at me with a curious expression. "Do you know Amelia's plans now that the tour is over?" she asks, her tone measured.

I shrug slightly. "I'm not sure. We planned to stay at the lake for a week or two to unwind."

Max nods thoughtfully. "We are in town for a few days. I would like to spend some time with her."

"I'm sure that'll be fine," I assure him. "We'll call you tomorrow and make some plans."

Satisfied with my answer, they exchange goodbyes and head off toward their car. I watch as they drive away before Alex steps up beside me, clapping a hand on my back.

"I'm glad everything worked out for you," Alex says, his tone warm and genuine.

"That puppy's so sweet," Natalie says. "I can't wait for Rose to meet her."

"My little *printessa* is going to love her new furry cousin."

"I have a feeling she's going to want a puppy of her own now," Natalie says.

"There's plenty of dogs in need of a good home," I reply with a knowing grin.

"I don't think I'm ready to take on two kids and a dog," he adds, shaking his head.

We share a quiet laugh before Alex and Natalie climb into their car. I watch them drive off, their taillights fading into the distance. Turning back, I head inside the bus.

The scene inside warms my heart. Amelia is fast asleep on the couch, her breathing soft and even. Nadiya is curled up behind her, nestled into the curve of her back.

After carefully setting up the puppy in her crate for the night, I return to the couch. For a moment, I watch Amelia as she sleeps. Her peaceful expression and the way her hair spills across the pillow make my chest tighten with emotion. I slide my arms under her, gently lifting her up.

She stirs slightly, her eyes fluttering open. "I was hoping this wasn't a dream," she whispers, her voice groggy but laced with emotion. "I was afraid I'd wake up, and you'd be gone."

"It's not a dream, *moya zirka*," I murmur. "I'm right here."

Her arms tighten around my neck as she relaxes against me, a small, contented smile playing on her lips. I lean down and press my lips to hers to show her how real this is. My tongue seeks access to her mouth, which she readily allows. I don't break our connection as I carry her to our bedroom, where I rid us of our clothing and worship her body, bringing her to orgasm several times.

"Please, Viktor. I need you," she begs.

I line myself up with her opening and push inside. My eyes

close from the intensity of the emotions. Amelia's my heart and soul. Without her, my world is dark and empty. I never want to experience life without her by my side again.

I move slowly, trying to prolong our shared pleasure. Hoping to make tonight last forever. But my self-control is slipping. I increase the speed and intensity of my movements. I want more—need to be deeper.

Pulling out, I flip Amelia onto her hands and knees. She looks at me over her shoulder and bites her bottom lip.

"Are you okay with this?"

"I am," she breathes.

Her consent is all I need to thrust back into her welcoming body. Her head drops as she mewls in pleasure. I hold onto her hips as I drive into her over and over. Her body begins to tense beneath mine. I know she's close. I reach around to her clit and rub my thumb over her sensitive area. The first waves of her orgasm begin, and she calls out my name. Then, I'm falling over the cliff with her. We soar on the wings of ecstasy until the last waves of pleasure subside, and we float to the ground.

Amelia's body collapses underneath mine. Not wanting to put my full weight on her, I roll over and lie next to her. She rests her head on my chest, and I hold her close.

"I'm sorry for the way I behaved. I shouldn't have shut you down so quickly," Amelia says quietly.

"I forgive you, *moya zirka*. We both need to learn how to communicate better." I rub her back gently. "The important thing is we figured it out and are here now."

"I never want to be away from you again."

I'm woken by the buzzing of my cell phone. Amelia's still sound asleep, her head on my chest and her leg tossed over mine. I reach over and grab my phone.

Charlotte: We're having a surprise party for Natalie tomorrow. We'd love for you and Amelia to be there.

Me: We wouldn't miss it. Just tell me when and where.

Charlotte gives me the address. When I look it up on the internet, I see it's at Water's Edge Bed and Breakfast. It's an odd place for a party, but I understand that it might be the only place to keep it a secret.

I set the phone back on the nightstand. I'm not in a hurry to go anywhere, but then I hear Nadiya whining. Carefully, I slide out from under Amelia and throw on a pair of pants and a shirt so I can take the puppy out for a walk.

Amelia

Yesterday, Viktor got us a rental car so we could drive to Northmeadow. My father's making arrangements for our Audi to be delivered to the lake house since we'll be spending a few weeks there.

I'm not due to be in California until mid-October. I'm looking forward to spending time alone with Viktor in one place.

This tour was incredible, and we were only the opening act. Knowing we'll be doing it next time as the headliner is unbelievable. But as fun as it was, waking up in a different city and state every day became tiresome. It'll be nice to be in the same place for a few weeks.

Today, we got up extra early. Viktor's finishing loading the car with all our stuff while I pack a doggie diaper bag for Nadiya. We have a nearly three-hour drive ahead of us. Traveling with a puppy is going to make the ride even longer since we'll have to make multiple stops.

"Are my girls ready to go?" Viktor asks when he comes back inside.

"I just finished packing her stuff."

Nadiya's running around the bus, dragging her leash behind

her. She's so excited even though she doesn't know what's happening.

"Let's get on the road." Viktor grabs the puppy's leash, and I take her bag.

We make our way out to the car, where Viktor buckles Nadiya into her puppy car seat. I do the important thing—take pictures of Viktor and our fur baby.

The guys left for home yesterday, and my parents and Lana flew down to Northmeadow two nights ago, so it's just us and my security team left. Thankfully, Dad gave them a few weeks off. We'll meet back up with them in California when we go back.

Viktor's already started looking for someplace for us to live since we told Dad it was okay to put the Long Beach house on the market. We'll spend most of our time in L.A., so we're looking for something closer.

It's a good thing we left early. We had to make more stops than we anticipated. For the most part, Nadiya did great on the drive, and four hours later, we're pulling up at the cottage. Natalie texted that she and Alex were spending the day with her parents, so they're not at the lake right now.

There's about an hour until the party, so we unpack the car and try to get everything settled inside before we have to leave for the bed and breakfast.

"It's a pretty cottage. But you didn't even hang up a picture?" I ask as I look around.

"Why would I?"

"To make it feel like a home."

"This place was only for work."

I walk over to the windows overlooking the lake. "Do you think Natalie and Alex would let us decorate it some?

"I don't think they'd have a problem with that." Viktor comes to stand behind me. "We can work on that tomorrow if you'd like."

I rest my head on his chest. "This view is beautiful. I might not ever want to leave."

"We'll make sure our new house has a view of the ocean."

"I'd love that, but I was also thinking about something else."

"What is it?"

I turn around to face him. "What if we had a place that had some land, and we could take in more rescue animals?" I study his face for a few seconds, hoping for a reaction. "I know we won't be able to be there all the time. Maybe we can hire someone to help care for the animals."

Viktor's mouth turns up in a smile. "You have the biggest heart of anyone I've ever met."

"Is that a yes?" I ask hopefully.

"Absolutely. That would be a great thing for us to do."

Standing on my tiptoes, I wrap my arms around his neck and plant a kiss on his lips. "Thank you."

"As much as I want to bring you to bed right now, we have to leave for the party."

"We'll have something to look forward to later."

The ride to the bed and breakfast is short. I couldn't figure out why Charlotte was having her party here, but now I see why. It's a beautiful place full of charm and character.

The three of us get out and walk around the house. The party's being held outside by the lake. Nadiya immediately spots my father and starts whining and pulling on her leash. Somehow, she charmed him, and they became best friends. I drop her leash and let her run to him. He stoops down, giving her lots of love, and takes her leash.

There's a bunch of people here that are unfamiliar. I'm assuming they're Natalie's friends from Northmeadow.

"I'm so glad you both made it." Leo comes over to us.

"So are we."

"Make yourselves at home. Charlotte texted. They'll be here in about five minutes."

Everyone's milling about inside a white gazebo that's decorated with lanterns and large, colorful hanging flower baskets.

"Congratulations on the tour and the record deal." Brandon, Lana's ex, comes over and gives me a hug.

"Thank you." I look over his shoulder and see Lana watching us. "Has she spoken to you at all?"

"A curt hello. But I'm not letting her leave without getting to the bottom of this."

It's been two years, but he's clearly not given up on them. I'm glad. Brandon's a genuinely sweet guy, and it's obvious he still loves my sister.

"Let me know if there's anything I can do to help," I offer.

"I will."

We make our way over to my parents. Dad insists that Nadiya stays with him and Mom. It makes me laugh, considering he couldn't wrap his head around the idea of why we got a dog just a few days ago.

While we wait for Natalie to get here, we stop and chat with Star and her sub, Jackson. Dimitri, Jessica, and Lana join us. It's so nice to see everyone in the same place. We're talking to Sam and Luna when Leo announces that Alex and Natalie are pulling in. Her parents told them they were coming here for an early dinner.

Everyone quiets while we wait for them to come around the building. As soon as they come into view, the group shouts a collective "Happy Birthday."

Natalie brings her hands to her mouth. "I don't know what to say." She enters the gazebo and looks around at everyone gathered here.

Leo steps over to Natalie and gives her a hug. "Your mom was instrumental in making this happen."

"Thank you both." Natalie looks between her mom and Leo. "I can't believe everyone's here. How did you do this?"

"Leo and I have an announcement to make." Anthony steps up next to his husband. "We'd like to tell everyone that we're now the proud owners of Water's Edge Bed and Breakfast."

Congratulations and applause come from all the guests. Rose sees Viktor and squeals as she runs over to him. He lifts her into his arms, planting kisses on both cheeks. Rose giggles in delight.

"We thought it very fitting for our first event to be a birthday party for Natalie. Especially since we would've never found this place without her."

"You guys bought it?" Natalie asks, shocked.

"We did," Tony says proudly. "To be fair, it was Leo and Charlotte who brought the idea up."

"We fell in love with the area when we were here for Natalie's wedding," Leo adds. "Mrs. Wilson let us know she was looking to sell the place so she could retire, and we were looking at getting out of the city and slowing down. So, we took the leap and purchased it." Leo motions to Natalie's mom. "Charlotte has been instrumental in helping us make some changes."

Charlotte and Leo have become very close. I think it has something to do with her regret over how they treated their son, Michael, before he passed away. Regardless of how or why, it's been a beautiful thing to see.

"Let's sit and eat," Anthony suggests.

I take Michael from Natalie so she can eat her meal uninterrupted.

We spend an enjoyable afternoon and evening with our friends and family.

It feels so good to be home.

Viktor

YESTERDAY, WE SPENT A WONDERFUL AFTERNOON WITH our friends and family. Nadiya was a big hit and fit right in with this eclectic group. But I'm equally as happy to be back at our quiet cottage. Just Amelia and me spending time together.

Tonight, like almost every night since we got here, we sit on our deck, a fire burning in the fire pit, while we watch the sun setting over the lake. Nadiya lays on her doggie bed next to us. It's quiet and relaxing.

The silence allows me to reflect on my life over the past few years. I've gone from a man who thought he had everything with Natalie and Rose to a man who found himself lost and alone.

There was a time when I didn't care about life. I actually wished I wouldn't be alive to see the next sunrise. I couldn't see it then, but the best part of my life was still to come. Thankfully, fate and my friends intervened.

Something happened to me that day in my bedroom when Amelia kissed me for the first time. Even though I pushed her away and gave her every reason we couldn't be together, I knew it was no use. The walls I'd erected around my heart crumbled. I knew there was no way I'd be able to resist this woman. Amelia's love is pure. When she looks at me, I'm all she sees. And for the first time in my life, I can admit that I deserve the love she gives me.

There's a lot on the radar for us. Amelia's career in the music industry is starting to take off. We'll be doing much more living from her tour bus.

We've also started taking the first steps toward opening Hope Ranch. A place for abused and neglected animals who need rehabilitation and love. Earlier today, we sent emails about some properties with plenty of land. We're also looking for staff who are well-versed in abused animals to help us with this endeavor.

Amelia owns my heart.

When I look at her, I see my forever.

I'm not sure what the future holds for us. What I am certain of is that whatever comes our way, we'll face it together.

Craving More Viktor and Amelia?

The story doesn't end here! Unlock an exclusive, never-before-seen bonus epilogue and discover what's next for Viktor and Amelia.

Scan the QR code to join my VIP Readers and get instant access to this special bonus content—completely free!

Don't miss out on the next chapter of their unforgettable love story!

Some love stories heal the broken pieces.

Others drag you willingly into the dark.

Continue the Fire & Ice series with Brandon and Lana in *Shattered Dreams*.

Or enter a darker romance...

Aoife Quigley was never meant to rule.

But the men around her forgot one very dangerous thing, underestimated women become powerful in all the worst ways.

And Aoife is willing to burn Ireland to the ground for the throne, the man she loves, and the life she was denied.

Enter the world of *Bound by Darkness*.

Find Tara's Books Here

About Tara

Bestselling author Tara Conrad writes where passion meets peril, crafting dark, spellbinding romances that blur the line between devotion and destruction.

Inspired by the haunting brilliance of Edgar Allan Poe, her stories reimagine Gothic tales with modern sensuality and power.

Within her pages, heroines rise unbroken, villains fall beautifully, and the darkness always tells the truth.

When she isn't writing, Tara travels with her husband, meeting readers who have found pieces of themselves in her worlds.

She believes love isn't always light. Sometimes, it's found in the dark. 🖤

Acknowledgments

To my husband, Dominant, and best friend George. I can't say thank you enough for everything you do to make my books gorgeous. I wouldn't want to be on this crazy adventure with anyone else. I love you with all my heart.

To all my kids: Thank you for always being my biggest cheering squad. I appreciate all your support. I love you guys.

To my readers: From Booktok to Instagram. Twitter to Face-book. And everything in between. Each one of you is so very important to me. Starting this journey, I was scared that no one would bother to read my books and even if they did, they'd hate them. You have all showed my so much love and support. I treasure every message and email from you. Thank you all for your support. I love you all!

Human Trafficking Resources

National Human Trafficking Resource Center 1-888-373-7888
TTY 711
Text HELP to 233733

ONLINE RESOURCES

www.dhs.gov/bluecampaign

polarisproject.org

humantraffickinghotline.org

327